EMILIE WAS ALIVE—OR AT LEAST SHE THOUGHT SHE WAS

But as she looked around at the lighthouse, she couldn't get her bearings. For a two-centuries-old building, the hinges looked new and free of rust. A beautiful quilt rested on a ladder-back chair, along with a blue coverlet. The walls had obviously received a recent coat of whitewash. The wooden staircase that led up to the tower seemed sturdy and solid. The dilapidated radar equipment was gone and in its place were a compass, a telescope and a copy of *Poor Richard's Almanac.*

There was something about all this that made the hair on the back of her neck rise. Could it be? No, things like that didn't happen in real life....

Her hands trembled as she looked at the first page. "Printed in the year of Our Lord 1776."

It was a first edition.

And it wasn't very old.

Barbara BRETTON

After a score of contemporary and historical novels, Barbara Bretton enjoys a warm place in the hearts of romance readers everywhere. She is the recipient of numerous writing awards, including Best Series Writer from *Romantic Times* and the Silver Pen Award from *Affaire de Coeur*. She is also listed in the prestigious *Foremost Women in the Twentieth Century*.

In her decade-long career, Ms. Bretton has written short stories, articles and novels. She is one of the original authors in the Harlequin American Romance line and continues to be one of the best loved. Hers is a voice of honest emotion that touches women the world over.

For Barbara the American colonial era is one of enormous interest. She has long been an admirer of the romance between John and Abigail Adams and has visited historic homes and Revolutionary battlesites throughout the northeast. Ms. Bretton now lives in the midst of the history she loves, in central New Jersey.

Barbara BRETTON

Somewhere IN TIME

Harlequin Books

TORONTO • NEW YORK • LONDON
AMSTERDAM • PARIS • SYDNEY • HAMBURG
STOCKHOLM • ATHENS • TOKYO • MILAN
MADRID • WARSAW • BUDAPEST • AUCKLAND

In memory of John and Abigail Adams,
who continue to show me what true love is all about

With special thanks to the following friends who
made the impossible possible:
Lass Small, who worried;
Susan C. Feldhake, who advised;
Sandra Marton, who understood;
Dallas Schulze, who gave me the
most valuable commodity a writer has—her time.

*License has been taken with the publication date of
Poor Richard's Almanac. All other historical data
are accurate.*

SOMEWHERE IN TIME

July 1992

ISBN 0-373-83246-X

"She was what a woman ought to be."

—Tombstone of one
Woman of Trenton,
late eighteenth century

PROLOGUE

Zane Grey Rutledge downshifted into second as he guided the black Porsche up the curving driveway toward Rutledge House. Gravel crunched beneath the tires, sending a fine spray across the lacquered surface of the hood and fenders. He swore softly as a pebble pinged against the windshield, leaving behind a spiderweb crack in the glass. He stopped the car behind a huge moving van and let out the clutch. The bricks had faded and the stones were worn smooth, but still the house stood, proud home to more generations of Rutledges than Zane had desire to count.

"One day it will matter to you," his grandmother Sara Jane had said to him not long before she died. "There's nothing more important than family."

Sara Jane had been dead now for three months and finally he was about to put the last of her estate to rights. Lately he'd had the feeling that she was watching him from somewhere in the shadows, shaking her head the way she used to when he was a boy and he'd been caught drinking beer with his friends from the wrong side of town.

He leaned back in his contoured leather seat and watched as the treasures of a lifetime were carried from the house by a parade of moving men. Winterhalter portraits of long-dead Rutledges, books and mementos that cataloged a nation's history as well as a family's.

His fingers drummed the steering wheel in a nervous rhythm. He'd done the right thing. Damn it, it was the *only* thing he could have done, given the circumstances. Playing curator to a museum masquerading as a house held little appeal for him. He wasn't about to change his way of life to suit a collection of inanimate objects just because they came with a pedigree as long as his. So far he'd done a pretty good job of escaping responsibility and he wasn't about to blow his reputation as the black sheep of the family at this late date.

Not that there was any family left to speak of. Sara Jane's death had seen to that. With her passing, the once-mighty Rutledges of Pennsylvania had only Zane to carry on the tradition of pride and patriotism that had begun back in the time of the revolutionary war. Too bad there was no one else around to appreciate the joke.

"Mr. Rutledge? Oh, Mr. Rutledge, it *is* you. I was so afraid I'd missed you."

He started at the sound of a woman's voice floating through the open window of the car.

"Olivia McRae," she said, smiling coyly. "We met last week."

He opened the door and unfolded himself from the sleek sports car. "I remember," he said, shaking the woman's birdlike hand. "Eastern Pennsylvania Preservation Society."

She dimpled, and Zane was struck by the fact that in her day Olivia McRae had probably been a looker.

"We have much to thank you for. I must tell you we feel as if Christmas has come early this year!"

He cast her a quizzical look. She was thanking him? In the past few days he had come to think of her as his own personal savior for taking Rutledge House and its contents off his hands.

"A pleasure," he said, relying on charm to cover his surprise.

"Oh, it's a fine day for Rutledge House," she said her tone upbeat. "I know your dear departed grandmother Sara Jane would heartily approve of your decision."

"'Approve' might be too strong a word," he said with a wry grin. "Accept is more like it." Bloodlines had been everything to Sara Jane Rutledge. No matter that the venerable old house had been tumbling down around her ears, in need of more help than even the family fortune could provide. So long as a Rutledge was in residence, all had been right with the world.

"Just you wait," said Olivia McRae, patting him on the forearm in a decidedly maternal gesture. "Next time you see it, this wonderful old house will be on its way to regaining its former glory."

"It's your business now, Olivia. Yours and the state of Pennsylvania." He'd never been one to bow down before the grandeur of history, family or otherwise. He didn't give a damn if he never saw Rutledge House again.

"We would welcome your input," the older woman said. "And we would most certainly like to have a Rutledge on the board of directors at the museum."

"Sorry," he said, perhaps a beat too quickly. "I think a clean break is better all around."

The woman's warm brown eyes misted over with tears. "How thoughtless of me! This must be dreadfully difficult, coming so soon after the loss of your beloved grandmother."

Zane looked away. Little in life unnerved him. Talk of his late grandmother did. "I have a plane to catch," he said gruffly. No matter that the plane didn't take off until tomorrow afternoon. As far as he was concerned, emotions were more dangerous than skydiving without a chute. "I'd better be on my way."

Olivia McRae peered into the car. "You do have the package, don't you?"

"Package?" His brows knotted. "I don't know anything about a package."

"Oh, Mr. Rutledge, you *must* have the package I set out for you." She looked at him curiously. "The uniform."

"Damn," he muttered under his breath. "I'd forgotten." *The oldest male child in each generation is entrusted with the uniform,* his grandmother had told him on his twelfth birthday when she'd handed him the carefully wrapped package. *Someday you'll hand it down to your son.*

Not if he could help it.

He hadn't forgotten about the uniform. He knew exactly where it was: in the attic under a thick layer of dust, as forgotten as the past should be—and usually was.

"You wait right here," said Mrs. McRae, turning back toward the house. "I'll fetch it for you."

He was tempted to get behind the wheel of the Porsche and be halfway to Manhattan before the woman crossed the threshold. For as long as he could remember, that damn uniform had been at the heart of Rutledge family lore. His grandmother had woven endless stories of derring-do and bravery and laid every single one of them at the feet of some long-dead relative who'd probably never done anything more courageous than shoot himself a duck for dinner.

Moments later Olivia McRae was back by his side.

"Here you are," she said, pressing a large, neatly wrapped package into his arms with the tenderness a mother would display toward her firstborn. "To think you almost left without it."

Zane looked at the package curiously. "Heavier than I thought it would be," he said. "You sure there isn't a musket in there with the uniform?"

Mrs. McRae's lined cheeks dimpled. "Oh, you! You always *were* a tease. Why, you must have seen this uniform a million times."

"Afraid I never paid much attention."

"That can't be true."

"I've never been much for antiques."

"This is more than an antique," said Mrs. McRae, obviously appalled. "This is a piece of American history...*your* history." She patted the parcel. "Open it, Mr. Rutledge. I'd love to see your face when you—"

"I will," he said, edging toward the Porsche, "but right now I have a plane to catch."

"Of course," she said, her smile fading. "I understand."

She looked at him and in her eyes Zane saw disappointment. But why should Mrs. McRae be any different? Disappointing people was what he did best. He tossed the package into the back seat and with a nod toward Olivia McRae roared back down the driveway and away from Rutledge House.

As always, Manhattan welcomed him with open arms. The anonymity of the crowded city soothed his restless nature in a way the security of hearth and home never could. Nobody expected anything of him in Manhattan, and he'd managed to live down to the lowest expectations.

Not even the dense traffic coming through the Lincoln Tunnel was enough to deter him, or the stop-and-go progress he made as he traveled from the west side to his co-op east of Fifth Avenue.

His apartment was on the thirtieth floor of a faceless high rise not far from UN Plaza. He'd bought it a few years earlier, flush from a great run at the baccarat table in Monte Carlo. *You can't put down roots in midair,* his grandmother had said, shaking her head in dismay. He'd smiled and told her that was exactly why he'd bought the place.

He didn't want a home, not in the way Sara Jane had meant it. That was one of the reasons for the failure of his marriage. The apartment was base camp, the place where he stowed his supplies and picked up his mail and made plans to move on to somewhere else. Running the bulls at Pamplona. Parasailing off the Kona coast. It didn't matter. The point was to keep moving.

He'd learned that lesson as a child and it was one lesson he never forgot. As soon as you grew attached to a place, you were in trouble. There was no gain to be found in getting comfortable.

"Afternoon, Mr. Rutledge." The liveried doorman tipped his hat to Zane. "Thought you were on your way to Australia."

"Tahiti," said Zane as he entered the gilt-and-marble lobby. "Tomorrow afternoon."

The doorman, a retired mechanic from Bensonhurst, sighed loudly. "Boy, that's the life," he said, massaging the small of his back. "You musta seen just about everything this world has to offer."

"Just about," said Zane. And a few things the gods would envy. Why it no longer seemed to be enough was a good question.

"Sorry to hear about your grandma. Hope her passing was easy."

"It was," said Zane, heading for the elevator. "Thanks for asking."

The elevator rose swiftly to the thirtieth floor, and moments later Zane let himself into his apartment. Cool, silvery-gray walls. An endless expanse of polished, bare wood floors. So relentlessly geared for function over style that it became stylish by default.

Not that he gave a damn, he thought, as he tossed the package containing the uniform onto an off-white leather-and-chrome chair. To be stylish you had to care and there were few things in his thirty-four years that Zane had cared much about.

Sara Jane, however, was one of them.

He yanked off his tie, slipped out of his jacket, then headed for the bottle of Scotch waiting for him atop the bar. Modern life had its benefits, but not even the wonders of the twentieth century could hold a candle to the sweet oblivion to be found in a bottle of good Scotch. He poured three fingers of the potent liquid into a heavy tumbler, paused, then poured some more.

Sara Jane Rutledge had lived ninety-three years, all but one of them in robust good health. When she'd found out she was dying, she had approached the inevitable with the same grace and fortitude for which she was known. He doubted if he would have been able to summon up as much courage as that tiny, white-haired woman had managed to do. "A new adventure," she'd told him during their last conversation. "In a strange way I'm looking forward to it."

He shook his head at the memory, then downed a long swallow of Scotch. There were people who said he courted death with his exploits. Race cars... cigarette boats with keels made to slice through the water...planes that climbed high and fast, then flung open their doors for him to challenge the wind. It wasn't death he was courting, not really. He had simply learned early on that if he kept moving he had at least a fighting chance to stay ahead of the loneliness.

Things came easily for him. They always had. Good grades when he'd needed them. Women when he wanted them. He'd been blessed with acute powers of observation and a damn good memory. He even walked away from car wrecks without a scratch. The only thing he'd failed at had been his marriage and he liked to think even that hadn't left a scar.

His gaze wandered to the package resting on the far edge of the bar. "I almost got out of there without you," he said, glaring at it. He'd noticed it the other day when he was up in the attic at Rutledge House, showing the moving men what to pack, and had assumed it would have been on its way to the museum by now with all the rest of the stuff.

So why hadn't he handed it right back to nice little Olivia McRae and been done with it? There wasn't a law against giving away family heirlooms. If there was, he wouldn't have been able to unload the portraits or the jewelry or the contents of Sara Jane's library, either.

You didn't think I was going to let you get away without a fight, did you, boy?

He started, spilling Scotch on the front of his shirt. Two gulps of booze and he was hearing Sara Jane's voice? Ridiculous. Probably his guilty conscience speaking. He would have given his grandmother anything, except the one thing she really wanted: a family to continue the Rutledge name.

It's not too late, Zane. Open your eyes to what's around you and your heart will soon follow....

He wasn't entirely certain he had one.

He put down his glass and stalked toward the other end of the bar and the wrapped package containing the uniform. Experience had taught him the best way to handle anything, from a hangover to a guilty conscience, was the hair of the dog that bit you.

"Okay," he said, unknotting the string, then folding back the brown paper. There was nothing scary about a moth-eaten hunk of cloth. "Let's take a look."

He pushed aside the buff-colored breeches and inspected the navy blue coat. Dark beige cuffs and lapels. A line of tarnished metal buttons. The only unusual thing about the garment was the decorative stitching inside the left cuff and under the collar. He looked again. He was surprised to note that the shoulders of the jacket seemed broad enough to fit him, and he was a man of above-average size. He didn't know all that much about history, but he vividly remembered diving off the Florida coast around the wreck of the Atocha some years back and noting the almost lilliputian scale.

What are you going to do, Zane, toss it in your closet and forget it the way you forgot everything else? You owe my memory more than that....

"This is getting weird," he said out loud. Next thing he knew he'd find himself breaking bread with a six-foot rabbit named Harvey. "I'm on my way to Tahiti. I don't have time for this."

Make time, boy! Wasn't I the only one who ever made time for you?

The truth hurt. Sara Jane was the one person he'd been able to count on when he was growing up, the only one who'd never let him down. This was the least he could do for her—even if it was too late to really matter.

Two hours later he climbed back behind the wheel of the Porsche. It wasn't possible. The odds were just too damn unbelievable.

Yet time and again he'd heard the same thing: "Emilie Crosse is the one for you." A Rutgers professor and two museum curators had all sung the praises of this woman with the old-fashioned name and outdated occupation. The woman who just happened to be his ex-wife.

"You play dirty, Sara Jane," he said as he headed across town toward the Lincoln Tunnel, "but it's not going to work. I'm dropping off the uniform and getting the hell out of there, understand?"

It's a start, boy. It's a start.

ONE

At the moment her life changed forever, Emilie was standing on a stepladder on her front porch watering a flowering begonia plant that had seen better days. She was considering whether or not to put the poor thing out of its misery when the roar of a car engine brought her up short.

She wasn't expecting anyone. The most traffic her street usually saw was the appearance of the red-white-and-blue U.S. mail jeep every morning, and the jeep's engine sputtered rather than roared.

She climbed down from the ladder and, wiping her hands on the sides of her pants, glanced toward the street. The sound grew closer. Then, to her amazement, a shiny black foreign car turned into her driveway. She didn't know too much about foreign cars, but it didn't take an automotive genius to figure out you could run the Crosse Harbor school system on what the driver had paid for that sleek beauty.

It roared up her driveway as if it were the home stretch of the Indianapolis 500, and she bristled with indignation when it screeched to a stop near her own sedate sedan.

She hated people who drove fancy cars as if they owned the road and everyone on it. As far as she was concerned, a car was nothing more than a hunk of metal, four rubber wheels and a lot of extra parts that broke down when you could least afford it.

A Porsche, she noted. Flashy, sexy, impossible to ignore.

She'd known only one person in her life who wouldn't be overshadowed by a car like that and she'd been crazy enough to marry him—and sane enough to divorce him six months later.

"It couldn't be," she said as she stood on the top step, doing her best to ignore the sudden jolt of excitement that urged her to fly down the porch steps and tear open the car door. Tinted windows should be outlawed, she thought wildly. It wasn't fair that the driver could see her while she—

The car door swung open and the driver of the Porsche climbed out.

She leaned against the railing for support, feeling as if she'd looked into the heart of the sun. Real men didn't look like that. He looked like the pirate hero on the cover of a romance novel, dangerous and compelling and totally out of this world.

She pinched herself sharply on the inside of her arm then looked again, but he didn't disappear the way dreams always did. Instead he started toward her, his long legs eating up the distance between them with powerful strides. She wanted to run. She wanted to hide. She wanted a crash course in 101 Reasons Why Divorce Was The Only Solution.

Hiding her trembling hands behind her back, she offered up an easy smile.

He didn't smile back. Why was it gorgeous men never smiled? She wondered if it was some code of honor or a congenital incapability.

He had a small cleft in his chin, a stubborn jaw and the most unabashedly sensual mouth she'd ever seen. She remembered how that mouth had felt pressed against—

"Been a long time, Emilie," he said in a voice so rich with testosterone that it made her knees buckle. "You look great."

"Don't tell me," she said. "Let me guess. You were in the neighborhood and decided to drop by." She snapped her fingers. "So what if it's been five years?"

"Still the feisty redhead. I'm glad some things never change."

"Did it ever occur to you to call first?"

"Why?" he countered. "You're here, aren't you?"

She glanced pointedly toward the watch on her left wrist then back at him. "Is there something I can do for you?"

"You're not going to ask me in?"

"I hadn't planned on it."

He flashed his movie-star grin. "You used to be a lot friendlier."

"And a lot dumber. You're here for a reason, Zane, and it isn't to talk about old times." She sounded cool and collected. He'd never in a million years suspect the way her heart was thundering inside her chest.

"I have a package in the car," he said. "I'd like you to take a look at it."

"I'd be happy to," she said, "but you'll have to make an appointment."

"But I'm leaving for Tahiti tomorrow afternoon."

"Then you can make an appointment for when you return." He'd always been on his way to Tahiti or the Hamptons or the Côte d'Azur, too busy looking for a good time to see that happiness had been right there for the asking.

And he'd always been able to do this to her, turn a sensible, intelligent woman into a hopeless romantic with a soft spot for happily ever after....

Don't give up so easily, boy. Convince her. Zane started at the sound of Sara Jane's voice in his ear. He hoped his grandmother was enjoying this encounter more than he was.

Sara Jane had to be enjoying it more than Emilie was. His ex-wife was glaring up at him with that redhead's intensity that had always been part of her appeal. The other part of her appeal was obvious. She was a beautiful woman—difficult, but beautiful. Their brief marriage had been a wild blend of sexual chemistry, romantic love and the absolute certainty that it could never last.

Still, the sight of her stirred something inside him, something he hadn't felt in a very long time.

Unfortunately she didn't seem to be feeling anything but impatient, and he pushed aside nostalgia in favor of the business at hand.

All it usually took was a sincere smile or two to win fair maiden. He had an address book filled with the names of women who enjoyed his company. How hard could it be to convince his ex-wife to look at a uniform?

"Look," he said, leaning forward, all charm and persistence, "this is important."

She started to protest, but he held up his hand to stop her.

"I made a promise to someone I care about and you're the only one who can help me."

"How do you know I'm the only one who can help you? If I remember right, you thought my career was a lot of nonsense."

"You've built yourself quite a reputation out there, Em. I called two museums and a professor at Rutgers and they all came back with the same name: yours." He upped the wattage on his smile. "I'm impressed."

"Don't be," she said. "It has nothing to do with you."

"I know," he said honestly. "And I'm still impressed."

"Well," she said, offering up her first smile of the encounter, "that's very flattering."

"It's meant to be." He gestured toward the car. "Will you take a look?"

"Five minutes," she said. "If I think I can help you, we'll work something out after you get back from your vacation."

Emilie waited on the top step while he jogged over to the car and retrieved a brown paper-wrapped parcel from the passenger seat. He cut a dashing figure in his tailored gray pants and white shirt of silky Egyptian cotton. Broad shoulders. Narrow hips.

Powerful legs. Definitely the poster boy for pirate fantasies.

Too bad her idea of marriage had entailed more than great sex and a well-worn passport.

"Okay," he said, thrusting the parcel at her as he mounted the porch steps. "Here it is. When do we start?"

She eyed the package. "What is it?"

"A uniform."

"How old?"

"Two hundred plus a decade or two."

She whistled low. "Bring it inside. We don't want to expose the uniform to any more light than necessary."

"Don't tell me you're one of those ozone-layer crazies."

She shot him a look. "Don't tell me you're one of those idiots who think all's well with the world."

"You can't turn back the clock," he said as she led him inside the house. "Technology's given us a hell of a lot more than it's taken away."

"Right," said Emilie, ushering him into her studio at the side of the house. "Acid rain... smog... shall I go on?"

"I should've known you'd become an Earth Day groupie," he said as he tossed the package down on the worktable. "Can't see the trees for the rain forest."

"Spare me your list of technological wonders," she snapped. "We could live without microwaves and computers. We can't live without clean water and fresh air."

"No wonder you're good with antiques," he shot back. "You always did think like one."

"Okay," said Emilie, folding her arms across her chest. *I don't care how gorgeous you are.* "That does it. Goodbye, Rutledge. It's been interesting, if not enjoyable."

He stared at her blankly. How anyone so good-looking could be so dense struck Emilie as a terrible waste of natural resources.

"What about the uniform?"

"That's your problem," she said with a dismissive look. *A uniform, Emilie! A two-hundred-year-old uniform. My God....* It took every ounce of will-power at her command to keep from ripping into the package. The last revolutionary-war-era uniform she'd actually worked on had come her way over four years ago and, unfortunately, it had proved to be a lost cause. Time and the elements had done damage not even Emilie could undo.

He glared at her from across the room. "You promised me five minutes."

"And I've already given you eight."

"You said you'd examine the uniform."

"Why bother? I know you, Zane. You've probably had it dry-cleaned three times and lined it with mink."

"Wrong again. Original equipment from collar to cuffs."

The temptation was more than she could bear. "All right," she said in her most businesslike tone of voice. "Let's take a look."

She approached the workbench with the edgy excitement of a high roller at a no-limits table. Except no high roller worth her weight in chips would have hands that trembled the way Emilie Crosse's trembled as she began to untie the string.

He would have liked to think it was his overwhelming male presence that brought about that reaction, but he had the feeling she really found this stuff exciting.

"Damn," she muttered under her breath as her slender fingers worked at the knot. He'd already noticed she didn't wear a wedding ring and cursed himself roundly for looking.

"Need some help?"

"Scissors," she said, gnawing at her full lower lip. "The red ones on the pegboard."

"Real authentic," he drawled as he handed her the scissors. "Didn't I see Made in Taiwan on the blade?"

"Very funny," she said, not looking at him. The string fell away at the first touch of the implement, then she moved to fold back the thick brown paper.

An odd sensation moved its way up his spine, raising the hairs on the back of his neck. *See, Zane! I told you so. It's starting to matter!* Sweat broke out at his temples. He felt as if he was standing at the end of a long pier and Circe herself was beckoning him into the floodwaters rushing past.

There was no reason for hearing voices—or for the almost unbearable sense of anticipation that gripped him by the throat and refused to let go.

Emilie's sharp exhalation of breath echoed throughout the room as the centuries came to life beneath her fingertips. *It's your imagination. You've read too many books.* . . . Still, there was no explaining the sound of drums beating cadence in her ears or the icy winds of Valley Forge raising goose bumps on her arms and legs.

I know this uniform, she thought. Each decision made by that long-ago tailor was one she would have made herself. The alterations had been skillfully rendered, made even more unusual by the fact that the sleeves had been altered to fit a shorter man.

Zane broke the silence. "So what do you think?"

She swung around to look at him, her eyes flashing fury. "If this is some kind of joke, so help me, I'll—"

"It's not a joke."

She traced the collar with her fingertips. She'd always favored that method of rolling a collar, although she'd never seen it used in colonial-era garments. "It's a reproduction—it has to be. The color is too rich . . . the weave is still tight. . . ."

"It's not a reproduction," he said. "It's the real thing."

"Believe me, two hundred years leave their mark on a garment. I've made a career out of undoing the damage time can cause."

"Okay, then prove it's a reproduction." She didn't expect him to leave so soon, did she? Damn it, he wanted to watch her breathe just a little while longer. . . .

She turned the uniform over and held the back seam up to the light. "Look at this," she ordered. "The fibers are long and supple. Very little stress on any of the stitches. This wasn't worn more than a handful of times."

"I suppose you're going to tell me the fabric is polyester?"

She shook her head. Okay, so she still didn't have a sense of humor. She was still beautiful.

"It's wool, all right. Tight weave...." The texture and weight and smell of the wool used in colonial army uniforms. The drum beat louder inside her head. "I just don't see how—"

"But it's possible?"

"Logically, no." She pressed the uniform to her nose, inhaling the heavy smell of wool and vegetable dye. It couldn't be...it simply couldn't.

"But?"

"There's one way to find out," she said, looking up at him. "If you could give me an hour, we'll know for sure."

"I don't have an hour. I have a long drive back to New York."

"And a plane to catch."

He looked at her sharply. "And a plane to catch."

"Then I can't give you an answer." She sounded cool and self-possessed, but inside, her stomach was twisted in sailor's knots. *Oh, God,* she thought. *You can't leave now. There's something happening here...something I don't understand.* Everything about the uniform seemed strangely familiar, from the braid of stitches that formed the buttonhole to the hand-finished seams.

He reached for the uniform and their fingers brushed. A brief spark flashed between them. She pulled her hand away as if burned.

"Static electricity," she said, ducking her head to hide her embarrassment. She still felt his touch reverberating through her body.

"Right," he said, totally unconvinced.

There was enough sexual electricity in that room to light Atlantic City and he found it impossible to believe she wasn't aware of it. She was close enough for him to catch the scent of spring flowers in her hair, and his blood quickened.

No way was he about to make that mistake again.

He glanced at his watch. "An hour's pushing it," he said. "Thirty minutes would be better."

"It's a deal. Just let me run a few tests on a fabric sample and see what we come up with." She pointed toward a wooden stool to the left of an enormous spinning wheel. "You can sit over there while I get started."

He took his first real look around him. The studio was a dizzying blend of color and texture and style. Colonial samplers vied for wall space with Erte prints and a Renoir poster of an extremely healthy female nude. Despite the twentieth-century intrusions, however, there was no mistaking the fact that the love of Emilie's life was the colonial era in American history. Back when they were first married he had teased her mercilessly about living in the past. Little did he know she'd end up doing it professionally.

"Do you really use this thing?" he asked, inclining his head in the direction of the spinning wheel.

"Of course I do," she said, casting a curious glance at him.

He spun the wheel, listening to the creak of wood. "Seems like a lot of work to make a piece of thread." He'd always believed if you couldn't find it in a store, you didn't really need it.

"It is a lot of work." She filled a basin with liquid from a brown bottle then stirred the mixture with a wooden spoon. "It's also a lot of fun."

He looked skeptical but Emilie ignored him. He hadn't understood her when they were married and there was no reason to assume he'd understand her now. He was a fast-food, fast-car type of man, while she longed for the days of butter churns and coaches-and-fours.

She worked quickly, easing open a seam and snipping a tiny swatch of fabric. She was painfully conscious of every detail in the room, from the scratchiness of the wool to the sound of his breathing to the way she couldn't quite shake the feeling that the adventure of a lifetime was about to begin.

Zane had no idea what the hell she was doing over there at the worktable and he didn't particularly care. He liked watching the way she moved, studying the graceful line of her shoulders and back, remembering how she had felt beneath him, all warm and open and ready....

He shifted position on the stool, grateful she had her back to him.

She wasn't particularly friendly, and she'd been anything but flirtatious; still, he found himself content to sit there and watch her fiddle around with inanimate objects as if she was a first-run movie and he was her captive audience.

But she'd always had that effect on him. The only thing they'd ever had in common was a major physical attraction, and they'd leaped headfirst into marriage, refusing to believe they'd ever need anything else.

The marriage was over.

He couldn't say the same thing about the physical attraction.

Maybe it was the fact that she seemed totally immune to his masculine charms that made her more alluring by the second. Was she in love with somebody? Not that it mattered to him, but he glanced around the workroom looking for clues. No photographs hanging on the walls. No men's clothes or shoes anywhere. He considered excusing himself to use the john and taking a quick look through the rest of the house for any telltale signs of an active love life, but, all things taken into account, he'd rather just sit there and watch her breathe.

Why on earth was he watching her so closely? Emilie could feel the heat of his gaze burning through the thin fabric of her shirt. For a man who seemed uninterested in the uniform she was examining, he hadn't taken his eyes from the proceedings...or from her.

"It's getting terribly hot in here." Emilie tossed her hair over her shoulder as she positioned a tiny scrap of fabric on a glass slide. She tried to sound matter-of-fact, but had the feeling she'd failed miserably. "Would you raise the air conditioning, please?"

She heard the scrape of the step stool against the tile floor, followed by Rutledge's footsteps as he walked across the room to the thermostat on the far wall.

"Thanks," she mumbled, not looking up. "Strange the way it got hotter after dusk, isn't it?"

"No," he said, his voice a rough caress. "Doesn't seem strange to me at all."

She waited for the sound of the stool scraping against the floor again as he sat back down, but it didn't come.

"I'll be a while longer," she said, struggling to sound casual and unconcerned. "Make yourself comfortable."

"I'm comfortable."

She jumped at the sound of his voice so close to her ear. "Don't stand over me like that, Zane. This is very precise work."

"I won't get in your way."

"You *are* in my way." She gestured toward the overhead fixtures. "You're blocking the light."

"I thought you were using the microscope."

"Would you please sit down?" she persisted, her voice unnaturally high. "This is serious business." And she was having a terrible time remembering that fact with him standing there next to her, close enough for her to breathe in the smell of his skin.

He retreated to the wooden stool. "Is this good enough?"

"It's fine."

"I don't want to get in your way."

"You're not in my way any longer."

"I'll just sit here and watch you."

"Great."

Not great. There was no way on earth the air-conditioning system could keep pace with the heat building inside her body. Damn it. They'd been divorced for five years. Wouldn't you think she'd be immune to him by now?

She cleared her throat. "I have a TV in the front room."

"I'll pass."

"You could catch the end of local news."

"Not interested." He glanced up at the clock. "You going to be much longer?"

"Just...another...minute." She bent over the uniform, squinting against the harsh glare of a high-intensity light clamped to the side of the worktable.

There was something happening in that room, something he didn't understand, but apparently he was the only one aware of it. He didn't like the way she made him feel, off balance and hungry for something he couldn't put a name to.

The hunger was soul deep and it scared the living hell out of him. It had always been like this. From the first moment he'd seen her, pinning a satin dress to a skin-and-bones model in a Hollywood costume studio, he'd known Emilie represented the one thing in the world he could never have.

That hadn't stopped him, however. Their courtship had been as swift and wild as a summer storm, and their impulsive wedding had been more the act of a desperate man, hell-bent on hanging on to something he really didn't understand.

She'd always managed to elude him. He'd known her body intimately but he'd never quite managed to touch her soul.

He brought himself up short. Introspection had never been his strong suit. This whole escapade had been a lousy idea and the sooner he escaped, the better he would feel.

"Look," he said, approaching the worktable, "I've run out of minutes. I've got a long drive ahead of me."

"What about the uniform?"

"I trust you," he said. "I'll pick it up when I get back."

"Don't trust me." She turned to face him. "I think it's the real thing."

He arched a brow. "I thought you said that was impossible."

"Lots of things are impossible. That doesn't mean they don't happen anyway." She smoothed her hands over the chest of the uniform jacket, palms tingling from the scratch of wool. "Try it on."

"Forget it."

"I need to see how it drapes."

He gestured toward a mannequin in the far corner of the room. This whole damn night was getting out of hand. "Let your pal try it on."

She shook her head. "Not good enough. I need some motion."

What are you afraid of, Zane? It's only a uniform.

"Shut up, Sara Jane," he mumbled.

"What was that?" asked Emilie.

"Nothing," he said, vaguely embarrassed. He reached for the uniform. "Let me try the damn thing on, then I'm out of here."

She held up the jacket for him to slip his arms into the sleeves. "I know it's none of my business anymore, but you really should do something about that attitude of yours."

"There's nothing wrong with my attitude." He rotated his shoulders, settling the regimental jacket into place, then changed the subject. "It fits."

Emilie's eyes widened. "Like it was made for you." She tugged at the cuffs, settling them over his wrist bones. The fit was perfect. "The odds of finding a uniform large enough for a man your size are—"

"A million to one?"

"Just about."

Of course it fits you, boy. You're a Rutledge, aren't you?

Emilie tilted her head and looked at him curiously. "Did you say something?"

He shook his head.

"I'm sure I heard something." Her brow furrowed and she looked at him even more closely. "Are you okay?"

"I'm fine."

"You don't look fine."

"I will once I get out of this thing."

"But I wanted you to try on the breeches."

"I don't wear tights." He yanked off the coat and handed it to her.

"They're not tights," she said, a grin tugging at her lush and beautiful mouth. "Spandex is a new invention."

"I don't give a damn if George Washington wore them. I don't."

"You'd probably look great in them. You always did have terrific legs."

"Forget it."

"Okay," she said. "I give up. I'll wrap the uniform back up and you can be on your way." She should have known better. She'd made this same mistake the first time they'd met, only she'd been younger and naive enough to believe in happy endings. That's why they were called fantasies; no woman in her right mind expected them to come true.

"You can keep the uniform."

"No," said Emilie. "This is a piece of history."

"History means nothing to me," he said bluntly. "You might as well keep the uniform for all the good it'll do me." *This isn't going the way I'd hoped, Zane....*

"If it doesn't matter to you," she shot back, "why did you come here?"

Again that odd sizzle of electricity in his veins, a rush of adrenaline with no place to go. How did you tell your ex-wife that your dead grandmother's voice had told you to come? She'd be dialing 911 before he reached the hallway. "It seemed like a good idea at the time."

"Remind me to tell Professor Attleman at Rutgers to recommend someone else next time around." She reached for the brown paper the uniform had been wrapped in.

"I wasn't kidding about the uniform. You can have it. It already means more to you than it ever will to me."

"If sentiment doesn't carry any weight with you, how about money? It's worth a small fortune."

"I'm rich. I won't miss it."

"Don't you care about anything?"

"Not if I can help it."

"You haven't changed a bit," she said with a shake of her head. "I feel sorry for you."

"Don't. I do what I want, go where I want, whenever I want. Most people would kill to have my life."

"You can't run forever," she said, not understanding why she cared. "Sooner or later you'll have to slow down long enough to figure out why you're so lonely."

He laughed out loud. "Lonely? Give me a break. You don't know a damn thing about my life anymore."

She looked at him as if she could see into his soul. "I'm right, aren't I?"

He bent down and kissed her hard and fast on the mouth, a kiss of anger and need and lost possibilities.

"Have a nice life, Emilie. I'm out of here."

TWO

One moment he was kissing her with more hunger and heat than she'd ever longed for.

The next moment he was walking out of her life as if nothing had happened.

Emilie stared out the window as Zane Grey Rutledge leaped into his fancy sports car, then vanished up the street the way all good fantasies were supposed to do.

She shook her head, trying to banish the memory of his mouth on hers. The last time he'd kissed her had been on the steps of the L.A. County Courthouse after they'd signed their divorce papers.

"I'm on my way to Australia," he'd said with that cocky grin of his. "Why don't you come with me?"

She'd barely restrained herself from kicking him in the shins. Their marriage had been an unqualified mistake, but there he was suggesting they fly off together to the other side of the world as if they were lovers.

And the truly awful thing was, deep down inside she was tempted. *Very* tempted.

Obviously nothing had changed.

Not his reckless attitude or, to her dismay, the way he made her feel. She'd been alive to his touch, filled with a sweet longing that seemed to promise something wonderful that was just beyond reach.

Five of the best seconds of her life. . . .

A full moon hung poised in the sky beyond her window, splashing silver on the turbulent waters. She should have known there'd be a full moon tonight. She'd felt crazy, out of control. With any encouragement she would have thrown her arms around his neck and begged him to make love to her right there on the floor in her workroom with the ghosts of the past all around them and only the stars to see.

The way he'd looked at her. The tone of his voice when he'd said her name. The signs had all been there, but she'd let the opportunity slip through her fingers and now she felt empty and very alone.

She turned away from the window, furious with herself for letting sexual chemistry cloud good, old-fashioned common sense.

If it wasn't for the uniform on the worktable, she might have believed she'd imagined the whole encounter. She crossed the room and picked up the jacket, holding it close to her chest. He'd worn it for only a few minutes but his scent, a blend of wind and rain and sea air, was everywhere.

He was everything she didn't want in a man, yet when she'd seen him striding up the driveway toward the house, she'd known the same sense of reckless excitement she'd experienced the very first time.

She'd been living in Hollywood at the time, working for a movie studio that specialized in big-budget films grounded in historical detail—especially when it came to the authenticity of the costumes.

Zane had been on the set visiting a stuntman pal of his who earned his salary by risking his neck. Zane, of course, was nothing like the stuntman.

Her ex-husband had been more than happy to risk his neck for nothing.

"Zane Grey Rutledge?" she'd said when he told her his name.

He'd shrugged with the casual ease of someone who'd never had to struggle for anything in his life. "My parents had a sense of humor," he'd said. "They were reading *Riders of the Purple Sage* in the labor room the night I was born."

Everything about him had been larger than life, from his movie-star looks to his relentless search for adventure. It had taken her a while to realize that his endless quest for the next thrill was a mask for a loneliness that went deeper than he'd ever admit.

He'd never been one to talk about the past, but she'd learned about his adventure-loving parents who had placed their five-year-old son in a fancy boarding school, then jetted off in search of their latest thrill. When they died on a mountain in Nepal, it took six months before Zane even realized they were gone. Only his grandmother, a Philadelphia mainline matron, had ever been there for him, but by then it had been a case of too little, too late.

Emilie had longed to fill the empty parts of his soul with her love but, like a shooting star, he was impossible to catch. He'd spent too many years alone to believe in happy endings.

They had nothing in common. She loved the past. He worshipped the future. He liked fast sports cars and trips to exotic locales, while she liked old quilts and museums. This miraculous wonder of a uniform meant less to him than a pair of sweat socks or a worn-out jockstrap.

He should have stayed in Tahiti or Manhattan or wherever it was he called home these days. She didn't need him in her life again, making her long for the impossible.

Lately she'd found herself pushing against the boundaries of the lazy town where she'd grown up. The kindhearted concern of her neighbors grated against her nerves. The cry of the gulls, the smell of salt air, the familiar routines of daily life all seemed alien to her, as if they belonged to someone else.

Just yesterday she'd raised her voice to Mrs. Willis at the market and told John Parker that no, she *didn't* like the way he'd wallpapered her powder room. She could still see the look of astonishment on the faces of those two nice people when she'd stormed out the door of the Stop'n'Shop with her quart of milk and half-dozen eggs.

"Poor Emilie," she'd heard Mrs. Willis say. "A girl so pretty shouldn't be alone."

Amazing how Mrs. Willis understood more about Emilie than Emilie did herself. She craved an adventure, a walk on the wild side of life. A jolt of electricity called excitement before she grew too old to care.

None of which was likely to be found in sleepy Crosse Harbor, New Jersey.

The one thing she hadn't needed, however, was her ex-husband roaring back into her life, reminding her that once upon a time she'd been naive enough to believe she could find adventure and security in his arms.

She turned, about to head for the kitchen, then stopped in her tracks. She tilted her head to the side, listening. The doorbell? It was almost eight o'clock at night. She had to be hearing things. The doorbell buzzed again, louder this time and more insistent.

She hurried through the house toward the front hall. "Who is it?" she called through the heavy wooden door.

"Zane."

The uniform...he's come back for the uniform....

She swung open the door.

"Took you long enough." He stood there in all his piratical glory, dark hair gleaming in the glow of the porch light. "Did I interrupt something?"

"What are you doing here?"

"Ask me in and I'll tell you."

"You're on your way to Tahiti," she said as her heart slammed into her rib cage.

He placed his hand on the door frame and grinned down at her. "I don't leave until tomorrow."

"Go home and pack."

"I will," he said, then paused a beat. "Will you?"

She couldn't breathe. His presence surrounded her, drawing her closer to the flame. *He's a game player, Emilie. Sophisticated, adult games with rules you never understood.* "I can't answer that," she managed finally.

"It would make it a lot easier on me if you could."

"Sorry. I've never been good at making life easy for men I used to be married to."

She sensed, rather than saw, the change in him, but the effect it had on her was profound. Behind his bravado hid the loneliness she'd recognized earlier, and it reached inside her heart and wouldn't let go.

"I got as far as the parkway," he said, "then I turned around."

"You came back for your uniform," she said, feeling terrified and thrilled and hopeful.

"No," he said, pushing past her into the dimly lit foyer. "I came back for you."

"There's no future in it," she said, devouring him with her eyes. "Nothing's changed. We're still the same people. Still—"

"There's no future in anything," he said. "There's only the moment...."

She was in his arms in a heartbeat. No questions. No second thoughts. *No promises.* Tilting her chin upward with his finger, he lowered his head and claimed the sweetness of her mouth with his. The kiss was gentle at first, a sweet melding of softness and strength, then just as she found herself wanting more, he slipped his tongue into her mouth and a fierce hunger rose up from the center of her soul.

Her hands rested against the hard wall of his chest and she felt the violent thudding of his heart against her palm. How could she have forgotten the feel of him and the smell, this explosion of pure sensation.

He swept her off her feet with one swift and unexpected motion. Instinctively she looped her arms around his neck, dizzy with longing. The amazing planes of his face...the high, almost cruel cheekbones, the proud nose of a warrior-prince. Those deep blue eyes shadowed by lashes as dark as the night. She could get lost in those eyes.

"The door," she whispered against his shoulder.

He kicked the door closed, shutting out the world and enclosing them in their own private world.

"Where?" he asked, his voice a husky, sensual growl.

"Through the hallway."

Her bedroom was the last door on the right.

He would have known it in the dark. The smell of her perfume, faint and evocative, was everywhere. For years he'd told himself he'd imagined that scent, but he hadn't. It was as real, as exciting, as the woman in his arms.

He remembered it all. The texture of her mouth. The silky flow of her hair against his cheek. The coiled female strength.

The thick feather mattress cradled them as they fell together into its softness.

"I can't believe this is happening," she said, touching his face with her fingertips.

"I couldn't leave," he said, running his hand along the proud curve of her hip. "I did my damnedest but I just couldn't leave you."

"I know," she whispered. "When I saw your car backing out of the driveway—" She shook her head. "I wanted you to come back." More than anything. More than air or sun or safety.

"No second thoughts?"

"No second thoughts." Did he have any idea how overwhelming he was? How beautiful?

He drew his hand across her flat belly, easing his fingertips under the soft fabric of her shirt, across her rib cage, to the lacy band of her bra. In an instant he undid the front hook, parting the wisps of lace, then cupping her breasts in the palms of his hands.

She felt his touch everywhere. In the fire that suddenly blazed to life in her belly and at the spot between her thighs. Slowly he drew the pads of his thumbs across her nipples until they grew hard and taut. She wanted his mouth on her, that hungry and sensual mouth, his lips hot and wet as he sucked on her nipples, drawing them into his mouth—

"That's it," he said, stripping her of her bra and shirt. "Let me hear you. Scream if you want to, Emilie. I want it all . . . everything you have to give."

A groan of pleasure, pagan and unbridled, broke free. The sound terrified her with its urgency even as it destroyed the last of her inhibitions with its pure, female power. It was all so strange yet so familiar, as if she'd been waiting for his touch to bring her back to life.

He lowered his mouth to her breasts, then slipped inside her heart and absorbed her fantasies. His mouth was hotter than flame against her skin. He captured one nipple between his teeth and she cried out again, not from pain but from a feeling so primitive and fierce that she wondered if she would survive another onslaught of sensation.

She was weightless, floating in the clouds, suspended in the throbbing darkness of an erotic dream. A rhythm, insistent and old as time, began to move inside her as her back arched, offering herself up to him on the altar of sensuality.

She'd waited forever for this moment. Dreamed about it. Longed for the only man who could take her on this journey.

And now she wanted more.

She wanted him to brand every part of her body with his mouth. She reached for the waistband on her white pants but he pushed her hands away and accomplished the task with a caress that brought her even closer to the edge of madness.

She was more beautiful than he'd remembered. Long slender legs, rounded hips, the dark red curls, wet with desire, that begged the touch of his tongue. The sounds she made as he touched her inflamed his soul.

She wanted to touch him, to reach out and place her hand against him and know that his power and heat belonged to her and her alone, if only for the night.

Again he seemed to understand what she wanted before she could translate desire into words. Rising from the bed, he stripped off his clothing. He didn't need the trappings of style to impress. His body was lean, powerfully muscled. A thick mat of dark hair furred his chest, narrowing down over his flat belly to—

He didn't disappoint. He'd never disappointed.

He was everything she'd remembered and more.

Tears sprang to her eyes and she blinked and looked away so he wouldn't notice.

But he did.

He dropped down onto the bed next to her and curled her body against his. "I want you," he said bluntly, "but as much as I want to make love to you, I've never taken an unwilling woman." He moved away so their bodies were no longer touching. "It's your choice, Emilie. Your decision."

She felt no shame. No guilt. This was a moment out of time. Her chance to taste life at its sweetest with no regrets to shadow her memories later on. She could be whoever she wanted to be tonight, captive or conqueror or both.

What she felt, what she wanted, went beyond words. She nodded, meeting his eyes, letting him touch her soul the way he'd touched her body.

He gathered her in his arms. They lay together on the bed, bodies pressed together, savoring the primitive feel of skin against skin. The pure, animal pleasure of it tumbled the last of her defenses.

She began to move against him, small, silken movements designed to tempt and tease. She felt as if she were spinning out of control and he was her anchor, the one real thing in a world she no longer recognized.

She was ready. He knew it by the sounds she made deep in her throat, by the moist heat of her when he cupped her with his hand, by the wild and hungry look in her green eyes when he parted her thighs and knelt between them.

He stroked her slowly at first, letting the need build between them to a fever pitch, then he deepened the motion until she cried out and he knew he could wait no longer.

"Now," she whispered against his mouth. "Now...now...now...."

Her words were all he needed.

She was softness and warmth, hesitant and passionate both. So small, so tight, that for a moment he feared he might hurt her with his power, but she urged him on, shuddering beneath him as she finally opened for him, sheathing him inside her welcoming body as if they had been made for each other by a benevolent god.

He had been the first man to know her body, to teach her the rites of lovemaking, and the thought that she had been with anyone else in the intervening years made him long to wipe their memory from her mind and brand her as his and his alone.

It was a fierce and primal call of the blood. She was all that he wanted—and more than he'd dreamed. He was a physical man and he knew a moment of pleasure with the woman he'd loved that ripped him apart then made him whole again.

And very soon he would come to understand that nothing about his life would ever be the same.

In the dark all things were possible.

That night she explored the wilder shores of sensuality with a man who understood her secrets before she gave them voice. As long as the moon cast its light upon them, the magic was theirs alone.

They napped briefly, then she brought a bottle of champagne to the bed, an old and dusty bottle she'd saved for a celebration that had never materialized.

"Cristal," he said, with an appreciative whistle. "I'm impressed."

"You should be," she said, climbing into the feather bed with him.

She eased the cork from the bottle and laughed as the resounding pop shattered the stillness of the bedroom. "I love that sound," she said, pouring the bubbly golden liquid into the cups. She placed the bottle down on the night table then raised her cup. "To unexpected guests."

He met her eyes. "To you."

She took a sip of champagne. "I suppose this is where we catch up on old times."

"I was hoping we'd talk about new times ahead."

She lay back against the pillows, eyes twinkling. "Suppose I tell you all about the Patriots' Day celebration the town's having tomorrow."

He groaned and she swatted him with a pillow sham.

"Laugh all you want," she said in mock outrage, "but it's big stuff here in Crosse Harbor. I'm sure you'll find this hilarious, but we all dress up in eighteenth-century costumes and drink cider and pretend the British are coming. Mayor Gold is playing Andrew McVie." McVie was Crosse Harbor's claim to fame, their one bona fide revolutionary war hero. Emilie had spent much of her childhood daydreaming about his daring rescue of General Washington not long before the Battle of Princeton.

She told him of the legend of the mysterious hero who had been cloaked all in black. Before a group of terrified onlookers, he'd vaulted onto Washington's horse and knocked the general to the ground, just as a musket ball split the air instead of the general's heart.

Emilie's family had always laid claim to the identity of the masked hero. Who else but a Crosse, they'd said, would have the fortitude to execute such a daring rescue? Everyone else credited Andrew McVie.

"Unfortunately, most of them were at a wedding celebration that day," she said with a laugh. "So much for family history."

"So who do you dress up as tomorrow?" he asked. "Betsy Ross?"

"No, smart guy, but I am the star of the show." Tomorrow morning, she told him, she would arrive at the village square for the festivities in a hot-air balloon.

"You're kidding!"

She crossed her heart. "Scout's honor. The research is faulty but it's great publicity for the historical society. How could I say no?"

"I wouldn't have had trouble."

"That's because you don't understand history and you never will."

"There are a few other things I do understand," he said, taking her champagne and placing it on the nightstand. "Why don't I tell you about them...."

They polished off the champagne afterward. Emilie padded back out to the kitchen, positive she had some more tucked away in the pantry.

"It's not Cristal," she apologized, "but I always say there's no such thing as bad champagne."

Zane, who had followed her into the kitchen, took the bottle from her.

Emilie disappeared back into the pantry and returned with a box of crackers, some peanut butter and a gift-sized jar of raspberry jelly. She arranged the items on an old lacquered tray she'd found at a yard sale the previous summer, then added two plates and a beautiful silver knife.

Back in her bed, she made a show of spreading the peanut butter and jelly on the tiny crackers, then presented each one to Zane with a flourish. He watched as she arranged the crackers along the edge of the plate in a semicircle. She'd always had the gift of turning straw into gold, he thought. Somehow she'd made the peanut butter and jelly taste like nectar of the gods.

"I haven't been to the market in ages," she said, refilling their cups, "or I would have made something wonderful for you. I *can* cook, in case you don't remember."

He grinned at her over his cup of champagne. "Don't mean to upset you, Emilie, but I never did give a damn if you could boil water."

Her eyes widened at first in dismay, then she laughed. "I guess it really doesn't matter, does it?"

"Not one damn bit." He pushed the plate aside. "Lie down."

"What?"

"Lie down," he repeated, more forcefully this time.

This was part of the fantasy. In that secret world, for just this one night, a man could command and a woman would obey.

The sheets felt cool and silky against her back. The champagne had softened the edges of her perception. It was difficult to tell where her body ended and the feather bed began. She was floating on a cloud, drifting along in a wonderful erotic haze—

"Zane!" She propped herself up on her elbows and stared at him. "What on earth—?"

"Trust me," he said with a piratical smile.

Her belly was warm. The champagne wasn't. She gasped at the sensation as it trickled toward her navel.

"You're crazy!" she said, laughing. "The sheets..."

The sheets, however, were in no danger. Drop by drop, inch by tantalizing inch, he licked the golden wine from her skin. Her navel...the slope of her belly...the juncture of her thighs...the sweet, sweet center of her being.

She threaded her fingers through his hair, holding him close to her, wanting this dark splendor to go on until she exploded into a thousand glittering pieces of gold.

But more than anything, she didn't want it to end.

Emilie sat up against the headboard the next morning and stared down at the man sleeping next to her. She'd been lying there for ages, eyes pressed tightly closed, listening to the slow and even ticking of the clock on her nightstand, praying she would wake up to discover she was all alone in her four-poster bed, same as she'd been every single night for the past five years.

She reached over and touched his shoulder. Hard muscle. Warm flesh. A living, breathing man.

Her ex-husband!

The gentle ache between her thighs...the delicious feeling of having been loved often and well...the sensation of standing at the edge of a high cliff and stepping out into space.

Vivid images of his mouth against her belly, his hands against the small of her back...she couldn't have imagined the deep, almost primal pleasures, no matter how hard she tried.

"Oh, God." She pulled the covers over her head and scooted to the edge of the mattress. She'd gone insane, that was it. Totally, completely mad.

Zane mumbled something and punched at his pillow. Emilie held her breath. He turned over and flung a hard, muscular leg across her hip, pressing up against her. She found herself leaning back into his warmth, wanting his strength....

"No!" she said out loud. Not again. She wasn't going to give in to the urge to throw caution to the winds again. Last night was last night. It was over, and if she had her way it would be forgotten as quickly as possible.

He wasn't her type of man and he never had been. He had no sense of history or continuity and he didn't feel the loss. Giving her heart to a man like Zane Rutledge was the romantic equivalent of tying herself to the railroad tracks and waiting for the next train to arrive. She'd escaped once with her heart intact. She'd be crazy to think she could escape a second time.

The magic that had existed between them yesterday couldn't possibly exist in the light of day. The sense of destiny, of being at the mercy of the fates—she'd blame it all on the full moon.

If you asked her, he seemed too darn comfortable sprawled out on her pale peach sheets with the satin duvet barely covering the essentials. He was tall and inordinately broad shouldered with powerful muscles that had felt like warm marble beneath her hands and—

Thinking like that would only get her in trouble.

Taking a deep breath, she took another look at him, determined to see only his shortcomings. Unfortunately, his shortcomings were not the first thing you noticed about Zane Rutledge. The packaging had always been impressive.

Wouldn't you think he'd have the decency to look out of place in such a frankly feminine setting? Instead, he looked as if he'd conquered her bedroom the same way he'd conquered her body.

The thought annoyed her and she poked his shoulder. "Zane." He stirred but he didn't awaken. "Zane, I have to leave in an hour."

"Mmph." He rolled over on his stomach and scrunched his face more deeply into the pillow.

She debated the wisdom of yanking at the corner of the duvet but the thought of all that naked male splendor was more than she could bear. She fled for the bathroom as if the hounds of hell were nipping at her heels, then closed the door behind her.

It was almost enough to make her laugh. Wasn't it the man who was supposed to be counting the seconds until he could make his escape? She read the women's magazines: she should be in the kitchen whipping up a delectable post-tryst breakfast of French roast coffee, fresh strawberries and cream while he calculated the distance between the bedroom and freedom.

Instead she found herself hiding in the bathroom, wondering if she could squeeze through the tiny window and vanish into the woods behind her house.

Quietly she padded into the dressing room off the bathroom, then slipped into a pair of leggings and an intricately laced bodice with ribbon ties that was part of her costume. It was too darned hot to wear the entire ensemble. She'd slip into the skirt and sash on the balloon.

She caught a glimpse of herself in the full-length mirror and stifled a laugh. She looked like *Mad Magazine*'s idea of an eighteenth-century streetwalker. An embroidered purse, faded with age, rested on the window ledge. She added a few dollar bills, two quarters, her driver's license and American Express card to the sewing kit inside, then tucked it into the waistband of her leggings. Sliding her feet into a pair of ballerina flats, she gathered up the flower-sprigged muslin skirt and draped it over her arm.

She glanced into the bedroom as she headed toward the kitchen. He was still asleep, sprawled diagonally across her bed as if he intended to stay awhile. It took a certain kind of person to get that comfortable that quickly. Emilie shook her head in dismay. Some things never changed.

A pad of hot pink Post-It notes rested atop the microwave. She scribbled a quick note with a bright green felt-tip pen, then stuck the note to the sugar bowl in the center of the scarred maple breakfast table. Her car keys hung from a hook near the door and she grabbed them on her way out.

Backing her car out of the driveway she absolutely refused to look at the sexy black Porsche parked there or think about its incredibly sexy owner.

She'd made a dreadful mistake. It was over.

She didn't intend to think about it again as long as she lived.

Langley Park was a good half-hour drive from her house. The morning was cool for late July and surprisingly clear. Although it was barely past dawn, the low-lying fog had already burned off. If it wasn't for the smell of auto exhaust mingling with the scent of salt air and summer flowers, it would be a perfect day.

She switched on the car radio, tapping her fingers on the wheel as an old Beach Boys' song came on. At twenty-nine she was too young to remember them in their prime, but there was something wonderful about their music that made it absolutely perfect for driving down a country lane on a beautiful summer morning.

Glancing in the rearview mirror she saw a jazzy black sports car making the left onto the main road. Impossible. The last she saw of him, he'd been sprawled across her bed sound asleep. She pressed down harder on the gas pedal but the sports car still trailed behind.

Gunning the engine, she made a sharp right onto a side road, only to see the black car follow suit a few moments later. Her heart lurched. Unless his Porsche had cloned a twin overnight, it was Zane. Maybe he'd lost his wallet or misplaced his watch. She slowed down, expecting him to pull even with her, but he maintained his distance. He looked grimly determined.

She turned back to the main road. He did the same. She considered trying to lose him, but the huge crimson balloon in which she'd soon be riding was a destination you couldn't hide. It hovered over the trees, gleaming bright red in the morning light, impossible to ignore.

"Stop tailgating," she muttered as she turned into the parking lot and swung into a spot. He'd always driven as if he had a death wish. She had half a mind to slam on the brakes then sue him for rear-ending her old sedan. It would serve him right.

He screeched to a stop behind her.

The Porsche's door swung open so fast it nearly popped its hinges. She considered locking her door and waiting out the storm but had the feeling he would peel the door open with his bare hands. He climbed from the sports car and stormed over to where she sat.

"Get out," he said through clenched teeth.

Some things an ex-wife never forgot. That tone of voice was one of them. Arguing with him seemed unwise.

She took a deep breath and swung her legs out of the sedan. He didn't offer any help. Not that she needed any, but it would have been a nice gesture.

In for a penny, in for a pound. She'd die rather than let him know the effect he had upon her.

"You made a wrong turn," she said airily, gesturing back toward the main road. "Manhattan's that-away."

At that moment he could cheerfully have wrung her neck. He'd been close to homicide a few other times in his life—most of them with Emilie—but this was the one time he could have legitimately labeled it a crime of passion.

"What the hell do you think you're doing?" he demanded.

She looked up at him, her grass-green eyes wide and innocent. "I'm afraid I don't know what you're talking about."

"The hell you don't."

Her gaze darted toward the crimson balloon, looming large in the open field. He grabbed her by the shoulders.

"A note on the kitchen table? You can do better than that, Em."

"Don't make such a big deal out of it." She looked up at him, the expression in her eyes all fire and heat. "I had to leave. I told you about Patriots' Day."

She pulled away and started toward the balloon.

He blocked her way. She tried to duck around him but failed. "Breakfast would've been a nice touch."

"Sorry if I'm not as experienced as the other women you've been with."

"You're out of milk," he said, "and you're real low on OJ. A man could starve to death."

"Thanks so much for the grocery update," she said, an edge to her voice. "I'll add them to my list."

"If I'd walked out on you like that, you'd call me a son of a bitch."

"I didn't walk out on you. I had an appointment."

"Bull. You ran for your life."

"Don't flatter yourself, Rutledge. I tried to wake you up but you were dead to the world." She ducked under his outstretched arm but he grabbed her again by the shoulder. "Don't you have a plane to catch?"

"This afternoon," he said. "That's why I'm here."

"Hey, Em!" Dan Walsh's voice carried across the parking lot. "Better get it in gear. We're ready to let 'er rip."

"I have to go," she said to Zane. "They rent those contraptions by the hour."

She started toward the balloon.

Rutledge was hard on her heels.

The roar of the propane gas tank sounded loud in the quiet morning air. Two young men sat in a yellow minivan, sipping coffee and stifling yawns.

"There's the rescue squad," said Rutledge, lifting his hand in greeting.

She winced. "What do you mean, rescue squad?"

"Spotters," he said. "The ground crew. They keep you in eyeshot in case you run into trouble."

"Don't say that! I've never been up in one of those things before."

"Nothing to it. You go where the winds take you."

"We're supposed to land near the village green."

"You will if nature cooperates."

"I suppose you've been up in a balloon before?"

He nodded, grinning broadly. "Balloons, gliders, ultralights."

"Have you ever considered gainful employment?" she drawled.

"Hey, Em," said Dan, looking from Emilie to Zane with open curiosity. "Baxter's ready to go." He pointed toward an overweight man in a red satin bomber jacket that had the logo Soul Man embroidered across the back. "He's grabbing a last cup of coffee before you take off."

Emilie took a good look at the cane gondola. It was about six feet wide with a large tank of propane secured to a support anchored to the centerpiece. "That's it?" she asked, swallowing.

"That's it," said Dan. "Just glad it's you and not me that's going up in that contraption. I told the missus you wouldn't get me going up in anything smaller than a DC-9."

Wise man. "How do I get in there?"

Zane grabbed her by the waist and swung her into the basket.

"Oh," she said, feeling very alone and very nervous. "My skirt," she said, pointing toward her car. "I'll need it when we land." The colonial hooker look wouldn't be appreciated at the Patriots' Day celebration.

"Do you mind?" Zane asked the older man. "We have a few things to settle."

Dan hesitated.

"It's okay," said Zane with a friendly smile. "Emilie and I are engaged."

"Well, whaddya know," said Dan as he turned to retrieve the skirt from Emilie's car.

"I could kill you!" Emilie leaned out of the basket and landed a punch on Zane's shoulder. "Why did you say something so stupid?"

"I didn't think you'd like it if I told him we were lovers."

"Why didn't you tell him the truth?"

"I told him the truth," he said with maddening male logic. "We were engaged . . . once."

"Now the whole town will be buzzing about it by the time we land."

"That we're engaged or that we're lovers?"

He was enjoying this altogether too much for her taste. "That I'm a total idiot."

"A touch of scandal never hurt anyone."

"You don't know Crosse Harbor."

"The hell with Crosse Harbor. Come with me today, Emilie." His smile was piratical, seductive. "We'll explore Tahiti, then I'll show you moonlight in Cairo and sunrise in Spain. We can breakfast in Paris and dine in Hawaii and make love in every city, port and country in between before we say goodbye."

Her heart thundered inside her chest as a fierce longing sprang to life. When she was old and gray and sitting on her front porch counting down the days, she'd have something to warm her soul besides an afghan and a pot of tea. The notion of walking away from reality and into a dream was extremely compelling.

"Absolutely not," she said over the insistent noise of the pilot burner.

"Last chance," he said, eyes narrowing.

"Forget it," she said. "I'm not going anywhere with you."

"Then I'll come with you."

She froze in place, shocked beyond description as he pulled up the two stakes anchoring the balloon to the ground then leaped into the gondola just as it started to rise.

"Hey!" Dan Walsh came running back from the parking lot, Emilie's skirt waving behind him like a muslin banner. "You come back here!"

"Do something!" Emilie shrieked. "Grab the ropes, Dan! Stop this thing!"

"Relax," said Zane, adjusting the flow of gas. "I'll get you to your celebration in one piece."

"Are you *crazy?*" she screamed over the roar of the propane tank that was propelling the balloon upward into the sky. "What do you think you're doing?"

"Taking you for a ride."

"You *are* crazy!" She backed away toward the edge of the basket. "Do you know how to fly this thing?"

"We'll find out soon enough." He fiddled with the control on the propane tank. "I've flown in hot-air balloons before."

"And I've flown in a 747. That doesn't mean I think I could fly one."

"That's the difference between us. I'm willing to give it a try." And the problem was he usually succeeded.

The flame shot upward while Emilie entertained visions of tangled power lines, and giant birds with very sharp beaks. The crimson silk balloon carried them higher and higher, leaving the safety of earth far below.

"I hope they arrest you for this," she said, struggling with a combination of fear and elation. He'd always been one for grand gestures and, fool that she was, she'd always been a sucker for them.

"Would you press charges?"

"Damn right. How dare you risk my life because you feel like pulling some crazy stunt!"

"Playing it safe has killed more people than craziness ever could."

"You think you can move mountains, don't you?"

Again that pirate's grin. "If there was something I wanted on the other side."

His meaning was unmistakable. She closed her eyes for a second against a flood of longing that went beyond sex to a place she'd thought existed only in her dreams. "I wish you hadn't done this," she whispered. "There's no point to it. Last night was last night. We both know there can't be a future for us." He was so perfectly gorgeous. Why couldn't he have the soul of a poet besides the face of a god? "I want more from a man than great sex. I want a man I can love."

"Most people would settle for great sex."

She shook her head and looked out at the panorama drifting by below them. If that had been enough they would still be married. "You never did understand."

"Are you sure *you* do?"

"What's that supposed to mean?"

"I get the feeling you're not as connected to that little town of yours as you'd like me to believe."

"I wish you wouldn't say things like that." She suppressed a shiver. He'd come too close to exposing her own fears. "Crosse Harbor is my home...my family helped build that town after the war was over."

"We're a lot alike," he said over her objections. "We're both looking for something we may never find."

"I'm not looking for anything." How false her words sounded. How empty. "I like my life the way it is."

"Like hell. You're an adventurer, Emilie. Admit it. You want more." His words, taunting and too close to home, broke the last of her control. She lurched across the swaying gondola and tried to land a punch. He grabbed her by the wrist then pinned her arm behind her, a wicked glint of amusement in his eye. She tried to pull away but each time she did, the gondola swayed alarmingly, sending her stomach into a roller-coaster dive.

"You got away with it once," he said, his tone holding a hint of steel. "I wouldn't push my luck."

Dangerous or not, she went to kick him in the shins but he pulled her up against his body and held her fast.

"Take a look, lady," he warned. "It's a long way down to earth."

She peered over the edge of the basket and gasped. They were sailing over the treetops, and into the clouds.

He saw the look of wonderment pass across her face, and his grip eased. "Impressive, isn't it?"

She nodded, unable to pull her gaze away from the panorama beneath her. "There's the main road into town," she said, pointing to a dark ribbon winding its way through the lush green countryside. "I never thought of it as beautiful before."

"Perspective is everything."

She shot him a sideways glance. "How cynical."

"Realistic."

"Isn't there anything in life that matters to you?"

"I thought you figured out the answer to that question last night."

"There's more to life than sex."

"Maybe," he said, "but there are few things that are better."

"I have to hand it to you," she said. "You always did know how to make the morning after as memorable as the night before. I wish—" She stopped. "My God, it's freezing." She wrapped her arms across her chest against the sudden drop in temperature. The sensation of movement had ceased. She felt as if the balloon was suspended in an icy, silver-gray cocoon. "Is this normal? It *is* normal, isn't it?"

The words were no sooner out of her mouth than the balloon and gondola dropped like an elevator shimmying between floors.

"It's okay," Zane said, raising the pilot flame to combat the sudden descent of the balloon. "Don't worry. Nothing's going to happen to us."

"There's something wrong, isn't there?"

"Those clouds." He pointed to the east. "A second ago it was dead clear. They blew in out of nowhere."

She started toward him as he worked with the sputtering tank of propane. The balloon shook like a platter of Jell-O, then dropped again.

"There's nothing to worry about," he said. "If I can just stabilize her, we can regain altitude once we clear this cloud cover."

He sounded so sure, so confident. One of the chosen few who could face down a tornado and live to tell about it. She wanted to believe him, but wicked crosswinds rocked the gondola and she was thrown against him as they plunged even deeper into the icy gray clouds.

He pushed her toward the floor. "Lie down," he barked. "I don't like—" His words were lost in the vicious gust of wind that roared in from the west.

The gondola tilted to the left like an amusement-park ride gone crazy, followed by the horrifying sound of the silk balloon ripping apart.

"Hold on, Emilie!" he shouted, as tatters of bright red silk drifted down from the sky. "We're going down!"

THREE

Emilie was alive—or at least she thought she was.

If she was dead she was fairly certain she wouldn't hurt as if someone had dragged her across five miles of bad road.

Her eyelids stung. Her shoulders ached. Knees, hands, face . . . every single part of her body, including the appendix she'd lost when she was three years old.

Champagne, she thought groggily. She had a vague recollection of a bottle of Cristal and—

And what?

She didn't know.

There must have been a good reason for polishing off a bottle of fancy French champagne but for the life of her she couldn't imagine what it was. If she'd had any idea what torture lay ahead of her, she would have reached for the diet soda instead.

She tried to pry open her eyelids but the sunlight was so intense that she just groaned and buried her face in the sand.

Wait just a minute. *The sand?* Spreading her fingers wide, she felt the area around her. Small pebbles, sharp pieces of shell, silky grains of beach sand—

"Dear God!" She pulled herself upright and opened her eyes. The sky overhead was an amazing, picture-postcard shade of blue, streaked with one or two snowy-white clouds. She found herself wishing she had a pair of sunglasses with her to shield her eyes from the glare bouncing up off the sand.

Gingerly she touched her face, her shoulders, wiggled her arms and legs. Nothing was broken, thank God. Her knees and hands were badly scraped, stinging each time the salt water lapped against the shore. She supposed she should be greatly relieved to be in such good shape, but she'd be even more relieved if she only knew how it was she'd come to be there on the beach.

With a groan she rose to her feet and looked about in an attempt to regain her bearings. The lighthouse rose from a rugged outcropping of rocks not thirty feet away from where she stood. She shuddered as she looked at the jagged boulders with the sharp edges and imagined what might have happened. Many a man had met his Maker along the shores of Eagle Island, the tiny spit of land across the harbor from her house.

"Think, Emilie," she said out loud, searching for a clue. "It's morning. You're near the lighthouse." She glanced down at her bizarre attire: an eighteenth-century bodice worn with black leggings and ballet flats. She was all in favor of mix-and-match but usually she tried to limit her choices to the same century.

A costume party, maybe?

If only she could think straight. Her brain felt as if it were filled with those Styrofoam peanuts that came tumbling out of packing boxes when you opened the lid. Not even the worst case of jet lag had made her feel so goofy and disoriented. She squinted down at her watch. The crystal was cracked but the second hand was still ticking. Nine in the morning on July twenty-fifth.

Suddenly the images came at her in a dizzying blur.

The sleek black foreign car with the lion's roar of an engine.

The uniform from a distant time.

A man with eyes the color of the deepest sapphire blue who'd held her close as the earth rushed up toward them and—

Zane!

She swayed on her feet as her center of gravity re-aligned itself. A mounting sense of panic gripped her by the chest, making it hard to breathe. Where was the gondola? The crimson silk of the balloon itself? Even the beach looked oddly different, as if all signs of life had been airbrushed away. No soda cans tossed into the dune grass. No bottles bobbing up and down at the water's edge. Not even a McDonald's wrapper or a Burger King bag, two of the most ubiquitous signs of human life.

But, worst of all, no sign of her ex-husband.

"Okay," she said out loud. "There has to be an answer to all of this." The sound of her own voice steadied her. "Just use your head, Emilie. You can figure it out."

Maybe it wasn't so confusing after all.

They'd drifted into some pretty weird cloud formations. She wasn't an expert in aeronautics, but everyone had heard stories about wind shear and crosscurrents and weird thermal down drafts that had vexed better pilots than Zane Grey Rutledge.

She remembered the stomach-churning sensation of vertigo as the gondola tumbled end-over-end after the balloon itself collapsed. She'd probably tumbled from the basket as they drifted past the beach, while Zane continued to struggle with the gas tank and the sputtering flame.

"The rowboat," she said, brightening. If she remembered right, the rowboat was tucked away near the east side of the lighthouse. All she had to do was jump into the boat, grab the oars, and she could be back on the mainland in fifteen minutes flat. She patted her waistband, amazed to discover that the embroidered purse with her car keys, American Express card and spare change was still there. A quick phone call to Crosse Harbor Taxi and she could make it to the celebration before they sent out the rescue squad to find her.

She turned, about to head toward the lighthouse and the rowboat, when something caught her attention. Shielding her eyes against the sun's glare, she scanned the shoreline. Everything seemed okay, but she could have sworn she'd seen a flash of crimson in the water.

"Yes!" she said, focusing all her attention on that point of color. There it was, something bobbing in the water about one hundred yards out. "Oh, my God! Zane!" He was struggling against the current and from the looks of it he was losing the battle.

She kicked off her shoes and raced for the water, trying desperately to keep him in sight, but he kept disappearing beneath the swells. *Hang on, Zane,* she pleaded silently as she plunged into the water. She was a strong swimmer, but the current presented a daunting challenge and each time he disappeared she thought her heart would stop beating.

"Zane!" she managed as she reached him. "Grab on to me!"

No response. A feeling of dread washed over her as she realized he had lost consciousness.

Working frantically, she rolled him onto his back, making sure his nose and mouth were clear of water. "You can do it," she urged. "Hang on to me."

Her words were as much for herself as they were for him. He was a big man, large boned and heavily muscled. She thanked God for the buoyancy of the salt water. Without it, they wouldn't have had a prayer.

The shoreline was growing closer and she rejoiced when her knees scraped against the sand. She stumbled to her feet in the calf-deep water, then continued pulling him toward safety. His eyes were closed. An ugly gash ran from the end of his right eyebrow down to his cheek. Blood mingled with salt water, leaving an ominous trail behind them.

"You can't be dead," she said as she struggled to haul him onto the sand. "You wouldn't dare do that to me." She tried to ignore the trail of blood, deeper and more frightening, that he'd left behind on the sand. He had to live, if only so she could tell him that he was the most arrogant, irresponsible, crazy excuse for a grown man she'd ever met.

She placed her ear to his chest but couldn't hear a thing. His color was dreadful. She pried open one lid, but he didn't stir. Her own breathing was rapid, ragged, and she willed herself to calm down before she hyperventilated, something that would do neither of them the slightest bit of good.

There was only one thing she could think of that might help and, straddling his chest, she began to administer CPR, praying the class she'd taken last year at the fire department had covered all the necessary bases.

"Breathe, damn you!" she ordered as she pounded his chest. "Breathe!"

It was like being trapped in a bad dream, the kind where you were running and running through an endless tunnel with no end in sight. But she couldn't stop, she couldn't just let him slip away, no matter how hopeless it seemed.

And then she heard it. Faint at first, then louder, stronger. He was coughing, spitting up seawater. And then the wonderful, miraculous sound of him breathing!

"I could kill you for this," she said, brushing away tears of relief. "You scared the living hell out of me."

When he came to, she intended to give him a piece of her mind, enough so that he felt guilty all the way to Tahiti. Her relief was short-lived, however, as her eyes were drawn again to the blood seeping into the sand. A man didn't bleed like that for no reason. She'd saved him from drowning, but what if there was something more serious wrong with him?

She was no doctor, but it occurred to her that the worst thing she could do was leave him lying on wet sand. He could go into shock or take some water into his lungs and end up with pneumonia. The thing to do was get him dry and warm, then call for help.

She glanced toward the lighthouse. She'd manage somehow to drag him through the sand but she wasn't entirely certain she'd be able to get him up the wooden stairs that led inside.

"You won't know unless you try," she said. The only thing she knew for sure was she couldn't leave him lying there on the sand. She retrieved her shoes, then approached him.

Gingerly she bent down and gripped him under the arms. He groaned loudly and she backed away, horrified that she'd obviously hurt him. She looked closely and noticed that his right arm was bent at an odd angle, one that made her insides twist into a knot.

She tried to favor his right side, but with his weight balanced unequally she felt as if she were dragging him around in circles.

"I know this hurts," she said apologetically, "but it's the only way."

Gripping him beneath both arms, she moved as quickly as her burden would allow, dragging him across the damp sand toward the bottom of the lighthouse steps.

She paused to catch her breath while she tried to figure out the best way to get Zane Rutledge up the stairs and into the lighthouse. She'd always believed wit and ingenuity could see a woman through any difficulty, but this time she had to admit that brute strength would have been a welcome addition.

"Zane." She touched his shoulder. "I need your help."

He mumbled something but didn't open his eyes.

"I have to get you inside," she persisted, "and I can't do it if you don't help me."

He opened his eyes and struggled to a sitting position.

"Do you know what I'm saying, Zane? I have to get you up those stairs."

He nodded. It was obvious even so small a motion as that caused him excruciating pain. Her heart ached for him but this wasn't the time for sympathy.

She moved to his left side. "Put your arm around me," she ordered in her most businesslike voice. "I'm going to help you stand."

His hold on consciousness was tenuous at best, but she managed to get his arm around her so she could use leverage to bring him to his feet. He tried to help. She could feel it in the way his weight shifted and in the sight of the beads of sweat breaking out across his handsome face.

"Too heavy," he said, ". . . forget—"

"Shut up," she ordered, not unkindly. "Keep your mouth shut and don't fight me. We'll get you up these stairs."

She'd spoken the words with great assurance, confident that her adrenaline would kick in and give her that little extra strength she'd need, and to her everlasting gratitude it did. They made it to the landing and she reached for the doorknob, overjoyed to discover that someone obligingly had left it unlocked.

That extra second might have spelled disaster.

They staggered together into the lighthouse as he once again lost consciousness. She tried to cushion his fall with her own body, wincing as his elbow caught her behind the ear.

What was one more bruise, she thought as she rolled him onto his back. She'd managed to get him up the stairs and into the lighthouse and now all she had to do was see to it that he was dry and warm. Then she could figure out a way to call for help.

"Now don't take this personally," she said with a wry smile as she reached for his belt. "This is all in your best interest."

He was as gorgeous today as he'd been last night. She felt like a pervert for even noticing. The poor man was in agony and she was admiring his pecs and abs. Still, you'd have to be blind not to notice.

Quickly she stripped him of his wet pants and shirt. She debated the wisdom of leaving his shorts on him, but decided that was ridiculous. A beautiful quilt rested on a ladder-back chair near the fireplace, along with a pale blue coverlet. She dried Zane with the coverlet, then used the quilt to wrap around his body for warmth.

She glanced around the front room of the lighthouse for a blanket or another quilt. It struck her as odd that these two beautiful specimens had been waiting for them here in the lighthouse. The place had been empty for more years than she could remember, and quilts as fine as these were collectibles that fetched impressive sums.

Sam Talmadge, one of the members of the Crosse Harbor Historical Society, was in charge of the light show that would be staged later tonight from the harbor. Could he have brought over the quilts to keep his grandkids warm while they watched the spectacle from the tower?

She'd never been inside the lighthouse before and she noted with interest that it looked anything but abandoned. The walls had obviously received a recent coat of whitewash. The wooden staircase that led up to the tower seemed sturdy and solid. The dilapidated radar equipment was gone and in its place were a compass, a telescope and a copy of *Poor Richard's Almanack*.

"Good for you, Sam," she murmured as she helped Zane to the trundle bed beneath the leaded-glass window. She'd always known Sam Talmadge was a great believer in period detail during these revolutionary war re-creations that Crosse Harbor was so fond of, but there was something about this that made the hairs on the back of her neck rise.

Maybe it was the silence. She tilted her head to one side, listening. Eagle Island was small, but it was never quiet. This morning all she could hear were the faint sounds of gulls circling overhead as they hunted for food.

Where were the sounds bouncing across the water from Crosse Harbor? Lawn mowers, the laughter of kids playing stickball, the putt-putt engines of the motorboat that cruised the waters in search of the ultimate fishing spot. Even the gnatlike buzz of small planes en route to the glitzier pleasures of the Atlantic City casinos was absent.

Apparently *everyone* was at the village green enjoying the celebration.

Or were they?

"Now you've really gone crazy," she said as she went back into the front room to check on Zane. Her imagination was running riot.

Her body had weathered the accident in good form; she was no longer so sure about her brain cells.

From the trundle bed Zane moaned loudly, bringing her back to the situation at hand.

"Oh, God," she murmured as she bent down to look at him. A huge purple bruise had blossomed over his right eye, which was almost swollen shut. She was positive his arm was broken and she wouldn't be at all surprised if he'd broken a rib or two in the bargain.

She sat next to him for a while as he drifted in and out of consciousness. It was almost noon. Her own clothes clung to her damply and her hair cascaded over her shoulders in a wild mane of wet curls and waves. Obviously no one had gone out looking for her. She had to do something. That broken arm wasn't going to set itself, and she knew that even a simple fractured rib could lead to complications.

There was only one thing she could do. She had to grab the small boat Sam Talmadge kept stashed behind the lighthouse and row back to the mainland for help.

"I'll be as fast as I possibly can," she said to Zane, who looked up at her with glassy eyes. "You have to stay in bed. Please, whatever you do, don't get up."

He nodded but she wasn't sure exactly how much he comprehended. He seemed to be in some kind of twilight zone, and it made her very apprehensive to see the self-confident Zane Grey Rutledge so vulnerable. She had visions of him tumbling down the stairs or something equally dreadful. If she had some rope she would even consider tying him in place, but there was nothing handy.

She made her way around to the back of the lighthouse. Funny thing, but she'd always thought there were beach roses on this side of the structure. Instead she found herself fighting her way through a veritable thicket of brush and untended shrubbery. She followed a stone path down toward the waterline where Sam kept his boat.

Only that wasn't Sam's boat bobbing gently in the water. Sam's boat was a small but jaunty metal vessel with a hot-pink heart painted along the starboard side and the name *Janine* emblazoned in throbbing Day-Glo purple. The rowboat bobbing in the water was enormous and built of wood with oars of a size to match.

Again that odd prickling sensation overtook Emilie, but she swallowed hard against it. Boats like that one hadn't been seen around Crosse Harbor for a very long time.

It's for the Patriots' Day celebration, she thought as she untied the boat then climbed into it. Sam Talmadge loved everything to do with holidays and he obviously was just making certain that all the revolutionary war re-creation details were right on the money.

She didn't know Sam all that well. For all she knew, he even raised his own turkeys for his Thanksgiving feast.

She hadn't rowed more than three feet before she found herself sorely regretting letting her membership at the health club lapse. The wooden oars were as heavy as they were huge and a few weeks of pumping iron would have been a welcome rehearsal for the enterprise.

"Think positive," she admonished herself as she struggled to move the oars through the water with firm, even strokes. She'd already done the impossible twice today when she'd saved Zane from drowning, then dragged him upstairs and into the lighthouse. Certainly she could manage to row a measly boat across the harbor and get help.

Lowering her head, she channeled all her concentration into the job at hand. Under normal circumstances a person could row across the harbor in fifteen minutes.

After a half hour, even Emilie had to admit that she was getting nowhere fast. Her arms trembled from the effort and she was starting to feel light-headed. At the rate she was going, she could row all day and all night and not see one of the usual landmarks.

But that was ridiculous. Still, there had to be some reason she was having so much trouble getting her bearings.

She stopped rowing and stared across at the shore-line she had known and loved all her life. Where was Brower's Dockside Restaurant? The marina with the brightly colored flags waving overhead in the sea breeze? The fishermen who should have been plying their trade for hours by now?

"Don't panic," she told herself. "There has to be a simple explanation."

Maybe this wasn't Eagle Island after all, and that wasn't Crosse Harbor.

Maybe she and Zane had floated down toward Cape May or up toward Long Branch.

Or maybe—

Her breath caught in her throat as she wondered why it had taken her so long to see what was right there in front of her very eyes. The water was crystal-line, the sky a blue so pure and deep that it reminded her of a Disney movie. The air had the sweet, fresh smell of a mountaintop. Where were the signs of modern life in the mid-twentieth century, the sludge and pollution and ever-present noise?

Her entire body jerked with the shock of realization. It couldn't be. Things like that didn't happen in real life. Peggy Sue and Marty McFly might travel through time but real people were bound by the laws of nature, not the whims of some Hollywood scriptwriter.

New strength filled her arms as she rowed back to the lighthouse, determined to unravel the mystery. She brought the rowboat into the dock, then tied it to a post.

The first thing she noticed when she reached the front door was the absence of a lock. In 1992? Not very likely. The hinges were new and free from rust. She burst into the front room and headed straight toward the window seat where she'd found the dog-eared copy of *Poor Richard's Almanack* that she had laughed at earlier.

Her hands trembled as she opened to the first page. *Printed in the year of Our Lord 1776.* No copyright. No reprint information. No mention of Doubleday or Simon & Schuster or McGraw-Hill.

Exhilaration rocketed through her.

It was a first edition.

And it wasn't very old.

FOUR

This couldn't be happening. There was no rational explanation for any of it, but Emilie couldn't deny the evidence right there before her eyes.

She'd seen enough reproductions in her day to know the difference, and this copy of *Poor Richard's Almanack* was the real thing.

She sank to the floor, her legs trembling too violently to support her weight.

No wonder Crosse Harbor had looked so different. The signs of progress had been erased as if they'd never happened.

At least, not *yet*.

A wave of dizziness spiraled through her body and she lowered her head, breathing in the clean salt air. The Industrial Revolution was yet to be born. Clean air, clear water—everything the citizens of the late twentieth century were struggling desperately to regain—were standard issue here.

Why on earth hadn't she realized it sooner? She lifted her head, then looked slowly around the cabin, trying to absorb the enormity of it all. No telephones. No electrical wiring anywhere to be seen. Amenities like indoor plumbing and refrigeration were still the stuff of dreams. She'd sensed something was different, but her eye had seen only what it was accustomed to seeing while her imagination had filled in the blanks.

Any reasonable woman would have been downright terrified to find herself catapulted back through the centuries. Fear of the unknown was one of the most basic human responses. Emilie, however, was galvanized with an almost supernatural energy that rocketed through her veins and flooded her mind with wonder.

Could it be that fate had had something planned for her, something more dangerous and exciting than even the adventure-loving Zane Rutledge had ever known?

"Oh, God," she murmured, glancing toward the man sleeping fitfully on the trundle bed by the window. He'd never believe it. No matter what evidence she paraded before him, he wasn't going to relinquish the world he knew.

Not without a fight.

Zane was a man comfortable in his own skin—and in his own time. The uncertainties and longings that had shadowed Emilie from the day she was born were alien to him. He took from life what he wanted and moved on when he'd had enough. How would he react when he found himself stripped of everything he knew and understood?

There had to be a logical answer, some combination of elements that would explain what had happened. She thought about that shimmering sense of destiny she'd experienced the first moment she saw Zane striding up the driveway.

How they had managed to end up back in the eighteenth century mattered less to her than *why,* but she knew he would never rest until he understood.

"What the—?" He opened his eyes and tried to prop himself on his right arm. "Jesus Christ!"

She was at his side in an instant. "Easy. Lie back down, Zane. You broke your arm."

He fell back on the bed, breathing heavily. "I'm either seeing two of you or you're the Doublemint twins."

His normally ruddy complexion seemed dangerously pale and she remembered the bloodstains on the sand. "There's only one of me," she said, struggling to keep her voice light and optimistic. "I'm right here." He tried to sit up but she placed a hand against his chest. "Don't."

"What happened?"

"Remember that stunt you pulled with the hot-air balloon?"

He nodded.

"Looks like we didn't make it to Langley Park in one piece." Or in the same century, but she'd save that nugget of information for another time.

"You . . . how are—?"

"A few bumps and bruises, but I'm okay. I'm afraid you took the worst of it."

"Good." Her heart turned over at that simple word. *He's in bad shape. You've got to do something!* The thought of setting his broken arm herself made her feel faint, but who else was there? She'd always prided herself on her knowledge of Crosse Harbor during this time period, but her mind was a blank. Until she gained her own bearings, she didn't dare risk searching for a doctor.

"How are you feeling?" she asked, leaning over him.

"Stupid," he said, wincing as he tried to shift position on the trundle bed. "Where are we?"

"The lighthouse," she said, truthfully enough.

"Where's the balloon?"

"I don't know. I woke up on the beach. You were in the water." And the balloon and gondola had both vanished without a trace.

"You saved my life?"

"I did what needed to be done."

"Remind me to thank you," he said, closing his eyes. "After I wake up...."

"Don't thank me yet, Zane," she whispered as he drifted back into sleep. Once he discovered where they were, he might not feel particularly grateful.

She'd survived the first round of questions, but the second round was bound to be her undoing. Wait until he asked her to dial 911 or arrange for an X ray or call his travel agent to change his flight to another day.

First things first. Survival was the order of the day. They needed water and they needed food. And if she could find some clean bedding and a smooth piece of wood to use as a splint she'd consider herself a very lucky woman.

She'd noticed a cellar door hidden beneath some wild strawberry vines when she was tying the rowboat to the dock after her aborted trip to the mainland. Hurrying outside, she elbowed her way past the thicket of vines and dune grass then breathed a sigh of relief.

There it was! The door was painted a dusty gray-ish blue, weathered only slightly by the salt air and water, and she was struck anew with the knowledge that the lighthouse was in its prime, not dilapidated and forgotten as it is—*was?*—now.

These hinges also were free of rust and she easily threw open the heavy door and made her way down the stone steps into the cool darkness of the cellar where, if her knowledge of colonial ways was half as good as she'd always believed, there was a better-than-even chance she'd locate a cache of preserved foods.

Ceramic pots of jams and preserved vegetables were lined neatly on wooden shelving, rough and un-finished, while a smoked ham hung from a hook sus-pended from the ceiling. It was far from an impressive display of goods but she couldn't have been happier if she'd been let loose in her local supermarket with a blank check.

"I hope you don't have a blood-pressure problem, Zane," she murmured as she made her selections. Without refrigeration, most people of the late eight-eenth century relied upon salt as a preservative. It was bound to be a shock to their modern palates, but beggars couldn't be choosers.

"We'll learn to adapt," she said, wishing she had a basket to carry her bounty. "We can—" She gasped as the food went flying and she found herself pinned face first against the damp stone wall of the cellar.

"State your business fast, lass," a man hissed as he held her against the wall, "or I'll slit your pretty throat from ear to ear." He was about her height and triple her strength and she wondered if she'd survived a lightning trip through the centuries only to meet her Maker in a musty root cellar.

She considered her options, her situation, the incredible happenings of the past twenty-four hours, then she did exactly what a proper eighteenth century woman would have done in her position: she fainted dead away.

Andrew McVie was many things, but a fool was not among them.

Ofttimes the enemy appeared in a comely package, designed to cloud a man's vision and lead him astray from the road he was sworn to travel.

These were dangerous times in which they lived. A wise man withheld his trust until a reason for that trust was offered.

But when the beautiful lass with the flaming red hair swooned at his feet, caution took second place to gentlemanly concern and he dropped his blade to the ground and sprang to her aid.

"Aye, you're a tall one," he said as he placed her on the stone bench near the door. Her shoulders were broad, her breasts rounded and full. She was a strapping woman, one a man could easily imagine warming his bed on a cold winter's night, but he started in surprise as he realized she wore not the usual maidenly array of skirts but a pair of black breeches much like his own.

If he'd seen a donkey walk like a man, he would not have been more surprised.

What manner of female was this? The cellar was bathed in shadows and he bent down to look more closely at her. No demure mobcap held back her fiery tresses; they cascaded freely about her face.

His eye was drawn to the hand at her throat and to the king's ransom he found there. On the middle finger of her right hand she wore a heavy ring of braided silver and gold and at her neck, on a fine golden chain, was a most amazing glass globe that seemed to have captured all the colors of the rainbow within its depths.

His gaze moved from the rise and fall of her breasts to the amazing display of wealth she carried on her person. He was uncertain which intrigued him more. He frowned as he followed the line of her limbs with his gaze. The black breeches were an affront to her womanliness. Surely she could afford to garb herself in clothing more pleasing to the eye.

He wondered if this lass might be part of the spy ring, but the notion was so absurd he laughed aloud. Who would believe such nonsense? No, this was probably the wife of one of the local fishermen, who had rowed across the inlet looking to steal a few potatoes for her children's supper. Times were difficult and the good woman could not be held accountable for doing what was necessary to keep their bellies filled. Yet, this woman looked as if she'd ne'er known hard times.

He remembered the early days of his marriage to Elspeth when he was struggling with his commitments to family and to his law practice in Boston and how, time after time, Elspeth and their son had suffered for his ambition. He had wanted so many things for them: a fine house and servants so Elspeth could sit by the leaded-glass windows and dream away the hours, a farm filled with produce instead of problems, a library stacked with the books necessary for the classical education he was determined his only son would enjoy.

Cinders now, all of it. Gone in the instant it took an ember from the hearth to ignite the blaze that had destroyed everything Andrew held dear while he pursued the almighty shilling.

Strange that the sight of this strapping woman should call to mind memories of his wife. Elspeth had been as delicate as a budding rose, but that fragile beauty had hidden a strength he had come to rely upon.

Mayhap too much, for Elspeth's strength had freed him to pursue the fleeting pleasures of life that had seemed so important at the time. That beautiful little boy they had created on a warm summer night had been more important than the accumulation of wealth. If only he had come to that realization while there was still time....

Today there was only the rebellion to give reason to his hours upon this earth and he intended to offer up his heart and spirit in the pursuit of independence, even if it ultimately meant nothing at all.

His last foray into English-held land on Manhattan Island had been for naught. He had come away with little but a sense of despair that grew stronger with each day that passed.

He had returned to the lighthouse, unlighted since the advent of war, hoping to find Josiah Blakelee awaiting him, but only silence had greeted his return. Blakelee, who owned a farm near Princeton, believed strongly in the cause of liberty and had offered his services in the pursuit of those blessings that flowed from independence.

Blakelee was one of those rare men whose demeanor and affability made him instantly welcome wherever he went. He also was possessed of a courage that took him many times into danger—perhaps for the last time some two months ago when he vanished north of Manhattan Island.

Andrew had intended to inflict upon Blakelee a sermon whose purpose was to impress upon the man the fleeting happiness to be found with family. Blakelee's disappearance tore at Andrew's soul, for it seemed to point out the ultimate hopeless nature of the struggle.

Family was all. Without it, even independence from the Crown meant little.

But Josiah Blakelee burned with the fires of liberty. For the past few months he had liberally quoted from Thomas Paine's *Common Sense,* and he understood what Sam Adams said better than Sam Adams did himself.

Last year, not long after Concord and Lexington, Andrew and Josiah had dined at Braintree with Samuel's redoubtable cousin John and John's wife, Abigail, and John Adams had given a vigorous discourse on the necessity to separate the colonies from the mother country.

Josiah had fair to boiled with the righteousness of the cause. There had been a time when Andrew, too, had known the same passionate commitment as shared by these two fine men, but that night he had only sat and listened, his mind on a time and place lost to him forever.

Mrs. Adams, a small and handsome woman whose powers of intellect were a match for those of her husband, seemed to sense that Andrew gave but lip service to the cause.

"There is a comfort to be found in a commitment to a cause," she'd said to Andrew over a pot of chicory-laced coffee. She and her husband had lost a child in infancy, and they took much solace in diverting their sorrows into pursuing a greater good.

And so it was that Andrew had joined forces with those who cared deeply about the pursuit of liberty.

Now he faced the unpleasant task of telling Blakelee's wife that her husband was still among the missing. A score of patriots had been rounded up near the Harlem Heights, and rumor had it they were on their way to one of the prison ships moored in Wallabout Bay in New York Harbor. A worse punishment could not be imagined, and it was Andrew's fond hope that Blakelee had been spared that fate.

The red-haired woman stirred, and his thoughts returned to the moment. The first order of business after she came around was to discover why the auburn-tressed woman had come to the root cellar—and what, if anything, she knew about his business.

If Emilie had fainted back home she would have found herself in the emergency room trying to explain her reaction to a pimply-faced intern with a fistful of forms and very little in the way of concern.

Instead she opened her eyes to find herself lying flat on a stone bench to the right of the cellar door. A man knelt on the floor next to her, a knife protruding from the waistband of his breeches. It took her less than a second to remember that, like Dorothy in *The Wizard of Oz,* she wasn't in Kansas anymore.

Sitting bolt upright she fixed him with her deadliest look. "Touch me once and you'll find yourself without a hand."

He rose to his feet. He was approximately her height, but much broader of chest and shoulders. He had the look of a solitary man, one who cared little for fancy clothing or grooming. His light brown hair was shaggy, drawn back into a ponytail and tied with a length of black fabric. His shirt was made of a rough cambric material in a natural color while his breeches were a faded tobacco brown. He looked oddly stylish to her modern eyes, yet totally in keeping with the time period.

"What brings you to this place, lass?" His accent was part Scottish brogue, part flat New England.

Would you believe a big red balloon? Withholding that particular nugget of information seemed the better part of valor. "Begging your pardon, sir, but I—I find myself in most difficult circumstances." She was horrified to find legitimate tears welling up in her eyes.

And elated to see the effect those tears had on this rough-looking man.

"Aye, now none of that," he said, his voice gruff.

"Begging your pardon, sir," she said, dabbing at her eyes. He handed her a rough square of cambric with the initial *A* in the corner. "Thanks."

Instantly she wished she had chosen her words with more care.

He looked at her, his thick, bushy eyebrows rising. "Thanks," he repeated. "What manner of speech is that?"

"It's—it's a family word," she said, stumbling badly over her white lie. "How foolish of me to use it with a stranger."

He nodded, outwardly accepting her explanation, but she had the feeling the warning bells were going off inside his head. *Watch yourself, Crosse! This isn't a man easily tricked.* She blessed her lifelong interest in the methods and mores of colonial America and prayed they'd be sufficient to see her through.

"Your most difficult circumstances—" he prodded.

I knew you'd come back to that. "My . . . my companion and I were partaking of a leisurely boating ride when a most unexpected storm swept us decidedly off course and onto your shores."

That flinty look reappeared in his hazel eyes. "And when did this aberration of nature occur?"

His word choice belied his rough-hewn appearance. The man was educated. This would be even more challenging than she had feared. "Before the noon hour," she said, praying her own word choice wouldn't give her away.

He nodded. That would explain why he had seen nothing untoward when he'd reached the lighthouse late last night. He had devoured a few slices of ham then dropped into a dreamless sleep, only to be roused by the sight of this redheaded woman helping herself to his cache of food.

"I see no evidence of a companion," he said, reminding himself that beauty and veracity did not always walk hand in hand.

"Inside the lighthouse," she said. "I fear he has a broken arm among other injuries."

He looked more closely at her. "Have you taken a full accounting of your own?"

She waved her hand and his eye was caught again by the glitter of gold and silver. "They do not matter."

Her gaze was as direct as a man's and Andrew found himself taken aback. "Would this man be your husband, then?"

"My friend," she said simply. "He has lost a great deal of blood, sir, and I—" Her voice caught and she lowered her gaze, but not before he saw the shimmer of tears.

"Take me to your friend, lass. I have not the skills of a doctor, but I can offer some assistance." He smiled, and his rawboned face was transformed. "'Twould be useful if I knew your Christian name."

"Emilie," she said, returning his smile. "Emilie Crosse." The name meant nothing to him, but it would be a few years yet before her family helped to build the town that would one day bear their name.

"'Tis odd circumstances under which we meet, mistress Emilie."

"You have me at a disadvantage, sir." *This is fun,* she thought. Like dancing a minuet with words instead of steps.

"Andrew," he said. "Andrew McVie." He reached for her. "Mistress Emilie, are you feeling faint?"

Mistress Emilie was just plain blown away.

Andrew McVie!

The man whose name had been on the lips of every Crosse Harbor schoolkid for the past two hundred years—the most wanted rebel of them all—was standing right here in front of her! Was it only last night that she had recounted McVie's story to Zane, glorying in the tale of courage and patriotism?

"It has been a long and difficult morning," she said at last, accepting McVie's hand as she rose to her feet. "I pray you will disregard my momentary weakness."

"Weakness in the fair sex is a most agreeable trait."

"Strength is more agreeable, no matter the sex," she returned. How disappointing it would be to discover her childhood hero was a male chauvinist pig. "Don't you agree?"

The woman was sharp-tongued and swift to voice her opinions. That would explain how it was that she remained unwed. "Take me to your companion," he said, ushering her toward the stairs that led out from the root cellar. "A broken arm left untended can rob a man of his ability to earn a living."

You don't know the half of it, thought Emilie as she climbed the steps, wincing at the assault of late-afternoon sunlight. Zane was a physical man. He was accustomed to pushing himself to the limit, then beyond. Being restricted in any way would drive him right up the wall.

Unfortunately, that was the least of their worries.

Andrew followed the redheaded woman along the stone pathway toward the front door of the lighthouse. Her abundant tresses seemed to capture the sun, then send its fire shooting back toward the sky. He wondered how she would look with her auburn waves piled neatly atop her head in the style the good women of his acquaintance favored.

Of course, her style of hairdress was not the only unusual thing about the woman. He allowed that her strange attire must be the result of the accident. Perhaps her skirt had been torn on the rocks or she had used the fabric to bind her companion's wounds.

She had no womanly embarrassment about her attire. She was neither coy nor modest. She walked before him with her head held high, unmindful of the shocking way her limbs were outlined for the world to see. The breeches fit her like a second skin. He wondered how or why she had knitted a pair designed to cling to her curves in quite so indecent a fashion. He could plainly see the shape and fullness of her buttocks, the slender shape of her thighs, the—

She stopped abruptly and turned to meet his eyes. He felt as if he had been caught stealing apples from an unsuspecting farmer's orchard.

"My companion isn't—he is not . . . thinking as himself since our boating accident."

McVie looked back toward the dock where the rowboat was tethered.

"That's not our boat," Emilie said quickly.

"Where is your boat?"

"I don't—I do not know."

"I see no sign of it anywhere."

"Of course you don't," she said, prepared to weave a tale of misfortune. "We found ourselves dashed against the rocks, torn apart by fearsome waves, then tossed into the ocean with naught but our wits to save us." She hadn't had this much fun since her honeymoon, and that was six years ago.

Or was it two hundred and ten years ahead? She wasn't entirely sure.

She would have continued spinning her tale of adventure and derring-do, but McVie threw back his head and started to laugh.

"That is unconscionably rude of you, Mr. McVie."

"I do not know what the truth is, lass, but this story of yours is most enjoyable."

"It's not a story," she protested. Well, maybe the part about the boat was, but that was picking nits. "I saved his life."

Were it any other but the strapping lass before him, Andrew would have had grievous doubts. He had never known a woman who was tall enough to look him straight in the eye before and the sensation was unsettling. However, it did explain her ability to save a grown man from drowning.

His Elspeth had been a tiny creature, barely reaching his shoulder even in her best shoes. She had made him feel strong and protective. Everything a man should feel about the woman he had taken to wife. Sometimes late at night when sleep danced just beyond reach, she came to him in the shadowy world of his imagination, and he could smell the scent of vanilla on her skin and hear the sweet sound of her laughter as she said, "Put aside the ledger, Andrew. The hour is late and our bed is warm."

No, this Emilie Crosse was a different type of woman and he found himself wondering what type of man would be a suitable companion.

Emilie approached the front door with trepidation. This wasn't going to work. She was crazy to think she had a chance of pulling it off. Here she was bringing a revolutionary war hero inside to talk to a man who thought he was still back home in the twentieth century.

Talk about a worst-case scenario.

She cast a glance over her shoulder at Andrew McVie. He was justly suspicious of her. The wonder of it was that he hadn't carted her off to the nearest representative of the law.

But wait until he met Zane. The minute Zane opened his mouth, McVie would know beyond a shadow of a doubt that something was amiss. She supposed she could explain Zane's "eccentricities" away by saying he'd suffered a blow to the head in their fictitious boating accident, but McVie wasn't likely to buy that for long.

Let Zane be asleep, she prayed silently as she reached for the doorknob. Maybe just a tad unconscious. She needed time to explain the situation—and he would need time to accept it.

What happened after that would be anybody's guess.

Zane paced the length of the front room, waiting for Emilie to return. His arm hurt like hell, he was sure he had the mother of all shiners over his right eye and he was hungry enough to eat sand.

He'd looked all over for a telephone, but to his surprise he couldn't find one anywhere. As a matter of fact, he hadn't been able to find a jack or wires or any other signs of human habitation. The place looked new. Rustic, but basically new. Emilie had mentioned something last night about renovations to the lighthouse. Maybe they just hadn't gotten around to rewiring the place.

He glanced at his watch. The damn thing must've taken as much of a beating as he had when the balloon collapsed on them. Too bad he hadn't bought a Timex. At least then he'd know if he had a prayer of getting to the airport on time. Let alone to a doctor for his arm.

Since Emilie had told him about the balloon accident, he'd racked his brain in an attempt to figure out what had gone wrong, but all he could come up with was a cloudy memory of watching the earth coming at him like a runaway train, and then nothing. The relief he'd felt when he saw Emilie had weathered the accident with nothing worse than a few bumps and bruises was still enough to make him consider a return to religion.

She'd said no when he'd asked her to throw caution to the wind and join him on his trip to Tahiti, but that was before they'd faced the grim reaper together. She'd always wondered what he found so seductive about courting disaster. Now that she'd experienced the ultimate thrill, maybe she'd understand.

He'd learned a long time ago that you were never more alive than you were when death was staring you in the eye. That adrenaline pumping through your veins...the white-hot certainty that you were running at top speed...the rush of pure elation when you met the challenge and emerged victorious.

Last night with Emilie in his arms he'd known the same sense of danger and renewal. He didn't believe in happy endings and he never would, but he couldn't help but wonder if maybe they should have fought harder to make it work—at least a little while longer.

Sara Jane used to say—

He stopped.

"That's it," he said out loud. That's what was different. For the past hour he'd been trying to figure out what had changed, and now he knew.

He wasn't hearing Sara Jane's voice any longer.

He didn't know exactly when it had happened, but sometime last night he'd stopped feeling as if his grandmother was inside his head, trying to tell him something.

But he knew when it was: when he'd taken Emilie in his arms and—

No way was he about to pursue that thought. What he and Emilie had found last night had been both real and powerful. He'd be the last person to deny that. She'd stirred something in his soul, a sense of wonder and yearning that he'd forgotten was even possible.

But to read anything more into it than a wonderful case of chemical attraction was to fall prey to the same romantic babble that had led to disappointment the first time around.

The rasp of the doorknob being turned brought him up short. Maybe she'd reconsidered Tahiti....

"He might be sleeping," Emilie said to Andrew McVie as the door to the lighthouse swung open. "We should—"

"What the hell took you so long?" Zane demanded as they entered the room. "If we're going to make that plane, we'd better—"

Poor Andrew stopped dead in his tracks and stared at Zane as if he'd encountered a hungry bear in his den. A hungry bear with a brightly colored quilt knotted at his waist. She could only imagine what Andrew must be thinking. Nervous laughter tugged at her, but she swallowed hard in an attempt to control it.

"This is Andrew McVie," said Emilie, forcing a pleasant smile and praying Zane would see the plea in her eyes. "I am afraid this is his home in which we have sought refuge."

Zane glanced around the room. "Monastic, isn't it?"

Andrew stepped forward. He seemed unconcerned at the difference in their heights and Emilie had the feeling that, appearances notwithstanding, the two men were more evenly matched than either might care to admit. "I have yet to learn your name, sir."

Emilie sensed rather than saw Zane's hesitation as he extended his left hand. Did he remember her stories about Andrew McVie's heroic exploits? *Please, God, let him forget....*

"Zane Grey Rutledge."

"What manner of name is Zane Grey?" asked Andrew, obviously puzzled. "Are you German?"

Zane met Emilie's eyes. "Is this guy kidding?"

She could only shake her head miserably.

Zane turned back to McVie. "I'm named after Zane Grey."

Andrew looked at him blankly.

"The writer," Zane persisted, apparently enjoying the other man's confusion. "He wrote Westerns. Cowboys...Indians...the last frontier."

McVie had yet to take Zane's outstretched hand. "Cowboys?"

"Okay, I give up." Zane backed away, shaking his head. He looked again toward Emilie. "What the hell's going on here?"

McVie glared at the taller man. "I must ask you to refrain from such language in front of mistress Emilie."

Zane's lips twitched as if he was about to laugh, but apparently he thought better of it. "Isn't this carrying the whole revolutionary war thing too far, McVie?"

Both men turned to Emilie, who wished quite fervently that she had disappeared along with the crimson balloon and the basket.

"I do not know what you mean, Zane," she said demurely, then turned toward Andrew. "I am afraid Mr. Rutledge hit his head upon the rocks when we ran aground. He is still discombobulated."

Andrew visibly relaxed.

Zane, however, was beyond understanding. Discombobulated? What the hell kind of word was *discombobulated?* He was one step away from going ballistic. "I don't know what in hell's going on around here, but if somebody doesn't give me some answers soon, I—"

"Leave the room, mistress Emilie," said Andrew, not taking his eyes from Zane. "Mr. Rutledge and I have a most pressing matter to discuss."

"The only thing I want to talk about is getting to the airport on time to make my plane."

"Air-port?" Andrew looked toward Emilie. "His injury may be more grave than you figured. He speaks nonsense."

Zane approached the smaller man, bristling with righteous male indignation. "Why don't you try saying that to my face, pal?"

Emilie stepped between the two men. "Please! We forget why we're here, gentlemen. Zane's arm needs tending and the hour grows late even as we stand here."

Zane looked down at her, his handsome features creased in puzzlement. "You sound weird."

"It must be your imagination."

"The hell it is."

McVie stepped forward. "Rutledge, I fear your manner is insulting to mistress Emilie."

Zane's mood slid from bad to worse. "If 'mistress Emilie' has a problem with my manner, she'll tell me."

"Your arm," said Emilie. "Please...."

"Lie down on the bed," McVie ordered Zane. "Mistress Emilie, bring me a thick branch from the stack of kindling near the cellar door."

"That guy's not laying a hand on me," Zane snapped, barring Emilie's departure. "Don't you have an emergency room in this town?"

"We will have," said Emilie.

"Emergency room?" said McVie. "Is this a new language he speaks or is it the blow to his head?"

"I'm going to land a blow to your head, if you don't butt out," Zane said to McVie.

McVie reached for his knife, wrapping his fingers around the hilt in a threatening gesture. Zane grabbed an andiron from the hearth and stared menacingly at the other man.

Emilie, at the end of her rope, knew there was only one option left to her.

"Gentlemen," she said, stepping between them, "we have to talk."

FIVE

"I've got a plane to catch," Zane said. "The only thing I want to talk about is whether or not you're coming with me." It was time to move on and he wanted Emilie with him.

"Sit down," she said, gesturing toward the trundle bed. "This is going to take some time."

Andrew McVie, still clutching the knife, glanced from Zane to Emilie. At first glance he had mistaken Rutledge for his compatriot Josiah Blakelee, and the similarity in size and physique still had him shaking his head in wonderment. It occurred to him that this could be part of an elaborately concocted scheme whose ultimate goal was the defeat of the thirteen united colonies.

"You can sit over there," said Emilie, pointing to the straight-back chair near the hearth.

He shook his head. "Nay, mistress. I think not." He took a position near the door. There was nothing about the situation that could be deemed normal and it was his intention to be prepared for any happenstance.

"Oh, God. . . ." Her words were exhaled on a sigh. She looked from one man to the other. "This is going to be tougher than I thought."

"Just spit it out," said Rutledge. "If we're going to make it to JFK, we'd better—"

"We're not going to JFK."

"You mean *you're* not going?"

She shook her head. "Nobody's going to JFK because there *is* no JFK." She laughed, but there was the sound of panic in her voice. "In fact, there are no airplanes, no automobiles, no computers. You name it and you won't find it here."

"What manner of object is a com-pu-turr?" asked Andrew.

Zane whirled toward the other man. "What's with you, McVie? You been living in a cave for the past twenty years?" *McVie...Andrew McVie...why does that name sound so damn familiar?*

"Don't you understand?" Emilie's expression was as intense as her tone of voice. "This isn't Crosse Harbor and it isn't 1992. We've gone back in time."

Zane's gut twisted. It was worse than he thought. She'd obviously lost her mind. He stood. "Listen, it's been a lousy morning. Why don't you lie down on the bed and get some rest. McVie can take me into town

to the doctor. A broken arm's no big deal. I'll be back
before you wake up from your nap—''

"Listen to me, Zane!'' Her voice filled the room.
"Look around you! This isn't the world you knew.''
She gestured toward McVie, who was standing, eyes
watchful, near the door. ''This is *his* world!''

Zane met McVie's eyes. ''Do you know what she's
talking about?''

McVie shook his head. He tapped the side of his
head with his forefinger in a gesture Zane recognized.

Unfortunately so did Emilie, and she let out a
shriek of exasperation.

"Where are the electrical outlets?'' she demanded, poking Zane in the chest. ''The telephone?
Refrigerator? Have you heard a car go by or seen an
airplane or motorboat? Where's the bathroom, for
God's sake, Zane?''

Sweat broke out on the back of his neck. ''You told
me last night that they were restoring the lighthouse,'' he said, evading the issue. ''They just haven't
gotten around to everything yet.''

"That's right,'' she said, meeting his eyes. ''It will
take another century or two to finish the job.''

He stormed through the lighthouse as a dark cloud
of fear settled itself around him. ''You're wrong,'' he
said, overturning tables and kicking open doors as he

searched for proof. "You don't go to sleep in one century then wake up in another." There had to be another explanation, some simple answer that they were overlooking.

Emilie was hard on his heels as he made his way up the winding staircase toward the lookout tower. "Remember the cloud cover that blew in on us? You said you'd never seen anything like it before."

"Shut up!" he roared. "I don't want to hear it. This whole thing is nuts. *You're* nuts!"

She laid a hand on his forearm. "I'm scared, too," she said, her voice soft. "It's normal to be—"

"It's bullshit," he said, pulling away from her.

"No, it isn't, Zane. You know it isn't."

"I'll prove it to you." He pulled himself up into the lookout tower, trying to ignore the sharp waves of pain radiating from his forearm to his shoulder and across his chest. "Most of the lighthouses today are automated."

"Not this one," said Emilie, popping up at his side.

"Bet me."

Emilie's heart ached for him. He was a man accustomed to being in control and this was a situation over which neither had anything resembling control. Beads of sweat poised over his upper lip and he held his arm at an odd angle, almost as if the appendage belonged to somebody else. Under normal circumstances

Zane's arm would be set by now and he'd have access to the painkillers almost everyone took for granted.

"This is a trick," he said, staring at the oil and wick that served as a beacon. "Some kind of practical joke."

"Look toward the west," she said quietly. "Toward the harbor. That's not the Crosse Harbor we left behind."

He didn't want to look. There was something in her tone of voice, some deeper note of truth, that was scaring the hell out of him.

He turned slowly, bracing himself, then looked around.

Maple trees, heavy with leaves, crowded the shore. The sky was a rich, deep blue streaked with a few high cirrus clouds. The water was clear, the air was fresh, the whole thing was impossible, but in his gut he knew Emilie was right.

"Beautiful, isn't it?" she whispered, coming up behind him.

He nodded. There was a certain wild magnificence to the sight before him but he refused to acknowledge it. Still, he found it impossible to turn away from the sight. "What year?"

"I'm not certain." She paused for a moment. "Around 1776, as near as I can tell."

His body jerked as if struck a blow. "How do you know?"

"*Poor Richard's Almanack.* I found it near the trundle bed."

Her face seemed lit from within, almost incandescent with the thrill of discovery, and it occurred to him that this woman wasn't like anyone he'd ever known. She wasn't afraid or angry or any of the hundred other emotions anyone else in their position would be feeling. The notion of being torn from the life she knew and thrust back in time seemed to fill her with excitement, as if she'd been waiting all her life for this moment.

Last night with her in his arms he'd felt they were on the brink of a new relationship, but he'd never imagined it would be anything like this.

"Zane." She moved into his line of vision. "Are you—"

"I'm okay," he said, not entirely convinced of that fact. "I just wish I'd paid more attention to high school history classes."

"I may not remember all the dates, but I paid close enough attention to everything else." Again she touched his arm and images from the night before seemed to shimmer in the air between them. "Think of it, Zane. The revolutionary war is going on and we're the only people on earth who know how it's going to end."

Andrew McVie had heard more than enough and he stepped from the shadows.

"Aye, 'tis talk like that that has led many a man to an early grave."

Emilie and Zane turned to see him standing at the top of the stairs, brandishing a wicked-looking knife.

"Oh, not again." Emilie motioned toward the weapon. "Come to your senses, Andrew. We're on your side."

He narrowed his eyes and looked from one to the other. "Lass, your countenance is most agreeable but I fear there is still much about you and your companion to cause me great affliction."

"You heard what I said, didn't you?" The mistress Emilie fixed him with a look from those huge green eyes of hers and it was almost his undoing.

"You spoke of war," he said, knife at the ready should they try to make an untoward escape. "What is it you know about the engagement?"

Mistress Emilie met her companion's eyes, then looked back toward Andrew. In television and movies there were rules that went hand in hand with time travel. Too bad she couldn't remember any of them at the moment. "I know that your cause will be victorious."

"And how is it you know to which cause I pledge my allegiance?" He'd been right to hold the couple in suspicion, and now the redheaded woman was about to betray her true convictions.

She hesitated.

"Aye, lass, it's as I thought. A noble ruse, I must admit, but one that will know an unhappy resolution."

"Wait a minute!" said the man with the inexplicable name. "What did you say your name was?"

It occurred to Andrew that he'd been a fool and more to have given his rightful name to these strangers. "McVie," he said with reluctance.

"That's it!" Zane Grey Rutledge looked unconscionably pleased with himself. "You're the one who saved George Washington from an assassination plot."

It took Andrew but an instant to react. He put the knife between his teeth, grabbed the redheaded woman, then held the knife to the softest part of her throat. "How is it you know anything about me?" he asked in a tone that brooked no argument. "Anything less than the truth and the lass will know the sting of my blade."

Zane lurched forward, ready to do battle, only to have the full fury of his broken arm drop him to his knees at the first swing of his fist.

"Touch her, McVie, and I'll kill you."

If Emilie felt anything more than surprise at the situation, she hid it well.

"I know this is difficult for you to believe, Andrew, but we're from the future."

Andrew's laugh echoed in the empty tower. "Witches no longer cast their spell in the colonies, mistress Emilie. Not even in Massachusetts."

"This isn't witchcraft or fortune-telling," she persisted in that oddly accented voice of hers. "We had an accident—"

"I know," he broke in. "On your boat."

"Well, not exactly." He released his hold on her, then spun her around by the shoulders so he could see her face. "It was a balloon accident."

He knew he must resemble the village idiot with his mouth agape, but her words were so preposterous that he could do naught but laugh. "You speak nonsense."

But she was not to be deterred. "I speak the truth. Zane and I were floating in a hot-air balloon. We sailed into bad weather and crashed to the ground." Her laugh was uneasy and it made him suddenly uncomfortable. "Only thing is, we misjudged our destination by about two hundred years."

He felt the way he had the last time he attempted to drown his prodigious sorrows in a tankard of ale at the Bunch of Grapes. "So you say you come from the future—from the year nineteen hundred and seventy-six?"

Emilie's mouth turned up in a smile. "Well, nineteen hundred and ninety-two, but who's counting?"

Andrew was. Every single unbelievable year. "I suppose you have proof of this phenomenon?"

She looked toward Zane. "Do you have anything?"

He shrugged. "I'm naked under this blanket, Emilie. How about you?"

"I don't—" She stopped. "Wait a minute. I think I *do* have something...."

Andrew watched with great caution as she reached into the waistband of her breeches and withdrew a heavily embroidered purse much like the ones the good women of his acquaintance carried on their person.

Emilie looked at the purse and tears of wonder sprang to her eyes. The faded silk threads were vibrant, pulsing with rich color. The worn spots on the outer edges were plush with texture. If she'd required more proof of their situation, this was it. She felt Zane's eyes on her as she untied the ribbon then withdrew a one-dollar bill.

She handed the single to McVie. "This should do it."

McVie took the bill from the redheaded woman. There was a linenlike texture to the note that felt substantial to his work-roughened fingers.

"Take a close look," she urged.

"Federal Reserve Note," he read from the top of the currency. "The United—" He blinked. Surely his eyes were playing tricks upon his brain.

"The United States of America," said Emilie. "And that's George Washington right there looking back at you."

It was more than Andrew could comprehend. "General Washington?"

Emilie smiled wide. "*President* Washington. The first president of the United States of America."

"This is— I cannot...." His words trailed off as he stared again at the currency in his hand. Indeed, the portrait of the white-haired man did seem to bear more than a passing resemblance to the likenesses he'd seen of His Excellency, the general. He read off a string of letters and numbers near the upper right-hand corner, then looked twice at the words beneath. "Washington Dee Cee. What does that mean?"

"District of Columbia," said Rutledge. "The capital of the fifty states."

"It's on the Potomac River," offered Emilie. "Near your Maryland and Virginia."

Her words were lost on Andrew. "*Fifty* states?"

"Thirteen colonies became fifty states," said Emilie, eyes shining. "From the Atlantic Ocean to the Pacific."

A green seal was positioned beneath the name of the nation's capital and within that seal were the words *Department of the Treasury 1789.*

Andrew dropped the bill as if it had suddenly caught fire. His chest felt tight, making it hard to draw sufficient breath into his lungs. He looked again at the redheaded woman and her tall companion. It would explain so much about them. Her strange attire, the king's ransom in precious metal that bedecked her person, the odd manner of speech they both affected.

There was no denying Rutledge's fury when the mistress Emilie related the story. The man had had the look about him of a wild animal caught in a trap. Andrew knew the feeling of being caught in circumstances not of his own design and, despite his better judgment, he well understood Rutledge's agitation.

But what then was he to make of mistress Emilie? Andrew recognized something of himself in the redheaded woman, as well, and that threw his mind into a whirlpool of confusion.

The patriots had been engaged in the battle against British tyranny for more than a year and still had not achieved a victory. His Excellency, General Washington, had sent numerous missives to the Continental Congress in Philadelphia, begging the good men of conscience to provide more troops, more food, more weapons to aid in their cause.

Andrew had seen the swift horror of Lexington and Concord. Little had happened since to raise the spirits of the patriots.

"You spoke of the general," he said, choosing his words with great deliberation. "Of some danger—?"

"A plot to assassinate him," said mistress Emilie. "In my day you are thought of as a hero."

He was many things, but a hero was not among them. "And what is it that I have done to deserve such praise?"

She told him quickly of a man, garbed all in black, who had risked his own life to save the commander of the Continental army.

"When did this happen?"

"In the summer of 1776."

Andrew grew quiet. July was all but gone. "Can you put a date and place to this event, mistress Emilie?"

"I wish I could, but there has always been a degree of uncertainty attached to the event." She hesitated, dropping her gaze in a most uncharacteristic fashion.

"Mark me well, mistress. I am not a man afraid of harsh news."

"The truth is that I have no news, Andrew. From that moment forward, you exist only in speculation." Her smile was gentle and for a moment he was reminded of his Elspeth. "I have always imagined that you retired to a life in the country with a wife and children and lived to be a very old man."

Her words struck a chord deep inside him, hidden away in that place where love had gone to die. For the past few years he had not felt himself long for the world. When Elspeth and their son had died, they had taken with them all that was fine and good in the world, leaving him behind to mark the days until he met his Maker.

Some men joined the militia because the fires of independence burned hot in their breasts. Those men became generals, leaders of men. Andrew had joined because he had nothing of value to lose. They made him a spy.

He looked at Emilie, who was standing near her companion. "How is it you come to know the ways of this time to such a degree?" Were he to find himself in Plimouth colony at the time of its beginnings, he would be without a clue as to proper behavior. "Sorcery, perhaps?"

"Nothing so exotic. I earn my living—Zane!"

Rutledge suddenly doubled over, clutching his right arm against his chest.

"He's in pain," she said, eyes wide as she looked at Andrew. "Can we fetch a doctor?"

"I cannot risk such an enterprise," he said. "My presence here cannot be revealed."

"I can risk it," said Emilie. "Tell me the best place to moor the rowboat and I can find my way into town."

"Over my dead body," said Zane, gritting his teeth. "I'm fine."

McVie slid his knife back into the waistband of his breeches and approached. "You are a fortunate man," he said, looking at Zane's right forearm, which had sustained a fracture. "If the bone had broken the skin, the cause would be lost."

"You're the local hero," Zane growled, "not the doctor."

"A physician would tell you same as I, Rutledge. You and your arm would be parting company."

Zane gestured toward McVie. "Keep him the hell away from me."

"We have to set that arm, Zane."

"I'll do it myself."

"You're talking like a fool."

"Hey, I'm not the one who says a balloon dropped us into the middle of the Revolution."

Emilie started to laugh. She couldn't help it. Maybe it was lack of food or the jet lag to end all jet lag. She didn't know. But whatever it was, the whole thing struck her as so absurd, so funny, that the laughter bubbled up and it wouldn't stop.

It took Zane all of about five seconds to catch the wave. He laughed until his sides hurt as much as his broken arm.

Emilie was draped over the bench, tears of mirth rolling down her cheeks, while Zane leaned against the wall and roared. McVie stood in the doorway, his expression perfectly deadpan. Each time they looked at him they laughed all the harder.

"I'm starving," said Emilie, holding her sides. "Let's call out for a pizza."

"Great idea," Zane managed. "Think it'll get here in thirty minutes?"

"Oh, no!" cried Emilie, wiping her eyes. "I left the water running in the kitchen."

"I can go you one better," said Zane. "I left the Porsche running."

Andrew watched them patiently from the doorway. He knew the words they spoke were English, but the meaning behind them was impossible for him to comprehend. All this talk about por-shuh and peetzah—what manner of world did they come from?

He glanced out the window, then cleared his throat. "It grows dark soon. We should tend to business while we can."

Both Emilie and Zane grew abruptly silent as reality once again rushed in on them.

"We have to do something about your arm," Emilie said at last. "The longer we wait..."

"I am no physician," said Andrew, "but I am skilled in certain basic remedies."

"I don't have a choice, do I?" asked Zane.

No one argued with him.

In silence they filed down the winding staircase to the front room where the blue light of dusk had begun to soften the stark simplicity of their surroundings.

Emilie borrowed McVie's knife and proceeded to rip into one of the beautiful quilts. They would need lengths of fabric to serve as a sling, as well as to bind the makeshift splint to Zane's forearm.

Andrew found a sturdy branch outside that he quickly broke down to a more manageable size.

Zane watched the proceedings with detached curiosity. The whole thing was beginning to take on an almost Kafkaesque quality and he half expected the alarm to ring and wake him up from the strangest dream he'd had in his entire life.

The two men locked eyes.

"The pain might be considerable," said Andrew, taking the other man's measure.

"Do it," was all Zane said.

McVie motioned for Emilie to stand at the head of the trundle bed. "Keep his shoulders down, mistress Emilie."

She nodded, biting her lip nervously. McVie placed one hand on Zane's wrist and another at his elbow. It was she and not Zane who cried out at the sound of bone against bone as McVie urged the broken pieces into the proper position.

Quickly he laid the splint along Zane's forearm, then instructed Emilie to bind the splint tightly in place. Zane's face was pale and his eyes were closed. A small muscle in his jaw worked furiously, but that was the only sign he gave that all was not right.

"You're very good at this," she observed as McVie finished his task.

McVie nodded. "I have always been so."

They listened to the sound of Zane's rapid breathing as he dozed on the trundle bed.

"I know I should be worrying about all sorts of dreadful things," said Emilie, "but right now all I can think about is food."

Andrew started for the door. "Come with me and I'll cut some ham for you and Rutledge."

He wasn't entirely certain what he was going to do with the two travelers through time, but he did know he wasn't about to let them out of his sight.

SIX

The ham was salty and tasted of wood smoke and the rum was potent, but Emilie polished off each with gusto. Zane awoke once in considerable pain and McVie pushed the bottle toward him. Zane didn't hesitate, and soon slept peacefully once again.

"The pain will ease by the morrow," said McVie from his spot near the door.

"I hope so," said Emilie, smoothing Zane's dark hair off his forehead with a gentle touch. McVie had helped her to dress the cuts on Zane's forehead and back and together they had used the rest of the quilt to bind his rib cage. She had thanked God that his ribs had been bruised and not broken. "I appreciate all you're doing for us, Andrew. I know this must seem more unbelievable to you than it does to us."

He tossed the quarter she'd given him into the air then caught it in his palm. "You have shown me some things that not even logic can disprove."

It was hard to see his expression clearly in the gathering darkness, but Emilie thought she caught a look of concern in his eyes.

"Is something wrong? Is there something about Zane's condition that I should know about?"

So that was the way the wind blew, thought Andrew. Her concern for Rutledge went deeper than perhaps even she realized.

"Nay, madam, I have kept nothing about Rutledge's infirmities from you. It is another, more distressing, matter that concerns me."

She nodded as if she knew. "You have to leave us," she said, in that oddly accented voice of hers. "I understand."

Andrew arched a brow in question. "That notion does not cause you alarm?"

"It doesn't thrill me," said Emilie, "but I know that you have a life of your own." *And a destiny to be met.* "I believe I can make a life for myself here."

Andrew gestured toward Rutledge, sleeping deeply on the trundle bed, his broken arm propped upon a pillow at his side.

"What of Rutledge?" he asked. "He does not strike me as a man willing to forego the world he left behind."

"Has he a choice? We're alive and we're here. The sooner we make our peace with that truth, the happier we'll be."

Andrew considered his words carefully. "And what of you, madam? Do you not feel the pull of friends and loved ones left behind?"

"There's no one," she said. "Not a soul."

He wondered about the bond between her and Rutledge but he refrained from asking. She obviously had affection for the giant of a man, but how deep that affection ran was beyond his knowing.

As for Rutledge, he had about him the look of a man who had made claim to a woman. A vivid image, shockingly explicit in its attention to detail, came to life and he closed his eyes against it. The mistress Emilie had said she and Rutledge were unwed, but Andrew was worldly enough to know that meant little when the blood ran hot.

He cast a curious glance toward her as she sat by Rutledge's side. She sat stitching the plain blue fabric from the coverlet into a skirt. She had an air of industry about her and he wondered if there was any goal she could not attain if she put her mind to it. She was a woman of bountiful charms, not the least of which was a most intriguing demeanor that was at once both fierce and agreeable.

He cleared his throat. "About your manner of dress," he began. "It appears to my eyes to be most...unusual attire."

For a moment she forgot what she'd been wearing when this whole thing began and she looked down to find herself clad in a demure eighteenth-century bodice and twentieth-century leggings. She quickly explained to him about the celebration and the outfit she'd intended to finish sewing while on the balloon ride to Langley Park.

Andrew gestured toward the apparel on her lower body. "Do others garb themselves in such fashion?"

"And worse!" she said, laughing at the expression on his face. "You would be scandalized if you could see the outfits, Andrew." She held aloft a cambric handkerchief she'd had tucked in her embroidered purse. "There are some women who wear as little as this."

Andrew's face flamed and he rose to his feet. "It grows dark," he announced unnecessarily. "You should sleep."

"I doubt if I'll ever sleep again," she said. "There's so much to do...so many things to think about."

"I bid you good night, mistress Emilie. Rest well."

"And you," she said.

With that he climbed the stairs to the lookout tower while Emilie laughed softly to herself, wondering how he would react when she told him about *Playboy*.

Zane awoke the next morning with the sun. His arm ached, as did his ribs, but all things considered he felt remarkably clearheaded and filled with resolve.

He climbed from the trundle bed, careful not to disturb Emilie, who slept on the smaller of the two mattresses. During the night he had come to terms with the reality of their situation. Although it went against all logic, he accepted the fact that he and Emilie had somehow tumbled through a rip in the fabric of time.

However, he was not about to accept the fact that the world he'd left behind was lost to him forever. If he did that he'd be saying that his entire life up until now hadn't been worth a damn, and that admission was too close to the bone for him to contemplate.

Besides, this world held little appeal. He liked everything modern life had to offer and was willing to accept the drawbacks as well as the benefits. Where was the challenge, living within boundaries that had been set by history long before he was born?

But there was one challenge on the horizon and it was probably the most important one he'd ever face.

He was going to find a way back to his own time.

And he was going to convince Emilie to come with him.

For years Emilie had prided herself on her love of the colonial era, but when she awoke that morning she realized how little she'd really known about the time. She could live without her electric sewing machine and her microwave oven, but indoor plumbing was another story entirely.

What on earth was she going to do?

Peering out the window she saw McVie and Zane engaged in animated conversation near the well. They looked as if they would be there for some time. Now if only she could find a chamber pot, maybe she could convince herself that the situation wasn't as dire as it was beginning to seem.

She scowled as she searched the lighthouse for the object. Did men have any idea how lucky they were? She doubted it. As a sex, they seemed to take for granted the ease with which they could perform necessary bodily functions. The thought of squatting down behind some prickly rosebush filled her with dismay, but the other alternative was even more appalling to consider.

Flinging open the front door, she stormed down the steps. "If either one of you comes anywhere near the rosebushes in the back, I will single-handedly see to it that neither of you reaches his next birthday."

With that she marched around the corner of the lighthouse and disappeared from view.

"Is she always thus?" McVie asked after Emilie had vanished from sight.

"She has a temper," said Zane. "No doubt about that."

McVie nodded. "She has the look of the Irish about her."

Zane knew McVie wanted to ask about the exact nature of Zane's relationship to Emilie, but his eighteenth-century caution kept him silent.

They had spent an interesting hour discussing the options open to both him and Emilie, and it was agreed that throwing in their lot with McVie—at least for the time being—was the wisest course of action.

Besides, there was the issue of McVie's obvious distrust. Emilie's eyes had shone bright with admiration each time she talked with McVie, and Zane had found his gut twisting with a jolt of white-hot jealousy, the likes of which he'd never experienced.

Only this time the jealousy wasn't directed toward a name in a dusty old history book, but a living, breathing man. Emilie's lifelong hero was more competition than he'd counted on bumping up against.

She saw McVie as a hero, the kind of man who would risk everything for the higher good. Funny thing, though: Zane had the distinct feeling that he and McVie had more in common than anyone, including Emilie, would think.

McVie was a risk taker, but it wasn't the higher good that concerned the man. McVie was running away from something, sure as hell, and Zane intended to find out what it was.

He looked at McVie. "So what's next?"

"We leave for the Blakelee farm when mistress Emilie returns," said McVie. "If luck is with us, we'll be at the edge of Milltown before night falls again."

The first thing Zane noticed on the mainland was the absence of sound. Back when he was in high school he'd read *Atlas Shrugged*. The mysterious John Galt had managed to stop the engine of the world and Zane finally understood what that was all about. It was gone, all of it. No planes, no cars, no computers, no machines, no constant low-level sizzle of electricity keeping the world on-line.

McVie tied the rowboat to a tree stump a few feet away from the waterline, then plunged into a thicket of branches and bushes, with Emilie and Zane bringing up the rear.

"Milltown lies some miles to the northwest," said McVie. "We'll make camp on the outskirts of town for tonight."

"We can't stay in the town itself?" asked Emilie. She had been thinking of a wonderful colonial inn, rich in atmosphere.

"Not Milltown," said McVie, glancing over his shoulder. "'Tis said the Britishers have made considerable inroads, and with your unusual attire we should draw too much untoward attention."

There was no arguing with his reasoning. McVie planned to make contact with his cohorts in the spy ring and obtain proper clothing for both Emilie and Zane before daybreak so they would blend in with the populace once they reached Princeton.

"How do we know you're not going to turn us in?" Zane asked.

"You do not," said McVie. "As I do not know with certainty if you intend to thwart my plans."

"You have our word," said Emilie.

"As you have mine," said McVie, "and I do not believe that is enough for any one of us."

They walked in silence for what seemed like hours. Emilie had feared McVie would plot a course through the swamplands that dotted the boundaries of modern-day Crosse Harbor, but he led them instead into a forest of maples and pine trees that towered so high overhead that she felt as if she'd entered a cathedral. Outside the forest the summer sun was blisteringly hot, but inside it was dark and cool. The forest floor was softly cushioned by fallen pine needles and dropped leaves and she found herself struck by the toll industrialization would soon take on the natural order of things.

They stopped by a stream to rest for a few minutes. McVie knelt down on the bank and leaned forward, cupping his hands to fill them with water.

"Don't do that!" Emilie said. "The water's probably—"

She stopped, glancing down at the crystal-clear reflections in the glassy surface.

"The water's clean," said Zane, sounding as amazed as she felt.

McVie looked at them both with curiosity. "You act as if clean water is an oddity."

"It is in our time," said Emilie. She told him about medical waste and acid rain, and the absurdity of designer bars where people paid good money for a cup of clean water.

McVie looked at Zane. "Why is it you wish to return to such a place?"

"Freedom," said Zane. "We can go anywhere we want, do anything we want. Hell, we've even been to the moon."

McVie turned toward Emilie. "He speaks nonsense."

"He speaks the truth," said Emilie, sipping the cool, fresh water. "The American flag flies on the surface of the moon."

McVie sat down on a mossy rock and looked up at the sky. "And how did the American flag reach the moon, mistress Emilie? A high-flying bird, perhaps, or an act of God?"

She shook her head. "Hard work, brain power and a dream."

Zane, however, understood what McVie was really asking. In broad terms he described the principles behind jet propulsion and outlined the development of the space program.

"I was a little girl when the Eagle landed, but I remember it as if it were yesterday," Emilie said.

"Neil Armstrong," said Zane. "For a while he was every boy's hero."

It sounded like a world of wondrous possibilities. Andrew's head swam with the notion of mortal men hurtling through the sky in a ball of flame, only to set foot upon the silvery surface of the moon. "And how is it you go about your daily business? In those... rockets you tell of?"

"All different ways," said Emilie, perching on a rock near him. "Some people walk to work, but most people drive."

"Horses?"

"Cars," said Zane.

McVie listened, eyes widening with surprise, as Rutledge described metal vehicles with wheels that were powered by controlled gas explosions. "I believe you are making sport at my expense."

Emilie shook her head. "He tells the truth, Andrew. The country is paved with roads and you can drive anywhere you want, any time you want." She reached into her waistband for her embroidered purse, then removed a hard and shiny piece of paper. "This is a driver's license," she said, handing it to him. "You take a test to prove your skill, then the state grants you the right to drive a car."

"What manner of substance is this?" McVie asked, tapping the license with his thumbnail.

"Plastic," said Zane with a grin. "It's everywhere."

McVie looked closely at the card. "'Tis your image, mistress Emilie. The artist was quite proficient."

"There was no artist," Emilie said. "That's what we call a photograph."

Zane started to explain the principles of photography, but McVie stood up abruptly. "Time passes. We must continue."

"So much for your lectures, Professor Rutledge," Emilie commented with a laugh.

"He kept your driver's license," Zane said as they fell into position behind McVie once again.

"I don't think I'll be needing it. Besides, if it helps him to believe us, he's welcome to it."

"We're going back one day," Zane said with great determination.

"I don't think so."

"We don't belong here."

"Speak for yourself."

"Come on, Emilie. I saw your face when you headed for the bushes this morning. You wanted porcelain, tile and running water."

"Too bad for me. I'll get used to it."

"Wait until December," he said. "You'll be praying for indoor plumbing."

"And so what if I do? That still doesn't change things. We're here and we're staying here."

"Not if I can help it."

"I don't think you can, Zane."

"It happened once," he said. "It can happen a second time."

"If you're planning to hijack another hot-air balloon, you'll have another seven years to wait until they're invented."

"We can build one."

"Why don't we build a spaceship while we're at it and go to Mars?"

"If it would get us the hell out of here, I'm all in favor of it."

He strode ahead, ostensibly to talk to McVie. Emilie bridled at his stubborn refusal to accept the fact that their lives had been changed irrevocably. He couldn't control this situation any more than he'd been able to control the hot-air balloon. For a man like Zane, that would be a difficult admission. Old rules no longer applied and the sooner he accepted that, the easier things would be for everyone.

"This is it?" asked Emilie two hours later when Andrew stopped for the night near an outcropping of rocks that overlooked a stream. "We're staying here?"

"There is a small cave beyond the lilac bushes where you may take shelter for the night."

"A cave?" Somehow her imagination hadn't taken her this far. "Bats sleep in caves."

It was Zane's turn to laugh. "You were expecting the Holiday Inn?"

"Oh, be quiet!" she snapped. "I'm only thinking of you."

Even McVie recognized the humor in that statement, and he barely knew her.

"The woods abound in game," McVie said. "Hunger should not be a problem."

Emilie determined that a shift to vegetarianism was in order.

"I'll need a pistol," Zane said to McVie, "unless you expect me to strangle something."

McVie retained his pistol but handed over his knife.

"You're leaving us?" Emilie asked as Zane carefully slid the knife into the waistband of his trousers.

"I'll return before dawn," he said.

"You won't let us down, will you?" Emilie implored.

McVie shook his head. "Nay, mistress. I will not."

The look on Emilie's face hit Zane like a slap. She followed McVie with her eyes until he disappeared, then turned back to Zane with obvious reluctance. She'd come to rely upon the rough-hewn patriot for a sense of security and that realization stung more than he cared to admit. He found himself wanting to reassure her that she was in good hands.

"If you're worried about starving out here, don't be. The broken arm'll slow me down, but it won't stop me." He'd done his share of roughing it up in Alaska and down in Peru. Central New Jersey shouldn't pose too much of a problem, no matter what the year.

"Don't kill anything on my account," Emilie said, gesturing toward the berry bushes and wildflowers growing everywhere. "These woods have a better selection of produce than my local supermarket."

He was just as glad she felt that way. Killing for sport had never done it for him. He knew he could kill if his life depended on it, but right now berries sounded fine to him, too.

Still, as he watched Emilie inspecting the berries and picking ripe specimens, he found himself wishing she was a little less self-sufficient. When he'd said he didn't belong, he'd only scratched the surface. Neither one of them belonged in that time and place, but he had the feeling he was the only one who realized it.

"Okay," said Zane as he stuck another branch on the stack. "All we need now is a match."

"Very funny," said Emilie. "I hope you have a lighter in your back pocket."

"You don't have any matches on you?"

"I don't smoke," she reminded him. "Don't you know how to start a fire without matches?"

"I was never the Boy Scout type," he drawled, "but I'd pay good money to see you rub two sticks together."

"Do you have any better ideas?"

"Different," he said, "but not better."

"It's a darned good thing you have me around," she said, metaphorically rolling up her sleeves. "You'd be lost here without me."

She'd tossed him a perfect straight line but the requisite wisecrack wouldn't come. She was right. Although it killed him to admit it even to himself, she was his guide in the strange new world in which they found themselves and he wondered how he would have managed without her.

They ate berries and picked at the dandelion grass, drank their fill of the stream's cold, clear water, then returned to the camp fire.

"I don't know about you," said Zane, "but I'd kill for a Big Mac."

"I thought the berries were delicious," said Emilie with a prim set to her mouth.

"Pizza," he continued. "Pepperoni with onions."

"The dandelion grass had a certain tang to it." She struggled to suppress a smile.

"Szechuan shrimp, hot and sour soup, all thirty-one flavors for dessert."

"You win," said Emilie, stifling a groan. "I'd give anything for a bowl of chili and a diet Coke."

"What the hell do they eat around here?" he asked, genuinely puzzled. "How did—how *do* they cook?"

"In the hearth, mostly. Beef roasts, game, lots of eggs and butter." She grinned. "The cardiac blue plate special."

"Great," he said, reaching for another handful of berries. "That gives me something to look forward to."

"It's not so bad, Zane," she said. "Not really."

"Tell me how it could be worse."

"We could be dead."

"In a way, we are," he said, his voice uncharacteristically flat. "And so is everything we knew."

"Maybe not," she said softly. Once again she sensed that deep chord of loneliness that she'd always suspected was part of his soul. "Maybe we're exactly where we're meant to be."

"That's a crock."

"I don't think so," she said, warming to the notion. "Haven't you wondered—even for a minute—if we aren't exactly where we're meant to be?"

"I know where I'm meant to be," he said grimly, "and it sure as hell isn't here."

When night came, it fell with a swiftness and finality that surprised them both. The temperature dropped, as well, and Emilie found herself drawing closer to the fire for warmth. They'd been inordinately proud of themselves when they'd coaxed fire from dry tinder by using a rock to strike a spark off the blade of McVie's knife.

If only she had a metal pot, she could have boiled water for herb tea. Indoor plumbing and a cup of tea, and she'd be a very happy woman. She was contemplating the inequities of life when Zane rose to his feet.

"Get inside," he commanded in a tone of voice she'd never heard before.

"Why?" She held her hands over the fire. "If you need privacy, go find yourself a spot behind the trees."

He grabbed her by the arm and yanked her to her feet. "Now!"

She stumbled toward the cave. What on earth had gotten into him? She crouched inside the mouth, listening. An owl hooted softly in the night breeze and from somewhere close by she heard the sound of leaves crunching.

Footsteps?

Maybe it's Andrew, she thought, wrapping her arms tightly around her chest. *Or maybe it's a bear.* They had bears in New Jersey in 1992. She could only imagine how many had lumbered through the woods before turnpikes and subdivisions.

All Zane had was a knife and a broken arm. He wouldn't stand a chance. She searched around the dark interior for something—anything—to help him. She grabbed a rock the size of a large cantaloupe and made her way carefully from the cave.

The fire was nothing but a pile of embers. Without the flames casting their light, she felt as if she were walking through a black hole in space. Her heart pounded loudly in her ears as she tried to decide which way Zane had headed.

It was quiet.

Too quiet.

Not even the owl was hooting.

She was so tense she could scarcely draw breath into her lungs. *Where are you, Zane?* She'd been in the cave only a minute or two. He couldn't have gone far in such a short period of time. Unless—

She screamed as a hand clamped down on her shoulder.

"What the hell are you doing here?" Zane growled in her ear. "I told you to stay put."

"I thought you might need help."

He tapped the rock with the hilt of the knife. "You were going to hit a bear in the head with that thing?"

"That was the idea."

"Next time do what I tell you."

"The hell I will," she said, bristling. "I suppose going *mano a mano* with a black bear makes more sense—especially with your broken arm?"

He dragged her back to the cave. "If I need help, I'll ask for it."

"For heaven's sake," she grumbled, dropping the rock to the floor of the cave, "I didn't mean to impugn your masculinity."

"You didn't." She heard the scuffle of dirt as he sat down. "But you did act like a jerk."

She glared into the darkness. "If I could find you, I'd kick you for that remark."

"You always were an original, Em. Another woman would be crying into her embroidered hanky, but you're out there looking for bear."

She found herself a spot to sit in his general vicinity. "Is that a compliment?"

"What do you think?"

"I'm not sure."

"It's a compliment," he said.

"Thank you." A pause. "So what *did* make the noise?"

He mumbled something.

"What was that?" she repeated.

"A skunk," he said. "It was a close call, but I was faster than he was."

"There is a God," she said wryly.

Again the rumbling laughter that had stirred her blood two nights ago. "You know, you never did answer my question," he said. "Would you have gone to Tahiti with me?"

She smiled into the darkness. "You'll never know."

"Come on," he said. "I won't hold you to it when we get back home."

"This is home, Zane," she said softly.

"Not for me."

"It doesn't seem as if you have a choice."

"There's always a choice, Emilie. Don't think otherwise."

His last remark brought her up short. The circumstances might change but the essence of the man remained the same. He'd never been a man for the long haul, not by any stretch of the imagination, and she'd be a total fool to think otherwise. As soon as he got his bearings, he'd be off in search of the eighteenth-century equivalent of Tahiti.

He shifted position and slid over closer to where she sat.

"Cold in here," he observed.

"Mmph." Late July and she was shivering.

"What happens if McVie doesn't come back for us?" Zane asked.

"He'll come back," she said. "He gave us his word."

Zane refrained from pointing out that many men gave their word but damn few managed to keep it.

She was almost thirty years old. If she didn't know that by now, it was time she learned.

"McVie said something interesting this morning," he went on. "He thinks we should pose as husband and wife."

A wave of heat rose up from the soles of her feet. "He may be right," she said after a long moment. "Women always traveled with a companion." And a man traveling alone would be viewed with suspicion, especially with the war raging. "Does he—did you tell him?"

"That we were married? Sure."

"Oh, God." She buried her face in her hands. "What on earth must Andrew be thinking? Divorce is practically unheard of."

"Who cares what he thinks? It's none of his business."

She knew McVie's opinion of her shouldn't matter, but it did. "I suppose you had to tell him."

"Glad you agree," Zane drawled, a definite edge to his voice.

"I wonder what he'll think we should do if we stay at an inn."

"If we're supposed to be married," Zane pointed out, "he'll expect us to share a room."

She narrowed her eyes and looked in his direction. "Did you put him up to this?"

"You've got to be kidding." He sounded sincere. She wished she could see if the expression on his face matched the sound of his voice.

"We need some ground rules," she said, doing her best to ignore the memory of the night they'd shared. "We'll share a room, but we won't share a bed."

He said nothing.

"Zane? Did you hear me?"

"I heard you."

"You didn't say anything."

"What do you want me to say?"

"That you understand what I'm talking about."

"I don't understand."

"We're not meant to be together," she explained. "If we were back home, we would have gone our separate ways. I refuse to be manipulated by circumstances."

"Don't worry," he snapped, visions of seduction vanishing before his eyes. "Your virtue's safe with me."

"Good," said Emilie.

"Great," said Zane.

She lay down and pillowed her head with her arms.

He leaned against the wall of the cave and closed his eyes.

It was a long time before either one slept.

SEVEN

"Godspeed, Andrew," said the buxom, dark-haired wench as she handed him the package. "Don't you be makin' yourself a stranger to us, now."

Andrew thanked the kindly woman with a kiss. "Mark me well, Prudence. You will be rewarded for your generosity."

Prudence made clucking noises with her teeth. "Keep your good self safe and well and that be all the generosity a body could wish for." She opened the front door. "Out with you. I'm a workin' lass, m'boy, and you cannot afford my favors."

"Treat those Redcoats kindly, Pru, for happy men are ofttimes careless."

Prudence kissed him on the mouth. "Maybe next time?"

He kissed her back. "With all certainty."

Thus far it had been a most profitable night. Prudence had performed a miracle and conjured up clothing for mistress Emilie. She had also filled a pillow slip with all manner of things that Prudence said a woman would love.

He had been too preoccupied to enjoy Pru's charms. He'd found himself thinking about the strange and wonderful inventions his new companions had told him about. Over a supper of mutton and ale, he'd asked Prudence if she believed man could ever fly through the sky like a bird. Prudence had laughed so hard she developed the hiccups.

He stepped to his right as a man on horseback galloped by, the animal's hooves kicking up a cloud of dust.

Rutledge had said that in his time men traveled by harnessing small explosions. He had drawn a picture in the dirt of a rectangular metal container on four wheels and Andrew had stared at it, trying to imagine thousands of those contraptions racing about at speeds he couldn't even begin to comprehend.

The word pictures Rutledge and mistress Emilie had painted for him were of such a fantastical nature that it was a wonder he did not commit them to the lunatic asylum on Manhattan Island.

Mayhap you are the one in need of the asylum, he thought as he neared the tavern. He had no reason to believe Rutledge and Emilie. As yet, he had not uncovered even a whisper of a plot against His Excellency, General Washington. In truth, he believed the general was in residence on Long Island with his troops, some one hundred miles from central New Jersey.

One thing distressed him, however. Rather than being pleased to know his life would merit even a sentence of mention in the books of the future, he found himself vaguely uneasy. Mistress Emilie said that he had vanished from the history books after the rescue of General Washington. Did he sink back into obscurity or had something more untoward happened to him?

The unforeseen always brought with it a healthy dose of apprehension. Living in the shadows, as he did, he tended to view every surprise as a possible calamity, which was why his acceptance of the two strangers amazed him.

The Black Dragon was crowded when he pushed through the door. Smoke from pipes and cigars filled the room, while the pungent smell of burning tobacco mingled with the smells of whiskey and ale and unwashed flesh. Tavern girls in tantalizing costumes swayed about the room dispensing tankards of ale and promising smiles. He glanced about the room for the man he'd been instructed to find, made eye contact, then claimed a table some ten feet away.

"Evenin', sir," said a spritely lass with big blue eyes and a plump bosom. "What would you be needin'?"

"A tankard of ale and some cheese," he said, his attention on the man he was to meet. "And a loaf of dark bread."

With a flip of her skirts the lass vanished toward the back room. Andrew rose from his chair to enter into a game of darts being played at the far side of the room. He passed close to his contact's table and the rotund man never missed a bite. He hefted his bread and cheese, took an enormous mouthful, then casually plucked the message from Andrew's hand in a movement so perfectly planned that it took Andrew a moment to realize the transfer had even occurred.

Two hours later Andrew approached the edge of the forest. He had gone out of his way to seek mention of a plot against the life of General Washington, but had heard nary a whisper. The thought occurred to him that his two mysterious traveling companions might have concocted the story from whole cloth, but again he found himself wanting to believe they spoke only the truth.

The forest enveloped him in its embrace as he left the town behind. His mind leaped with the images mistress Emilie and Rutledge had conjured of men who walked on the moon, of fire-breathing contraptions that raced across the wilderness on roads that people paid money to use. He'd spent a goodly amount of time staring at the green currency with the general's countenance set upon it, and he'd known a hunger for knowledge that defied place and time.

Ever since losing Elspeth and their child, he had been courting danger at every turn, all in the name of patriotic fervor, caring little for the outcome of the battle. In truth, it was well and good that his work with the spy ring was beneficial to the patriots, but he went where others dared not because he had nothing of value left to lose.

He had no trouble finding the spot where he had left them. The embers from their fire had long since been extinguished but the pile of ashes gave it away. He wondered if Emilie had merely snapped her fingers and called forth a flame from the accumulated branches and twigs. Little would surprise him. They had come from a time of great wonderment and he understood full well how it was that Rutledge fought against the boundaries of the world Andrew was part of.

He slipped beside the cave as the first light of dawn limned the tops of the trees. It took a moment for his eyes to adjust to the absolute darkness inside. The sight that revealed itself to him caused him a sharp stab of pain. Emilie lay curled against Rutledge, her head resting on his chest. The skirt she had wrought from the lighthouse coverlet was draped over their sleeping forms. Rutledge sat with his back against the wall of the cave, his broken arm resting across his stomach.

There was no denying the way they fit together. They had the look of contentment about them as if—

He had no wish to pursue the thought.

Apparently Rutledge slept lightly. His eyes opened and he met Andrew's gaze across the dim light of the cave.

"How goes it?" Rutledge asked, his voice husky with sleep.

Andrew tossed down a sack. "I cannot vouch for the fit of the garments, but I believe mistress Emilie will be well pleased." He found his gaze drawn again and again to the rise and fall of her breasts against the other man's chest. Since Elspeth, he had not wanted for the companionship of a woman, and he wondered why it was this strapping lass had such an uncommon effect upon him, body and soul. "We leave for Princeton after daybreak."

Zane watched as McVie left the cave. There had been no mistaking the tension between them, and he was certain he knew the cause.

Zane had sensed the other man's fascination with Emilie from the start. What man wouldn't react to a beautiful redhead with a body to match? What bothered Zane was her reaction to McVie.

Back on his own turf Zane could've given the guy a run for his money, but here in the middle of nowhere he was stumped. How did you compete with a woman's hero? Zane had money, freedom and entrée to the best of everything the world had to offer, and none of it mattered a damn.

This wasn't his world, it was McVie's.

For thirty-four years he'd charted his singular course through life, needing nothing and no one but himself.

Stripped of all the trappings of modern life, he felt naked. He had dodged bombs and bar stools and more bad tempers than a man twice his age, but he had never faced his own limitations, in the way he was doing now.

He hated feeling anything less than in total control of himself and his situation. The broken arm was an unpleasant reminder that he was only human. The way Emilie made him feel went even deeper.

Is this what you wanted, Sara Jane? he asked, wondering if his grandmother was somewhere laughing at the predicament in which he found himself. *You told me there was more to life.... Is this what you had in mind?*

He waited, but there was no answer.

As they followed Andrew on their journey north to Princeton, both Emilie and Zane were moved to stunned silence by the beauty of the land. The dense forests gently gave way to rolling meadows dotted with wildflowers, peach orchards and small springs that sparkled with water as sweet and clear as liquid diamonds.

"You went to school in Princeton," Emilie said as they crested a small hill. "I wonder if you'll recognize anything."

Zane looked at her as if she were crazy. "I don't think Marita's Cantina's been around that long." Then a thought struck him. "You know, Nassau Hall's pretty damn old."

"And the old governor's mansion on Stockton Street—"

"Morven," he said, shaking his head. Buildings he'd walked by every day for four years and never noticed were taking on monumental importance in his life. The whole thing was enough to make him think longingly of a bottle of Scotch and sweet oblivion.

"At least we're dressed for it," Emilie said, gesturing toward her mint green outfit with the snugly laced bodice.

Zane looked down at her, taking careful note of the deep valley between her breasts. "Can you breathe in that thing?"

"Barely," she said with a groan. "I suppose I should thank my lucky stars Andrew was able to find anything at all."

Zane scowled. "I feel like a jerk."

"You look great." Andrew had been unable to find clothes that would fit a man of Zane's size, but they had managed to cobble together a passable imitation of period clothing by combining Zane's twentieth-century garments with a dark gold cape. Emilie had combed his hair back and tied it with a length of black ribbon. If they could change his attitude, she'd be very happy.

"It's hot as hell under this damn thing."

"You'll survive."

"Right."

"It's a different world, Zane," she reminded him. "I'm wearing more layers of clothing than the flying nun and you don't hear me complaining."

"That's because you like this kind of thing."

"No," she said, "it's because I can accept it."

"I don't see the difference."

"I know," said Emilie, "and that's always been our problem."

The Post Road, formerly known as the King's Highway, led into the heart of town.

"This can't be real," said Emilie as she stared at the horses and livestock, the peddlers and merchants, the crowds of people choking the thoroughfare. Men in white powdered wigs and silk brocade jackets in vibrant oranges and reds strolled up the road, rubbing elbows with milkmaids wearing homespun skirts and plain bodices and street porters whose laced shoes bespoke their lowly station in life. "I feel like I'm on a movie set."

A blacksmith shop sat next to a printing establishment. There was a silversmith's shop across the street, and that was adjacent to a wigmaker, which was near the barber's storefront.

A woman carrying a basket of lemons approached, a hopeful look upon her face. "Fine lemons to cool you on a summer day," she said, extending the basket. "Brought up from Jamaica by my very own husband this Saturday past."

Emilie reached for a lemon, savoring the smoothness. "Oh, I'd love some."

"Two pence the half dozen," said the woman, her smile revealing two missing front teeth.

Emilie looked to Zane, who shook his head. Andrew stared at her, his expression impassive.

"I'm sorry," Emilie said to the woman, replacing the lemon in the basket. "I cannot, after all."

The woman's eyes flashed fire. "'Tis a dreadful thing, wasting a good wife's time with idle promises."

"I should truly love to buy one," said Emilie, trying to match the woman's speech patterns, "but I fear I am not able."

The woman's gaze took in Emilie's braided ring and crystal pendant. "A basket of lemons for one of those trinkets would be a fair trade."

Andrew took Emilie by the arm and propelled her up the street to where Zane stood near the door of the Plumed Rooster.

"Engage in no idle talk with tradespeople, mistress Emilie, or you will find your pockets picked before you reach the other side of the street."

"It's the same way back home," Emilie marveled as they caught up with Zane. "Only we call them flea markets."

"Fleas?" The expression on Andrew's face made both Emilie and Zane laugh out loud.

"It's a long story," said Zane. "We'll explain it to you some day."

Andrew gestured toward the Plumed Rooster. "I have business to attend inside and then on to the Blakelee farm."

"Fine," said Emilie. "We'll come with you." She started for the door to the pub.

"Nay," said Andrew, barring her way.

"Don't be ridiculous," said Emilie. "Move away, Andrew."

"''Tis not proper.''

"What isn't?"

"You would not be welcome in the Plumed Rooster."

"Because I'm a stranger?"

"No," said Zane. "Because you're a woman."

For a moment she'd forgotten the inequality of the eighteenth century. She turned to Andrew. "Surely I can—"

Andrew shook his head. He'd never seen such fire before on a woman's countenance. It both intrigued and alarmed him. "''Tis but one kind of woman who frequents the Rooster," he said, trusting she would infer his meaning from his words.

"Oh, God," she groaned, shaking her head in dismay.

Andrew glanced toward Zane. "Do you understand the cause of her distress?"

"Equal rights," said Zane.

Andrew looked relieved. "A notion put forth by the Continental Congress in Philadelphia a few short weeks ago. It is one with which I am familiar."

"Of course you are," said Emilie, still smarting. "All *men* are created equal."

"I do not understand your dismay, mistress Emilie. Certainly the notion of equality is one appreciated in your time."

Zane snickered audibly and Emilie whirled about. "Stop that!" she ordered. "You know exactly what I'm talking about."

"Women's liberation," Zane said to a wide-eyed McVie. "Equal pay for equal work."

"A major consideration for a man," Andrew acknowledged, "but surely a wife does not expect recompense for her services."

Emilie strangled on a scream of frustration. "Women do more than cook and clean for a man in the future," she snapped. "We fly planes and own companies and even rule countries."

Andrew laughed. "For a moment I did not realize you were jesting."

Emilie's hand clenched into a fist and Zane stepped between his ex-wife and her girlhood hero. "I'd shut up if I were you, McVie. She's got a great left hook."

Emilie, however, had more to say on the subject. "In our time, a woman ruled Great Britain."

"That is not difficult to believe," said Andrew, "for Good Queen Bess inherited the throne two centuries ago upon the death of her father."

"Well, there is another Queen Elizabeth on the throne of England," said Emilie, "but her power is only ceremonial. I speak of someone else."

Andrew's rugged face was split by a wide and knowing grin. "Aye, it's a cunning lass you are, mistress. Her powers are ceremonial for it is her husband the king who rules, is it not?''

"Wrong again," said Emilie, beginning to wonder if this whole discussion had been such a great idea after all. She would have been much happier not knowing Andrew McVie was a male chauvinist—a term she had no intention explaining to him. "England is governed by a parliament presided over by a prime minister." She paused. "For many years that job belonged to a woman."

"Nay," said Andrew, "that cannot be." How could she expect him, an intelligent and worldly man, to believe such nonsense?

"It's true," Emilie persisted.

Andrew again looked toward Zane.

Zane almost felt sorry for the guy. He himself still had trouble with the notion of women's equality and all it entailed, and he'd lived through that particular revolution. McVie had to be completely dumbfounded.

"It's true," Zane said. "One day a woman will probably be president of the United States."

"I have heard enough," said Andrew. "I will finish my business and meet you at this spot shortly." He disappeared inside the Plumed Rooster.

"Poor guy," said Zane as the door swung closed behind McVie. "He couldn't wait to get away. We'll be lucky if we ever see him again."

"Was I that bad?"

"He didn't know what hit him."

"I just couldn't believe his attitude," Emilie said. "It was Neanderthal."

"Take a look around, Em. You won't find a copy of *Ms.* magazine anywhere. If you're looking for equality you're about two hundred years too soon."

His words hit Emilie hard. Women had played an important part in the war for independence. She could recite tales of wives who had followed their husbands into battle, mothers who'd risked their lives to further the cause of freedom for their fighting sons.

To hear McVie talk, they'd done nothing but sit by the fire and dream.

"Serpent in paradise?" Zane asked, grinning.

"Oh, shut up." She started off down the street, picking her way through the crowd of fishmongers, vegetable grocers and assorted livestock.

"Careful where you walk," Zane said, catching up with her. "Pooper scoopers haven't been invented yet."

She was about to snap out a sharp retort when a hen raced across the road, followed by a yipping dog.

She stopped abruptly, almost tumbling into Zane's waiting grasp.

"Told you to be careful where you walked."

"Am I crazy," said Emilie, regaining her balance, "or is it as busy here now as it is in the future?"

"You won't get an argument from me." He glanced across the street, then cupped her elbow with his left hand in a protective gesture. "Keep looking at me, Em," he ordered.

Her eyes widened. She made to turn toward the street but he gripped her more tightly and propelled her back toward the Plumed Rooster. "What's wrong?" she asked.

"Soldiers," he said, "and I don't think they're on our side."

The urge to stop and stare was almost irresistible. If Zane hadn't looked so stern, she was sure she would have made a show of herself.

"They're watching us," Zane said as they waited for Andrew to come out.

"We're not doing anything wrong," she said indignantly. "What can they do to us?"

"Anything they want," said Zane, struck by that knowledge. "Isn't that what the war was about?"

EIGHT

The Blakelee farm was situated a mile north of town. Cows grazed in the meadow near the weathered red barn, while a flock of sheep wandered about the front yard in the waning light of late afternoon.

At fifty acres the farm wasn't overly large, but it did afford the Blakelees a comfortable living—or at least it had before the advent of war.

The farmhouse itself was a two-story clapboard structure, unadorned by shutters or flower boxes. The only decorative touch was the red roses blooming to the right of the front door.

As they walked up the lane toward the house, Emilie's heartbeat accelerated and her hands began to tremble.

Andrew had explained little of his involvement with the Blakelees but both Emilie and Zane had deduced that they were somehow linked to the spy ring of which McVie was a part. They did know that the man, Josiah, was missing, but beyond that they were in the dark.

Andrew stopped a few yards from the front door and turned to them. "'Twould be best if the Blakelees think of you as a wedded couple."

"We've already covered that," said Zane. He knew all about eighteeth-century sensibilities and was more than willing to play along. He glanced at Emilie standing beside him. At least, in this instance he was.

McVie had more to say. "You should be average in every way possible."

Emilie nodded. "Don't worry. We'll be careful."

"I don't know if I can pull it off," Zane said to Emilie as McVie climbed the steps to the front door.

"I can," said Emilie, switching her silver-and-gold ring from her right hand to her left. "Just pretend you're the strong, silent type and follow my lead. You can—" She stopped abruptly as the door to the farmhouse swung open and a tiny brown-haired woman appeared in the doorway. She wore a simple dress in a dark beige color. A white mobcap sat atop her head.

Mrs. Blakelee looked at Andrew then her gaze slid past him and landed on Zane, whose back was turned to her.

"Oh, sweet merciful heavens!" the woman exclaimed, hurrying down the steps. "Josiah!"

Andrew grabbed the woman by the shoulder. "Nay, Rebekah. It is not Josiah."

Zane turned to see what had caused the commotion, and the good woman's narrow face lost the glow of happiness.

The woman looked back at Andrew. "I had so hoped Josiah would be with you."

"As I had hoped to find him safe at home. I fear we are both doomed to disappointment."

"Nine weeks and nary a word," said Rebekah Blakelee, wiping her eyes with the edge of her apron.

"He lives," said Andrew, comforting the woman with awkward pats on the back. "It cannot be otherwise." The specter of the dreaded British prison ships in Wallabout Bay rose before him, but he steadfastly refused to acknowledge its presence.

A child of about three years appeared at Rebekah's side. He held a small wooden hoop in his plump hand. Rebekah was too distraught to acknowledge his presence, even as he tugged at her skirts. From the front window came the sound of an infant crying. Emilie could only imagine how trapped and alone the woman must feel with so much responsibility on her slender shoulders.

Andrew spoke low to the farm woman. She nodded, then glanced toward Emilie and Zane.

"These are the Rutledges," Andrew said. "I discovered mistress Emilie in a most dreadful situation and have endeavored to lend aid until such time as her spouse is mended."

Zane shot McVie a deadly look. *Spouse* was bad enough. *Mended* made him sound like a canary with a broken wing. He started to say something to that effect, but a subtle poke in his ribs, courtesy of his ex-wife, made him reconsider.

Emilie stepped forward. "We shall endeavor to be a help and not a burden to your good family."

The woman's narrow face was transformed by her smile. "My Christian name is Rebekah."

"And I am Emilie." She gestured toward Zane. "This is my hus—" She stumbled over the word. "This is Zane."

He inclined his head toward the good woman and smiled. Emilie watched, both amused and somewhat piqued, as high color rose to Rebekah's cheeks and her smile deepened, making her plain face almost pretty.

"Zane," Rebekah said. "What manner of name is that?"

"It's a family name," he said easily.

Emilie breathed a sigh of relief that he had bypassed his *Riders of the Purple Sage* explanation.

Rebekah ran a hand across her forehead, smoothing the wispy strands of hair that had fallen toward her eyes. "I am sorry that you see my home in a time of turmoil." Her brown eyes filled with tears but she did not acknowledge their presence. "Without Josiah the farm has suffered greatly."

Twice her farmhouse had been commandeered, once by British officers and once by the Continental army, neither group exhibiting any concern for her well-being or that of her family.

"We are in need of lodging," Andrew said simply. "Rutledge has a broken arm and mistress Emilie—"

"Not another word," said Rebekah. "My husband holds you in high esteem. It is an honor to have you in my home."

Rebekah Blakelee was a practical woman. No sooner had she extended her generous invitation than she put Andrew and Zane to work bringing in more wood for the kitchen hearth and extra buckets of water.

Emilie followed the woman into a cool and spacious sitting room that ran from the front of the house to the back. Emilie instantly gravitated toward the spinning wheel situated near the stone fireplace. A basket of knitting rested next to a comfortable-looking wing chair by the window, while another basket, this one piled high with mending, sat atop the ledge. Military uniforms, in various states of completion, were stacked on a gateleg table in the corner.

"I am proficient at the wheel," Emilie said, turning to face Rebekah. "I would be honored to be of assistance."

"My daughter will be delighted to hear of your generous offer," said Rebekah, "for Charity is a most unwilling participant."

As if on cue, a pretty, dark-haired girl of about sixteen swayed into the room in a flurry of flowered skirts. "How can I embroider my wedding linens, Mother, if I am forever enslaved to that dreaded wheel?"

"This is Charity," said Rebekah with a rueful shake of her head. "My outspoken oldest child." She turned to her daughter. "Mistress Emilie and her spouse, Mr. Rutledge, will be spending some time with us."

Charity did not receive the news with any particular degree of interest. *A typical teenager,* thought Emilie. It was comforting to know that some things never changed.

"Charity is to be married a few weeks hence," said Rebekah as Charity sat down by the window with a child's shirt she'd been working on. "A most agreeable young man from a fine family north of here. I had so hoped Josiah..." Her words trailed off and she glanced away.

Impulsively Emilie reached for the woman's hand and took it in her own. "Everything will work out," she said earnestly. "I am certain of it." She tilted her head at the sound of a baby crying. "Have you an infant?"

Rebekah nodded. "A hungry one. Let me pour a pitcher of cider for you and your husband and then I shall tend to Aaron."

"Let me," said Emilie, then caught herself with a laugh. No bottles and formula here. "Not with Aaron, of course, but with the cider."

Rebekah was not accustomed to accepting help from guests in her home, but Emilie insisted. She wanted to see and experience everything she possibly could. For years she'd been insufferably proud of her knowledge of colonial ways. It would be interesting to see if her conceit was merited.

The kitchen was situated in the rear of the house. It was a large room with a high, beamed ceiling, dominated by an enormous hearth, some ten feet wide and over five feet high. As was the custom, the main meal had been served at midday and the fire was banked now. Emilie peered curiously at the two keeping ovens built into the bricks on the sides of the hearth and at the assortment of iron pots and copper pans that hung from hooks overhead.

It was all so perfect—and so perfectly wonderful—that she threw back her head and laughed with joy.

Zane looked out at the farmland from the bedroom window on the second floor. Acre after acre of pastoral tranquillity luminous in the fierce light of the setting sun. Throughout history men had lived and died to hang on to the land, bound to it through mysterious ties of blood and dreams.

No matter how hard he tried to understand that longing for roots and stability, the secret eluded him. Things that had been impossible for him to understand in 1992 were just as impossible in 1776.

He wasn't entirely sure what that said about him, but for the first time in his life he felt a sense of lost possibilities that had nothing to do with fast cars and exotic cities.

Downstairs Emilie sat in the front room, cradling Rebekah Blakelee's infant son. He and McVie had just come in from inspecting the barn and root cellar for any indications of foul play that Rebekah might have missed, when the sound of a baby's laughter had caught the men's attention.

McVie had stood in the entranceway, transfixed at the sight of Emilie with the laughing infant cradled in her arms. There was something so intimate, so ethereal about the scene that Zane had found it difficult to look at the expression of wonder on his ex-wife's beautiful face, and he'd turned away.

For all he knew McVie was still down there, staring at Emilie as if she held the secrets of the universe in her arms.

"So what's it to you, Rutledge?" he mumbled as he looked out at the bucolic scene. None of this mattered. All he had to do was bide his time and stay alert to possibilities and he was certain he'd find a way to get back to the world he'd left behind.

The image of Emilie gazing down at the infant cradled against her chest rose up again before his eyes, more vivid than the sight beyond the window. She'd always wanted a child. Even though their courtship had been brief and their marriage short-lived, that one fact had been painfully clear. She'd longed to cast her lot in with the future, while Zane had wanted to live for the moment with no regard for the past.

Children deserved more than biological parents. They deserved all the time and love and energy a mother and father could give. He knew firsthand what happened when parents cared more for their own happiness than for the new life they had created. If you couldn't make that kind of wholehearted commitment, you had no damn business bringing a kid into the world.

Even if the thought of a baby with her eyes and her smile made something strange happen inside his chest.

He turned away from the window, his gaze resting briefly on the wooden rocking chair in the corner, the highboy near the door... the narrow bed pushed up against the wall.

They'd never had any trouble in bed. If they'd been half as good at talking as they were at making love, they'd be celebrating their sixth anniversary. It struck him as a damn shame that two people who'd had so much going for them had let it all slip through their fingers without so much as putting up a fight.

Rebekah served a hearty supper of cold meat, bread and cheese with cider. The rest of her family joined them at the table and Emilie was amazed that the slender woman had borne Josiah Blakelee five sons and a daughter. The eldest son, Isaac, was fifteen and eager to throw in his lot with the patriots. The boy listened with rapt attention to Andrew's description of the situation at the Harlem Heights and Long Island.

"General Washington has but ten thousand troops against the hordes of British regulars and Hessians."

He took a drink of cider. "The Harbor is choked with British vessels."

"The cause seems lost," said Rebekah with a sigh. "Such a miracle as independency has never been done in the history of civilization. We were foolish to believe it could be done now by sheer power of will alone."

Isaac leaped from his seat, his face alight with determination. "I'm going, Mother! I'll join the general's troops like Sam'l Pearce did. We'll drive those Redcoats into the ocean!"

"Sit down, you fool!" snapped his sister, Charity. "Pa may never come back. You have to stay here and run the farm."

"Half the army has broken rank and gone home," Andrew observed. "'Tis hard to leave fields that need ploughing and crops that need tending when circumstances ahead may require much in the way of supplies."

Emilie noted the look of gratitude on Rebekah's drawn face. Before today she would have imagined that every mother's dream was to have her son serve the cause with distinction. But these were a practical people, their forebears, as concerned with growing crops as with securing independence from the Crown.

"The soldiers are a dreadful lot," Charity said, casting a look toward Zane, who was eating in silence. "Just last month they tore down our fences and commandeered our horses without so much as a by-your-leave."

"The British soldiers have been here?" asked Emilie.

"Our soldiers," the girl replied. "Five officers moved into the old Whittaker place and stole sugar and flour and all the silverware."

Zane looked up from his plate. "Is that true?" he asked Rebekah.

"That and more," said the good woman. "Dreadful things have happened from Trenton to New York. We buried our silverware and pewter in the herb garden. Without Josiah, I fear for our safety."

The Blakelees were held under a cloud of suspicion by the Tories, who speculated, correctly, that Josiah was a spy, while the patriots claimed the man had been too friendly with the enemy.

First thing tomorrow Andrew would head back into Princeton and begin his search anew. He'd learned much this afternoon at the Plumed Rooster. New intrigues were afoot. The British were planning mischief in Trenton to the south, while Hessian troops waited to cross the Hudson to the north. He found himself weary of the endless speculation and the absence of resolution.

Time and again his mind wandered to the stories Rutledge and mistress Emilie had told him and he wished with all his heart he could leave this place and find that other world that existed somewhere in the future.

Emilie excused herself immediately after supper, claiming dreadful fatigue.

"After your ordeal you must long for a hot bath," said Rebekah, who had been told the same story about a boating accident that Emilie originally had told Andrew.

"I must admit the notion holds considerable charm," said Emilie, holding back a yawn.

"Then a bath you will have," Rebekah declared. "There are few luxuries left to us. A hot bath is one I shall not forsake without a fight."

Amen to that, thought Emilie a half hour later as she sank blissfully into the warm water.

Rebekah had commandeered her children into setting up the copper tub in Emilie's room, then seeing that it was filled with plenty of warm, scented water. Rebekah hoarded attar of roses, which she doled out in minuscule portions for her weekly soak. Emilie had been touched that the woman would share her bounty with a stranger.

The copper tub was meant for soaking, not reclining, and try as she might Emilie could not submerge her knees or shoulders beneath the water at the same time. It was a small quibble. A marble bath the size of a swimming pool couldn't have been more appreciated.

She closed her eyes, letting her head fall back against the edge of the tub. She ached from toes to eyelids. In the past two days she'd walked more than in the past twenty years. Funny how you could know so much about a time period, understand the customs and the history, and still be surprised by the most basic differences.

All the Jazzercise classes and StairMaster sessions in the world hadn't prepared her for life without a car. No wonder the average life expectancy had been lower. People were just plain exhausted.

How did Rebekah manage, she wondered, with a home to take care of and a farm to run, not to mention six children of varying temperaments and needs. Large families had always held a certain appeal for Emilie and she had been charmed by them all, from about-to-be-wed Charity right down to six-month-old Aaron with the big brown eyes and tufts of blond hair.

She could still feel him cuddled against her chest, his plump baby hands pressing into her breasts. And that smell—was anyone immune to that sweetly seductive smell? She knew it was all part of a plot engineered by Mother Nature, designed to ensure the survival of the species, but that didn't matter.

Once again, Mother Nature was successful. The fierce yearning for a child that she had experienced during her brief marriage to Zane swooped in on her with the primal force of the tides.

She took a deep breath, then tried to think of something else. The red roses in the front yard, for example. Charity's wedding plans.

Or the beautiful sapphire blue of Zane's eyes.

As if on cue, the door swung open and Zane strode into the room.

"Zane!" She crossed her arms over her breasts and tried to slide lower in the tub. "You should have knocked."

"I tried to call," he said, sitting down on the edge of the bed, "but the phone's out of order."

"Very funny." She gave him a fierce look. "I was here first."

His gaze swept over her like a hot breeze. "So I see."

"Hand me a towel," she said, gesturing toward the stack resting next to him. "And stop looking at me like that." She was struggling to maintain a detached composure and the struggle grew more difficult with each second that passed.

"Don't get out on my account," he said, grinning. "I'm enjoying the view." More than she could imagine.

"That's exactly what we have to talk about." She tried to look authoritative but found it difficult given the circumstances. "Just because we—I mean, we made a mistake the other night and I don't intend to compound it."

He leaned back on the mattress, looking as comfortable as you please. "I couldn't agree more. Pretending to be married was McVie's idea, not mine."

"You agreed to it."

"Why not? You'd already stripped me down to the skin. He probably figured there weren't many surprises left."

Emilie cringed at the thought. "Between that and the divorce I can just imagine what he must be thinking."

Zane sat up straighter. "Who gives a damn what he thinks?"

"We should if we expect his help."

"You sure there isn't more to it than that?"

"I don't know what you mean."

Zane leaned forward. "The guy's your childhood hero and he's about fifty years younger than a childhood hero should be. Think about it."

"Really, Zane," she said, feigning nonchalance. "You sound like an idiot."

"I think you're falling for him."

"Ridiculous!"

"Is it?"

"Absolutely." She rose from the tub and reached for one of the towels stacked on the bed next to Zane. For an instant, as she leaned forward for the towel, she stood naked before him and the air seemed to shimmer between them. The towel didn't cover much, she noted with dismay, but it did manage to shield the essentials.

"McVie is serious and patriotic," Zane said, "just the kind of guy you always wanted."

"You don't know anything about what kind of man I want."

"I know you're looking at the kind of man you don't want."

His words stung, and she didn't know exactly why. She stepped from the tub. "This is a ridiculous conversation. There are more important things to think about." She reached for a cotton wrapper Rebekah had been kind enough to supply. "Like what we're going to do after we wear out our welcome with the Blakelees."

"Ask McVie. He seems to be the answer man around here."

There it was again, thought Emilie. The sound of jealousy. She couldn't believe her ears. "We're the ones with the answers," she pointed out, "and we have to decide which ones we're going to provide."

"You can't change history."

"I don't intend to," said Emilie. "Just give it a push in the right direction."

"If it's already happened, why would it need our help?"

"Did it ever occur to you that maybe we're part of the bigger picture?"

"No," he said. "Not for a second."

She stood by the window, brushing her hair with a large tortoiseshell comb. "There's a reason for everything that happens," she said, "and I can't help thinking we've been sent here for a purpose."

"Where's Shirley MacLaine when you need her?"

She sighed and put down the comb. "I didn't think you'd understand."

"There's no reason, Em," he said, walking toward her. "It just happened and now we have to find a way to get back where we belong."

Her gaze was drawn to the bed pushed up against the far wall.

"You should be in Tahiti," she said, meeting his eyes. "You would have been if you hadn't hijacked that balloon."

"Would you call it fate?"

"I call it temporary insanity."

He drew her close, draping his left arm around her shoulders. "You shouldn't have taken off the way you did."

She tried to move away, but he held her fast. "I made a mistake," she said softly. "There was no point to pretending otherwise."

"It didn't feel like a mistake."

"No," she said, "but that doesn't change things. We want different things from life, Zane. We need different things. Not even traveling two hundred years through time can change that."

He understood her meaning. "I'd sleep on the couch," he said, "but they don't have one."

"You don't have to sleep on the couch. We'll manage."

He looked at the narrow bed. "I doubt it."

"It is kind of small, isn't it?"

"Turn over once and we're talking conjugal rights." He reached for the closure on his trousers.

"What are you doing?"

"What do you think I'm doing?"

"I think you're taking your pants off." Hadn't he understood a single word she'd said?

"Best way to take a bath." He gestured toward the tub in the middle of the room. "Is the water still warm?"

She nodded.

"Great." Even with his broken arm he managed to divest himself of his clothing in record time. He placed his gold watch on the window ledge. "You'll scrub my back, won't you, Em?"

"Zane, you really don't want to get into that tub."

"Look," he said, "I'm tired and hot and grubby. If we're going to share a bed, I need the tub."

"But the water—"

"Is just right," he said, lowering his impressive body into the small tub. He frowned, sniffing the air. "What the hell is that smell?"

"Roses," said Emilie.

"From the front yard?"

"From the bathwater," she said, starting to giggle.

"You're kidding me."

"Afraid not. Rebekah gave me some attar of roses to put in the water."

"Why the hell didn't you tell me?"

"I was trying to. You were too fast for me."

"I'm going to smell like a damn bridal bouquet."

"Nobody'll notice."

The look on his face spoke volumes.

She approached the tub, clutching a flannel wash-rag. "Would you like your back scrubbed?" she asked sweetly.

He grunted.

"Once for yes, twice for no."

"Don't push it, Emilie," he warned.

She knelt down behind him then leaned forward, dipping the washrag into the scented water. "Keep your arm out of the water," she advised. "You don't want to get the splint wet."

"I don't give a damn about the splint."

"You will if it ends up smelling like rosewater."

She noticed with a smile that he made a point of keeping his right arm well out of the reach of the bathwater. The only light in the room came from a candle set upon the nightstand. Its light sent shadows flickering across the wooden floor. Slowly she drew the wet, warm cloth over the muscles of his back and shoulders, watching the drops of water glisten in the candlelight.

The feel of his skin beneath her hands was both strange and familiar, and once again she felt that dark need building inside her. It had always been like this. The sound of his voice, the touch of his hand, the way his hair always smelled of sunshine and sea breezes— any one of those things was enough to send her foolish heart into a spin.

If only she didn't want him. This whole ridiculous mess would be so much easier if she didn't yearn for him. She hated feeling so open, so vulnerable, wanting the one thing on earth she shouldn't have.

Thank God she wasn't still in love with him, that what she felt was nothing more than lust.

"That's great," Zane murmured, letting his head drop forward as she kneaded the muscles of his neck and upper back. "Down there...yeah, that's it...."

She watched, mesmerized, as a bead of water inched its way down his spine, fighting the urge to follow its trail with her tongue.

This was the life, thought Zane as Emilie ministered to him. A warm bath—even if the water did stink of roses. Candlelight. A beautiful woman and a waiting bed. He had the feeling all of the elements were about to come together.

For the first time since he'd hijacked that damn balloon, he felt hopeful.

"Well," said Emilie, rising and moving away from the tub. "Your back is as clean as it's going to get. I think I'll go to bed."

Zane's thoughts exactly. The feel of her hands against him had focused all his attention on the same idea.

She threw back the covers and climbed into the narrow bed. He noticed she was still wearing the pale blue robe, and he grinned. He'd always liked helping her undress.

He watched, amazed, as she yawned, scooted down beneath the covers and closed her eyes.

"You're going to sleep?"

She nodded, eyes still closed. "Of course."

That's what he got for having an overactive imagination. She'd told him she wasn't interested in continuing where they'd left off two hundred years from now. He'd have to remember his ex-wife was one of the few women in the world who meant exactly what she said.

Not that it made the situation any easier. Climbing into that narrow bed and staying on his own side of the mattress would be a major-league test of willpower, and where Emilie was concerned he'd never had much of that commodity.

"A deal's a deal," he muttered as he climbed out of the tub.

Emilie peered at him through the flickering candlelight. "Did you say something?"

"Not me," he said, grabbing for the scratchy tissues that passed for early-American towels. "You must have heard me yawn."

"Mmm," said Emilie, not sounding terribly convinced. "That must have been it." She turned on her side and closed her eyes. "Last one in bed blows out the candle."

It was going to be a very long night.

NINE

From sunup until sundown the Blakelee farm was a hotbed of activity. Andrew and the boys set out for the fields soon after dawn, returning to the farmhouse only for food and drink.

Emilie was swept up into the household routine that was uniquely the province of females. She swept the bare wood floors, beat the rugs when necessary, mended stockings and repaired worn trousers. She helped Rebekah with kitchen chores, shuddering at the sight of an unplucked chicken lying on the table, and she was again struck by the realization that knowing about a way of life and actually experiencing that way of life were two totally different things.

Still, there was something exhilarating about being tested to the limits of your knowledge and ability, and as they began their second week in this strange new world, Emilie found herself more confident that she could find a way to make a life for herself.

Unfortunately Zane was finding it difficult to carve a place for himself. Day after day he watched McVie and the Blakelee boys working in the fields while he sat on the top porch step and waited for some sign, some indication that he'd find a way back to the world where he belonged.

He was a coiled mass of energy, a taut mainspring ready to snap. The damn broken arm kept him from burning off his tensions with hard work. His usual diversions of fast cars and bright lights were unavailable. Pretending he and Emilie were married was easy enough during the day but at night, when she was only a heartbeat away, he burned for her.

In desperation he had taken to sleeping on the floor and, he noted wryly, she had offered no protest. He had only his thoughts for company and as the days passed those thoughts grew increasingly dark.

All around him the talk was of independence, but to Zane independence would begin only when he regained financial freedom. Back in his time he'd never had to worry about things like earning a living. He'd been born into money and all that entailed, and the pursuits of lesser mortals had always seemed murky at best. McVie had said that once Zane's arm healed he would be an asset in the fields. "Josiah was a large man such as you," Andrew said, "capable of lifting his weight and more."

Pumping iron was one thing. Baling hay was something else again.

He supposed he could get work as a fortune-teller, but that was probably the best way to insure his place as first in line at the gallows. In his pocket his hand rested on the wristwatch he'd refused to hide with Emilie's twentieth century booty. You could probably feed the Continental army for a year on what he'd paid for the damn thing—and on top of everything else, it no longer worked.

"Wait a minute," he said out loud as he slipped the watch off his wrist. Times may have changed but gold remained constant. If he removed the watchface and separated the band into segments, independence might no longer be as far away as it seemed.

Money could make the difference. He could repay Rebekah Blakelee for her generosity, then purchase a horse and carriage so he and Emilie could return to the lighthouse. He had the feeling that if they were to have any chance at all of returning to the future, they would have to be waiting for that chance at the place where the future began.

As for Andrew, he was faring no better than his counterpart from the future.

Each day he worked the farm with vigor.

Each night he slipped from the quiet house to meet with the other members of the spy ring. A spy ring whose numbers were dwindling away faster than the coins in his pocket. First Blakelee. Now Fleming. Arrest warrants had been issued for Miller and Quick.

Papers had fallen into the wrong hands and, to everyone's dismay, invisible ink had proven to be less than reliable. There must be a better means of achieving the desired end, but neither Andrew nor the other members of the spy ring could discover what it might be.

Rumors abounded about British troop movements on Long Island and anarchy in the Hudson River valley. Militiamen in Pennsylvania and New Jersey had laid down their arms and returned home to farms and families in desperate need, with promises to return to the front once the harvest was past.

Andrew listened with a keen ear for any mention of a new plot against the life of General Washington, but there was none.

To his puzzlement, he found himself both relieved and disappointed. He wished no danger upon the head of His Excellency, but he wanted to believe that all mistress Emilie and Rutledge had told him was true. If the general faced no threat to his life, did that mean that the other stories his companions had told him were so much whole cloth?

He had spent much time considering the curious bond between the beautiful red-haired lass and Rutledge. They had once been wed, had stood before man and God and repeated those sacred vows that he and Elspeth had repeated on that long-ago summer's day. *Until death...* they had promised, and only death's finality could have torn Elspeth from his side.

He had little experience or knowledge of divorce. He knew that it existed, but beyond that the notion was as foreign as it was distasteful. Doubtless it had been Rutledge who instigated the separation. There was much of the rogue about the man. He had not the aspect of stability that a woman found important in the man she would wed.

Of course, he reminded himself, they came from a time and place unknown to him where men watched moving images on giant screens and made a fortune in gold tossing a leather ball through a hoop. Perhaps in that world divorce was an everyday occurrence, but still he found that impossible to believe. He wondered what manner of difficulties he had visited upon the lass by forcing her to share a room with the man who had turned away from their conjugal vows.

And he wondered how it was that any man could turn away from such a beautiful woman....

One morning, in the third week of their stay with the Blakelees, Emilie was in the kitchen kneading a batch of bread. Rebekah stood at the open hearth, stirring the stewpot, while Aaron slept soundly in his cradle beneath the window.

Isaac and two of his younger brothers had gone into the fields to work with Andrew. Charity was in the sitting room working diligently on the pillow slips she would take to her marriage bed two weeks from now.

Zane had been gone when Emilie woke up, and she found herself vaguely disturbed that no one had seen him yet today. Not that his whereabouts were any of her concern. They lived in edgy proximity in the small second-floor bedroom, married in name but not in fact. That would have been hard enough for any man and woman but, given their volatile history, it was rapidly becoming impossible.

That first night alone in the second-floor bedroom had been the turning point. The urge to give in to temptation once again had been strong, but she had been stronger. Strange how little pleasure that fact afforded her.

They were polite to each other, and considerate, but that was where it ended. Passion still simmered beneath the surface, and she was determined that was where the passion would remain. It would be too easy to make the same mistake over again, settling for lust when what she wanted was the whole, incredible, wonderful package: lust and love and a future that included a home and family.

All the things Zane had never wanted—and probably never would.

She glanced toward baby Aaron asleep in his cradle.

"You're a lucky woman," she said to Rebekah as she divided the bread dough into four portions.

Rebekah looked at Emilie, then at her infant son. "I thank the Almighty everyday," she said simply. "Josiah and I lost two daughters to the pox three springs past. A day does not go by where I do not think of their beloved faces."

Emilie spoke without thinking. "Surely you had your children inoculated?"

"'Tis a dangerous and painful process," Rebekah said, looking at Emilie's obvious curiosity. "We would have had to uproot the children and spend many uneasy days in Philadelphia while we waited to see if the pox would come."

"I'm sorry," Emilie said, flustered by her own thoughtlessness. What miracles they took for granted in the twentieth century. "You owe me no explanation."

"Nor do you, Emilie, but there is a question that has plagued me now for days."

Emilie directed her attention to the bread dough. "You may ask me anything."

Rebekah wiped her hands on her apron, then walked over to the table where Emilie was working. "This is a most delicate matter but one to which I must address myself."

Oh, God, thought Emilie, heart pounding inside her chest. Could Rebekah possibly suspect that Emilie and Zane were not what they seemed to be? She had cut the zipper from Zane's trousers and buried it behind the barn with her American Express card. To her knowledge, Andrew still had her driver's license. She prayed he hadn't decided to share their secret with Rebekah Blakelee.

"Speak your mind," Emilie said with more serenity than she was feeling.

Rebekah's cheeks were flushed with high color. Emilie watched, unnerved, as the small-boned woman squared her shoulders, then met her eyes. "'Tis about Andrew McVie I speak. He is a fine man, you will agree."

"I agree," said Emilie, puzzled. "He is a man of honor and principle and I—"

Rebekah raised her hand. "He is also a man in love."

The tension rushed from Emilie's body and she laughed. "How wonderful!" she said. "Who is the object of his affections?"

Rebekah's brows slid together in a frown. "You are."

"Rebekah! That is ridiculous. I am—I am a married woman."

"That may be so, but I have seen the way he looks at you when he believes no one is about, and I fear the signs are clear."

Emilie abandoned all pretense. "He scarcely knows me," she said. "Love does not grow in such a short span of time."

"Love does not set its pace by the clock, Emilie. I am a woman and I know what I see. Andrew loves you."

"This is dreadful," she said. "Certainly I have done nothing to encourage such a thing." She wiped her hands on her apron. "I must find Andrew and settle this matter immediately."

"No!" Rebekah grabbed her by the arm and held her fast. "You mustn't! It has been a very long time since I have seen Andrew smile. He would be much embarrassed if he knew we read his thoughts."

Andrew McVie—*her childhood hero!*—in love with her? "Surely it is a temporary thing," Emilie said, twisting the gold-and-silver ring on her left hand.

"He—he knows that Zane and I..." Her words trailed off. Andrew knew the truth. The entire truth. If he had fallen in love with her as Rebekah believed, it was with the full knowledge that a future between them was within the realm of possibility.

"He has known great sorrow these few years past," Rebekah was saying. "Since losing his wife—"

Emilie's head snapped up. "His wife?"

"I did not know Elspeth," Rebekah said, "but I believe he loved her and their son with his heart and soul."

"Is his son—?"

Rebekah nodded, her brown eyes glistening with tears. "A terrible fire," she said, shaking her head. "He lost them both ... he lost everything."

A cold chill rose up Emilie's spine. She shivered and wrapped her arms around her chest. "I'd always wondered," she murmured. "There'd never been any mention of a family."

Rebekah looked at her. "I thought your acquaintanceship was of a short duration."

For one crazy moment she considered telling Rebekah the truth, that she and Zane were not only divorced, but from the future. Then reason returned and she caught herself before she made a dreadful mistake.

"What should I do?" she asked the brown-eyed woman, who was watching her closely. "How shall I handle him?"

"Gently," said Rebekah. "Without harshness or idle encouragement." There was the faintest reproach in her tone, almost as if she'd felt Emilie had been leading him on.

"I—I would never do anything to hurt him."

"He is a good man," said Rebekah once again.

Emilie gazed out the window toward the fields. In the distance she could just make out Andrew's wiry figure and she looked away, her chest tight.

"Your husband is a fine-looking man," Rebekah said. "How long have you been wed?"

"Five—no, six years," Emilie said. "Yes. Six years."

Rebekah smiled. "The years pass swiftly."

"Faster than you could ever imagine," said Emilie.

"You have been blessed with children?"

Emilie shook her head. "Not yet."

Rebekah's smile faded and she reached out to pat Emilie's hand in a sympathetic gesture. "You are young. I am certain you will be blessed."

"I'm afraid I'm not *that* young," Emilie said with a small laugh. "Thirty years old my next birthday."

"You jest," said Rebekah.

"I haven't been sleeping well," said Emilie, gesturing toward the circles beneath her eyes, "but in truth I will turn thirty in December."

"That cannot be."

"Rebekah!" Emilie's voice rose in indignation. "Do I look that unwell?"

"It's just—I mean to say, you look so young. I did not think it possible that you were—" She shook her head. "I hesitate to stand next to you, for I appear old enough to be your mother and I am but three years your senior."

Emilie made polite noises of disagreement but, in truth, the difference in their appearance was startling. "I have had a gentle life," Emilie said.

Rebekah sighed deeply. "I cannot say the same."

Childbirth and toil aged a woman in ways the years could not. Emilie experienced a moment of fear, primal and inarticulate, as she thought of the life she'd left behind. Why had she never realized the depth of ease, of privilege, that the most average of women enjoyed as a matter of course? She wondered what Rebekah would think if she told the woman about microwaves and washing machines, about face-lifts and birth control pills.

It won't always be so hard to be a woman, she thought, but that knowledge wouldn't help Rebekah—or herself. The realization was sudden and overwhelming.

Retin-A, cosmetic surgery, the wonders to be found in Estée Lauder and Elizabeth Arden—gone, all of it. This was a rougher world, harsh and unyielding. A woman's beauty was as short-lived as a rose in winter. She had always talked a good show about superficiality and the cult of youth but, when push came to shove, would she be able to face the uncompromising truths that her mirror would soon reveal?

By two o'clock Zane had still not returned. Neither Emilie nor Rebekah had any idea where he had disappeared to. Emilie briefly considered walking out into the fields to ask Andrew or Isaac if they knew where Zane had gone, but Rebekah's words lingered in her ears and she stayed away.

Andrew did not come in for dinner, but continued working.

The two women shared the meal of slaw, hot rolls and mutton with the Blakelee children, except for Isaac who remained in the fields with Andrew. Charity and her mother had much to consider as the day of the wedding celebration swiftly approached, and Emilie found herself drifting along on a wave of bittersweet longing.

Baby Aaron slept contentedly in his cradle near his mother's chair. Benjamin and Stephen, eight-year-old twins, teased each other mercilessly, while the toddler, Ethan, entertained Emilie with tales of his imaginary friend, John the Flying Dog.

It was a simple meal, served in a simple way and shared with people she barely knew, yet Emilie experienced a sharp stab of envy. It seemed so little to ask for: a home of her own, a husband to love, children to care for. Somehow that most basic of dreams had always managed to elude her. Leave it to her to find the man of her dreams, only to discover her husband had no interest in any of it.

He loves you, Emilie, Rebekah had said about Andrew. *I see the way he looks at you....*

She couldn't imagine the despair Andrew had felt when he lost his wife and child. It explained so much about him. That haunted look in his hazel eyes. The sense of restlessness. The depth of his commitment to the cause of independence. He was the kind of man a woman could admire: strong and loyal and—

She stopped, shocked by the direction her thoughts were taking her. What on earth had come over her? Surely she wasn't attracted to him—not in the fiery way she was attracted to Zane.

But how would it feel to cast your lot with a man who wanted the same things you wanted, home and family and happy endings? Maybe that type of wild and passionate love was, by its very nature, doomed to failure. Certainly it had been with her marriage to Zane. She'd had such high and shining hopes for their future, only to discover he cared more for adventure than he ever could for her.

After the meal, Emilie helped Rebekah with cleaning up.

"You are looking pale," Rebekah observed, placing her palm against Emilie's forehead. "Are you unwell?"

"Tired," Emilie said.

"You should rest."

Emilie shook her head. The last thing she wanted was to be trapped in a room with her tangled thoughts. "I think I'll sit outside and work on the mending."

Rebekah grew thoughtful. "Is there a chance that perhaps you are with child?"

"No!" Emilie took a deep breath. She laughed nervously as vivid images of that one magical night heated her blood. "I mean, I don't believe so."

"It will happen," Rebekah said with a gentle smile as she took Aaron from his cradle and prepared to nurse him.

Emilie fled before the woman could say any more.

Emilie found a shady spot beneath an old maple tree and settled down with the mending a few minutes later. Her fingers shook as she unfolded the man's shirt and searched for the worn spots in need of repair. Rebekah was a practical woman and she was seeing to it that her husband's garments were in perfect shape for his return.

This had to be the strangest day she'd had since this whole adventure began. First Rebekah told her that Andrew loved her and now Rebekah asked if she might be pregnant. It was enough to make Emilie throw her hands in the air and flee.

Which, it occurred to her, was exactly what it seemed Zane had done.

There was no telling where his thirst for adventure might take him. This was probably the longest period of time he'd ever spent in one place since he was in diapers. In another week or two his arm would be healed, and she wouldn't hazard a guess what course of action he would take after that.

He still talked about finding his way back to their old lives. She'd caught him once, drawing designs in the dirt with a stick. "Our escape hatch," he'd said when she asked what he was doing. A hot-air balloon. "Great," she'd said, shaking her head. "Now all you have to do is manufacture a propane tank and you're all set."

Obviously he was still unable to accept the reality of their situation. For all she knew he was out scouring the countryside in search of a wicker gondola and a few thousand square yards of silk.

"Rebekah told me I would find you here."

Emilie jumped, pricking herself with the steel needle. "Andrew!" She popped her finger into her mouth, and looked up at him. "You snuck up on me."

He squatted down next to her. "I have not heard that expression before."

She grinned. "Consider yourself lucky. We've done terrible things to the language in my time. You would be appalled."

"Yesterday you told Rutledge that his socks would be knocked off by Rebekah's apple betty. I spent much time trying to envision that occurrence but came up wanting."

"It's slang," she said, noting the touch of green in his hazel eyes.

"What does it mean?"

She thought for a moment. "Overwhelmed, but in the best possible way."

"And if the situation was dire?"

"You'd be bummed out," said Emilie. "Of course, that only applies if you're a surfer—or from California."

He looked at her blankly. "Those words mean nothing to me."

"California is the state that curves along the western coast. They found gold there in 1848 and that really put it on the map." She told him about the perfect climate, the perfect beaches and the perfect specimens who rode the waves.

"I don't believe I understand it correctly," Andrew said, considering her words. "A man stands on a wooden board and sails through the waves?"

"Women do it, as well."

"This world of yours," he said, sitting down a few feet away from her. "Rutledge would sell his soul to Beelzebub to return, but you—" He stopped abruptly.

"I don't seem to care if I go back. You're right. I don't." There. She'd said it. She hadn't intended to, but now that she'd given voice to the words she felt as if she'd crossed into alien territory.

"I do not understand. All the wonder you've left behind." He shook his head in bewilderment.

"We've told you only about the wonders, Andrew. There is much wrong in our time. Many people fear that the earth will not survive."

The world he knew was one of bounty, of clear skies and clean water. She tried to explain the differences to him, but when she came to garbage dumps the size of mountains he started to laugh.

"Forget it," she said, laughing too. "What difference does it make? Maybe it'll never happen."

"But you have seen them with your own eyes, have you not?"

"I've also seen myself pulled back two centuries through time. Who knows what else is possible?"

"You are unlike any woman I have ever known, lass."

"Given the circumstances, I'd have to agree." She tried to sound bright and breezy, the opposite of the way she felt.

"You are so full of life, so strong and—"

"Andrew." She placed a hand on his forearm. "Please don't."

He placed a hand over hers. "I cannot stop, lass. There is so much I have to say and I fear that time is my enemy."

She made to withdraw her hand but he would not allow it. "Andrew, you must believe it is just the circumstances that make you feel this way. It has nothing to do with me."

"It has everything to do with you."

"We shouldn't be talking like this."

"Do you love him still?"

"Andrew!"

"'Tis a logical question."

"We're divorced," she said. "Whatever existed between us is long gone." It was less than the truth but not quite a lie.

It was also the best she could do.

"He abandoned you and still you are friends. I find it easier to comprehend a man walking on the moon."

"So do I. The truth is a little more complicated than that." She hesitated. "Actually, I walked out on Zane, not the other way around."

"Do not try to shield him."

"Andrew, I'm not trying to shield him. I'm telling you the truth. We wanted different things from marriage. I was very unhappy, and so I left him."

"And he allowed this?"

"It's a free country," she said. "Or at least it will be in a few years."

"Did he beat you?"

"If he'd tried it he'd be walking funny today."

Andrew's face turned beet red. "Then why was it that you left him?"

Emilie sighed deeply. "I wanted a home. He didn't. I wanted a family. He didn't."

"You speak as if there are choices to be made. Only the Almighty can decide when a couple will start a family."

She wasn't up to a discussion on birth control. She cleared her throat and changed the subject. "Have you uncovered anything about the assassination plot?''

It took Andrew a moment to regain his emotional balance. ''Nay, I have not. Our troubles have been of a more personal nature.''

''Tell me.'' Emilie moved her needle and thread through the fabric of Josiah's shirt as Andrew told her of Fleming's disappearance, and of the arrest warrants issued against two more members of the spy ring. ''And what of the messages you've been passing through to General Mercer?''

''It grows more difficult with each day.'' An important dispatch of a very sensitive nature had fallen into British hands two nights ago and Andrew feared the Jersey spy ring might be coming to the end of its usefulness.

Emilie watched the rhythmic motion of the sewing needle as she pushed then pulled it through the fabric of Josiah's shirt. ''Maybe you're going about it wrong,'' she said thoughtfully. ''Letters can be stolen.''

''And what alternative is there, lass?''

Sunlight glittered off the silvery needle. ''Embroidery,'' she said, meeting his eyes. ''A message could be embroidered onto a garment then handed over to a courier without arousing undue interest.''

Andrew frowned. "No man would wear a school-girl's sampler on his back."

"Not a sampler," she said. "What I'm thinking about would be tiny." Quickly she rethreaded her needle, then stitched her name along the seam of the shirt.

"'Tis no bigger than a grain of rice."

"Exactly. An entire message could be embroidered beneath a collar or inside a cuff."

"Not many are skilled enough to do such work."

"I am," she said without hesitation.

His heart felt light inside his chest. Surely there was more to her eagerness than patriotic fervor.

"The thinnest floss of tan or gray will disappear..."

Her voice carried the sound of angels.

"Inside seams or on the underside of a lining..."

Her eyes flashed with the fire of priceless emeralds.

"...work clothes or uniforms or even a baby's blanket..."

Her skin smelled sweeter than the roses blooming by the front door.

She looked up at him and smiled. "I think it will be wonderful, don't you?"

"Aye, lass," he said, his heart soaring. "Wonderful."

TEN

"Are you going to tell Ma?"

Zane looked down at the lanky youth. "I don't know, Isaac. What do you think I should do?"

Isaac Blakelee, carrying a parcel of muslin fabric for his mother, considered the question with almost comical deliberation. "I think it should remain a secret between men."

Zane had to bite his lip to keep from laughing. The boy was still wet behind the ears. Barely fifteen years old and already burning with the righteous fires of independence, both personal and patriotic. Rebekah had sent the boy into town for fabric with strict orders to return home without delay. Isaac, however, had been unable to pass the Plumed Rooster without paying a visit.

He cleared his throat and struggled to look stern. "Next time I would avoid rum, Isaac, and stick with ale."

Zane felt better than he had in weeks. Money might not be able to buy you happiness but it went a long way toward buying a man his freedom. Those chunks of gold from his watchband had translated into a considerable stack of notes, like the New Jersey three-shilling with the warning To Counterfeit is Death printed on the front. His pockets bulged with coins, most of which bore the likeness of King George II and dates in the 1740s.

If he had had any doubts as to the reality of his situation, they were gone now.

He and Isaac walked together in silence for a while. Zane had been enjoying a tankard of ale in the Plumed Rooster, with the mixed clientele of farmers and Continental soldiers, when he noticed Isaac engaged in an altercation with the proprietor. The boy had been vigorously defending his father's honor, but the owner of the pub had been having none of it.

"Out with you, boy. I'll not be servin' a traitor's son."

Zane had stepped in, settled Isaac's tab, then dragged the hot-tempered teenager out into the sunshine and pointed him in the direction of home.

"Feel like talking?" he said as they waited for a coach and driver to rumble past.

Isaac shrugged his narrow shoulders. "They think my pa's a traitor but I know that ain't so."

"People say a lot of lousy things," Zane said. "Sometimes you have to forget them."

"I can't forget my pa," the boy snapped. "Old man Carpenter's a Tory and he says my pa and the others are in jail by Little Rocky Hill and next week they're going t'be moving the lot of them up to the Hell Ship."

Zane's interest was piqued. "What's the Hell Ship?"

"Floating prisons," said Isaac. "They say Wallabout Bay's fillin' up with bodies of dead prisoners." The boy's eyes glistened with tears but he fiercely blinked them away. "We ain't got enough soldiers to stand against the Lobsterbacks. My ma's got to—"

"Forget it," said Zane. "She needs you with her, Isaac. At least until your father comes back."

"What if my pa don't come back?" the boy asked, voice trembling. "What then?"

There was, of course, no answer for a question like that, and there never would be an answer for it, at least not in either of Zane's lifetimes.

Isaac looked up at him with curiosity. "The army'd be needing lots of help. I know my pa will join sooner or later. How about you?"

"I don't think I'm military material."

"Neither's my pa, but he says you do what you can to help."

"It's something to think about." And he'd been thinking about it a lot lately as he watched McVie and the Blakelees and Emilie strive toward a goal they couldn't see or hear or touch but knew was as necessary as air and water.

He draped an arm around the kid's shoulders and they walked the rest of the way home in companionable silence.

"One of the cows has been feelin' poorly," Isaac said as they started up the lane that led to the farmhouse. "Would you give this to Ma so I can go straightaway t'the barn?"

Zane motioned for the parcel and Isaac tossed it to him.

"Much obliged," the boy said, then dashed off in the direction of the barn.

Isaac was a good kid, filled with energy and loyalty and high ideals. Zane couldn't help but wonder how life would treat him. Sooner or later Isaac would make good his threat to join the Continental army, and he found himself hoping that fate would treat the boy with kindness.

He climbed the front steps and was about to go inside when the sound of Emilie's laughter, sweet and high, drifted toward him on the heavy summer air. He glanced across the front yard, expecting to see her walking toward him.

Instead he found her sitting in the shade of an enormous maple tree, smiling at that damn McVie as if they shared a secret.

He placed the parcel of muslin on the porch railing, then headed over to where Emilie and Andrew sat.

"Zane!" Her eyes widened as he approached. "We've been wondering where you were." She motioned for him, to join them beneath the tree.

"I had some business to take care of." He looked from Emilie to Andrew and didn't like what he saw. Not one damn bit.

"Business?" Her eyes widened some more. "What business could you possibly have?"

"I'll tell you later." No way was he going to let McVie know he had a king's ransom stuffed in his pockets. He didn't trust the guy as far as he could throw him.

"Where did you go?" asked McVie.

"Princeton."

McVie looked surprised. "How was it you were able to find the town without a guide?"

Zane started to say something both profane and right on target, but Emilie leaped into the fray.

"Zane has the most amazing memory," she said brightly. "People, places, conversations—" She laughed. "It's almost scary."

No, thought Zane, what was scary was the way she looked. Edgy with excitement. Soft and beautiful and female.

"So what's going on here?" he asked. "You two looked thick as thieves."

Emilie's face reddened and she looked down at the sewing in her lap.

McVie, however, met his eyes. "Mistress Emilie has provided a way to transport messages that will greatly aid our cause."

Great, thought Zane. Next thing he knew she'd be leading a protest march at Independence Hall.

"Yeah," he said, "she's another Betsy Ross."

"I'll explain it to you later," Emilie said to Andrew, who'd been about to ask.

"So what's the big idea, or is it a state secret?"

She looked toward Andrew who nodded. "I'm going to embroider the messages right on the messengers' clothing."

"That's it?" he asked. "Why don't you have them carrying billboards while you're at it?"

"We're not stupid," she snapped. She handed him a shirt. "Take a look at this and tell me what you see."

He glanced at the garment. "Other than a hole on the elbow, nothing."

She crossed her arms over her chest. "I rest my case."

"Take careful note of the underside of the collar," McVie said. "Mistress Emilie has embroidered her name."

"I'll be damned," said Zane as he held the garment up for closer examination. "That's microscopic."

"Mi-kro-scoppik?" McVie repeated.

"Tiny," said Emilie. "And that's the point, Zane. If I use the right shade of floss, you'd only know it was there if you were looking for it."

"Great idea," he said, "but what happens once they figure it out?"

"Then we'll come up with something else," she said.

McVie was watching them both with avid interest.

"Built-in obsolescence," Zane drawled. "It's what made America great. Why not throw a few roadblocks in their way from the outset?"

"I suppose you have a brilliant suggestion."

"Damn right. Use a secret code."

Both Emilie and McVie burst into laughter.

"What's so funny?"

They told him that secret codes were far from a revolutionary idea.

"Sorry," said Emilie. "It just proves there's nothing new under the sun."

"Depends on the code," he said, not cracking a smile.

McVie leaned forward. "Explain."

Zane grinned. McVie was a lot of things, but stupid wasn't one of them. "What if the key to the code was unbreakable?"

"Such a thing does not exist," said McVie.

"It does if the key comes from 1992."

Emilie's sharp intake of breath was audible. McVie's attention was directed solely on Zane.

"It doesn't matter what you use," Zane continued. "The Gettysburg Address, an old Beach Boys song. There's an endless supply and, unless I miss my bet, Emilie and I are the only people around who could break it."

"My God," said Emilie, heart pounding. "It's perfect!"

"I know," said Zane. "I thought the same thing when I first came up with the idea back in grade school."

"What song did you use?" she asked.

He grinned. " 'Twist and Shout.' The Beatles' version."

Emilie launched into a rousing version of the old rock-and-roll hit that had McVie staring at her as if she'd grown a second head.

"Sorry," said Emilie after two verses. "I always loved that song."

"Are there many such songs?" McVie asked.

Emilie and Zane looked at each other and laughed.

"Don't worry," said Emilie. "Plenty to last until the end of the war."

"You have told me the resolution will be favorable to our cause," said McVie, "but will that resolution be a long time in coming?"

How did you tell a man that another five bloody years would pass before Lord Cornwallis and the British troops surrendered at Yorktown?

Emilie finally broke the awkward silence. "It will be a long time coming," was all she said.

Emilie was too excited to eat supper. Her stomach felt shaky, as if she'd taken one ride too many on an amusement-park roller coaster. She excused herself and sat down by the window in the front room, embroidering a message into the underside of McVie's collar.

It was a simple message and a simple code. She and Zane had decided "Jingle Bells" was a good way to start. Zane wrote out the words for Andrew on a piece of foolscap, muttering loudly about the quill pen.

As it turned out he needn't have bothered, for Andrew quickly memorized the song, and they determined that each of the next three nights would key into a different stanza of the old Christmas carol.

She wondered if the day would come when she and Zane taught a group of colonial spies the lyrics to "Doo Wah Diddy." Apparently there were a lot of things that didn't make it into the history books.

Two hours later she said goodbye to McVie in the doorway. She had worked diligently to embroider the message into the underside of his collar with stitches as fine as the web of a spider, and she was pleased with her accomplishment.

"I wish I could come with you," she said, admiring her handiwork as she smoothed down his collar. "This is incredibly exciting."

The look in his eyes made her step back, flustered. He'd made his feelings clear this afternoon beneath the maple tree. Apparently he had spoken the truth. Be kind to him, Rebekah had warned, for he'd known his own brand of heartbreak.

"Wish me Godspeed," he said, his voice both rough and caressing.

"Godspeed," she said. "And be careful."

He turned and left the farmhouse.

She stood in the doorway for a long while, staring out into the darkness. Her thoughts were scattered, as if she were caught in one of those crazy dreams where people changed shape and nothing was quite the way it seemed.

"You're tired," she told herself, turning away from the door. That's all it was. After a good night's sleep, everything would seem normal once more—or whatever passed for normal these days.

As she climbed the stairs to the bedroom, it occurred to her that this was why television had been invented: for nights like these when being alone with your thoughts was too awful to contemplate.

Zane was standing by the window when she entered the room. He was naked from the waist up, his torso illuminated only by the starlight twinkling above. His hair had grown longer. She'd come to love that ponytail, but Zane swore he never would.

"Did McVie leave?" he asked.

She nodded, sidestepping the enormous tub set up in the middle of the room. "I'll come back after you've taken your bath."

"I'm finished," he said.

She sniffed the air. "Roses?"

He didn't meet her eyes. "This tub's for you."

She chuckled softly at the reference as her heart slid into her rib cage. "Thank you, Zane."

He nodded, then turned away from the window. "I'll sit on the porch until you're done."

"Zane." She touched his arm. "You look exhausted. Haven't you been sleeping?"

He shrugged. "It's too damn quiet around here. I miss noise."

She took a deep breath. "I'm going to take a *very* long bath," she said, gesturing toward the bed. "Why don't you sleep?"

He didn't need to be convinced. "Thanks," he said, stretching out on the narrow bed. "Kick me out when you're done."

"I will."

He closed his eyes, and conversation ended. She stood there watching him, wondering if she should admonish him to *keep* his eyes closed while she bathed, but he didn't show the slightest degree of interest in her activities.

She considered forgoing the pleasure of a warm bath, but the temptation was more than she could stand. A candle flickered on the highboy and she quietly crossed the room to blow it out. The room abruptly plunged into darkness. She wondered if she'd ever grow accustomed to this total and complete absence of light, so different from the nights she'd known in that other, faraway world.

Zane's breathing was the only sound in the room. She fumbled with the laces on her bodice, acutely aware of the enforced intimacy of the situation. She took off the pale green dress, the petticoats and her cotton hose, then laid them over the back of the rocking chair.

The scent of roses enveloped her senses as she slipped into the tub. Sighing, she leaned back and closed her eyes, willing herself to clear her mind of everything but the blissful sensation of warm, silky water caressing her body.

If only her mind would cooperate. Not even the seductive pleasures of the warm tub could compete with the tangled thoughts vying for her attention. Why couldn't life be easy, she wondered. You met someone, you fell in love. You married and built a life together. Case closed. Maybe there was something to be said for the days when you expected nothing more from marriage than a united front to present to the world and children to move that world into the future.

Sex only confused things. Andrew McVie seemed to be everything she'd ever wanted in a husband, yet she didn't feel that inexplicable jolt of electricity that she experienced every time she looked at Zane. Her heart ached for Andrew and the family he'd lost. How empty his world must seem without his wife and son. You could see the yearning in his eyes each time he looked at baby Aaron or little Stephen, and she could only imagine how he must long for a home and family of his own.

Isn't that what marriage should be, a union of like minds with a single goal? Wouldn't that be enough for one lifetime. . . .

"You can do it," he said, supporting her shoulders. "Just a little longer. . . ."

"No!" She bit her lip as another wave of pain tore through her midsection. "I can't . . . I just can't do it anymore."

"Push, Emilie!" urged the midwife positioned at the foot of the bed. "The head's crowning."

"C'mon, Em," he urged. "We're almost there."

Her scream ricocheted off the walls then lodged itself between her legs. Pain . . . more pain than she'd imagined existed in the world . . . then the overwhelming, irresistible urge to push and then that sound . . . that incredible sound of life beginning right there before their very eyes.

"Oh, God!" she cried out. "We did it. We have a son!"

She touched his cheek, feeling his tears against her skin.

"I love you," she said, her words mingling with her own tears. "More than you'll ever know...."

"I love you...." The voice came toward him from a great distance. "More than you'll ever know."

Zane woke up, completely alert to his surroundings. The nightstand to his left. The window open wide to the night air.

Emilie asleep in the copper tub.

He rose from the bed and walked toward her.

"Wake up, Em. You're dreaming."

She murmured something he couldn't understand and sank more deeply into the tub.

"C'mon. That water's getting cold."

Her breathing was slow and regular. Trying to wake her up seemed cruel. He leaned forward and scooped her into his arms. His movements, hampered by the splint on his right arm, were clumsy. She barely noticed.

Zane, however, couldn't say the same.

Her naked body was warm and supple as he held her against his bare chest. He scarcely noticed the water dripping from her hair and skin onto his, except to register a deep sensual thrill that stirred his blood.

Slowly he carried her to the bed, laying her down gently on the horsehair mattress. He wanted to light a candle against the dark so he could see the splendor of her naked form, but the truth was he knew exactly how she looked, every spectacular inch of her.

She shivered slightly and he remembered that she was wet from her bath. Two towels rested on the seat of the rocking chair and he brought them back to the bed. Kneeling down, he took her right foot in his hands and pressed a towel to the instep and arch, the elegant toes. Her ankle was narrow, delicately made. The muscles of her calf were strong and firm, yet still extremely feminine.

He shifted position, aware of the way his blood was pounding inside his head. She managed to combine delicacy with strength, the most beguiling combination imaginable. He drew the towel over her knee, then slowly dried his way up the length of her thigh. Her performed the same actions on the other leg.

She moaned low in her throat.

He waited.

She sank again into sleep.

The curls between her thighs were damp, fragrant with roses and the smell of a woman. Her smell. He leaned forward and pressed his mouth against her for an instant, branding her.

Branding himself.

It would be easy to lose himself in her, to take her before she awakened enough to protest, and prove that whatever problems they'd had, this powerful physical desire wasn't one of them. This was the best thing life had to offer, the one chance human beings got to walk with the gods.

But, damn it, there were some things you didn't do no matter how much you—

She shivered again, despite the warm summer air drifting through the open window. He took a deep, steadying breath and drew the cloth over her hips and belly. He relished the female softness of her flesh.

Her waist was narrow and he could feel the flare of her rib cage. He sensed the fullness and warmth of her breasts before he touched them. He cupped them in his palms, savoring their weight.

He was enjoying this too much.

Swiftly he dried her chest and throat. He tried to gather her hair together in a makeshift ponytail, but failed.

The coverlet was folded at the foot of the bed. He opened it, then placed it over her body.

"I love you...." Her voice was low, that faraway voice of someone deep in a dream.

"Who do you love, Emilie?" he asked as he lay down on the bed next to her and gathered her gently into his arms.

He was almost glad when she didn't answer.

ELEVEN

When Emilie awoke the next morning she was alone in the second-floor bedroom.

She was also naked.

She sat up, holding the coverlet to her breasts, then glanced around. Everything looked normal. The tub was pushed against the far wall, same as it had been last night. She smelled like roses, so she must have finished her bath, but she didn't remember anything beyond settling into the warm water and closing her eyes.

Either she was the world's only sleepwalking bather or Zane had plucked her from the tub and deposited her beneath the covers.

A long, slow heat slid along the insides of her thighs. Surely she'd know if something had happened. But she remembered nothing save an odd series of dreams that had left her feeling sad and hopeful and everything in between.

Last night she'd given birth to a baby. At least, she had in her dreams. If she closed her eyes she could still feel the crushing pain that was followed by a wave of pure joy that made all that had come before it seem meaningless.

And he'd been there with her. Holding her hand. Whispering encouragement. Sharing that miraculous moment when the visible proof of their love entered the world.

She felt empty now. Her arms ached for her child.

Her heart yearned for the man who had helped create the child.

If only she had seen his face.

The next few days passed in a blur of activity. The embroidery method of transmitting messages was a rousing success, and Andrew grew more daring. Zane, watching from the sidelines, found himself growing restless. His life seemed to be at an impasse and he knew the time was approaching when he would have to make some difficult decisions.

As for Emilie, her confusion manifested itself in a fatigue that seemed to sap the energy from her very bones. She'd fall asleep instantly at night, then awaken in the morning feeling as if she'd barely slept at all. She'd never mustered up the nerve to ask Zane what had happened the night he'd lifted her from the bath. In truth, she didn't really want to know. Either way, she had the feeling she would lose.

Why couldn't life be as simple and clear-cut as one of those TV dating games that she'd left behind?

Two men.

Two choices.

They were as different as night and day. Choosing between them shouldn't be difficult.

But then, who said they both wanted her? She knew in her heart that Andrew cared and she had little doubt he would welcome a chance to build a life with her. She wasn't vain enough to believe it was her beauty that held his interest; she brought with her the secrets of the future, and that had to be a potent attraction.

And then there was Zane. He'd been so distant lately, so preoccupied that some nights he hadn't bothered to come to bed. She tried not to imagine where he might be spending his time, but heated visions of him making love to some tavern wench from town made her stomach knot in jealousy.

It occurred to her that he no longer needed her the way he had when they'd first discovered themselves in this strange new world. He might not like eighteenth-century living, but he was a survivor and he'd adapted to it better, in some ways, than Emilie had.

Now that he had traded the gold from his watch-band for usable currency, he didn't need her to help him find his way. He was fully capable of charting a course for himself. After all, she had made it clear that she refused to allow circumstance to dictate her future.

Who'd expected him to suddenly take her at her word?

Things were changing quickly and Emilie only wished she had the energy to change along with them.

For the first time in days, everyone was gathered at the Blakelees' pine trestle table for the main meal. Andrew and Isaac were caught up on the work in the fields and, for a change, they came in to join everyone else. Even Zane, who had taken to keeping himself distant from the others, took his chair opposite Emilie.

The house was beginning to take on a festive air as the final preparations for Charity's wedding were being completed. The simple dark pine furniture gleamed after being rubbed with oil and polished to a high sheen. The curtains were freshly washed and hung smartly at the windows. Rebekah was putting the finishing touches on her daughter's wedding dress, while Emilie worked on the soldiers' uniforms in the morning and work for the spy ring in the afternoon.

The only thing missing was Josiah Blakelee himself and, unfortunately, hope was fading quickly that he would be home in time for the wedding. Each day brought a different rumor as to his whereabouts. The most ridiculous was that he had joined the Tory cause; the most frightening, that he was imprisoned aboard the *Jersey* in New York Harbor.

Rebekah, however, was determined that their daughter's marriage not be postponed. Life was short and the sooner you embraced the future, the better. It was a lesson not lost on anyone at the table that August afternoon.

Indeed, the air in the room was charged, the same way it was before a storm.

Andrew thought it was his own dissatisfactions making themselves evident.

Zane was sure it was the power he'd gained with the acquisition of money.

Emilie was positive it was her own state of confusion.

None of the Blakelees noticed a thing amiss. They were too busy running a house, tending a farm and planning a wedding.

"The sugarloaf!" Charity exclaimed, leaping from her chair. "We must have a sugarloaf or Timothy's parents will think we're poor as church mice."

"Would I forget such an important item?" said Rebekah with a laugh.

"And the sugar-scissors?" the bride-to-be asked.

"Don't worry," her mother said. "Things are well in hand. Why don't you—"

Her words were interrupted by the sound of horses' hooves in the distance.

The four adults at the table looked at one another.

"Are you expecting visitors?" Andrew asked Rebekah.

Rebekah shook her head.

Andrew pushed back his chair and stood up. "Behave naturally. I will wait in the pantry." He collected his plate, utensils and cup, then disappeared.

Emilie's heart lodged in her throat and she found it difficult to draw a full breath into her lungs. Rebekah's face went pale, and the children grew ominously silent. It was Zane who took charge of the situation.

"Do as McVie said," he ordered, resuming his meal.

The fricassee of chicken tasted like straw but Emilie forced down a bite. The others at the table did the same.

The hoofbeats drew closer and the drinking glass at Emilie's place trembled with the vibrations.

"I can't stand it," Emilie mumbled.

"Shut up," Zane snapped. "This isn't a game."

Emilie's cheeks flamed. Rebekah had heard every word.

Moments later someone pounded on the door.

Rebekah rose to her feet to answer it.

The dining room was cloaked in silence.

"Talk," Zane said.

"What about?" asked Isaac.

"It doesn't matter. Just do it."

Small conversations broke out like random brushfires. Nobody paid any attention to the words because everyone's attention was focused on the front door and the unexpected guest.

Rebekah returned to the room with a stocky, red-haired man dressed in the uniform of a Continental soldier. He introduced himself as Benjamin Fellowes. His manner was affable, but Emilie saw the way he seemed to notice every inconsequential detail in the room.

Rebekah's face was composed, but she fingered the ties on her apron with a nervous gesture. "You will see for yourself, Lieutenant Fellowes, that we are a simple family eating a simple meal."

"So it would seem," said Fellowes. His glance swept the table. "And you are certain you have not seen Andrew McVie?"

Rebekah did not so much as blink. "As I told you, Lieutenant, I have not seen the man since my beloved Josiah disappeared and if this Andrew McVie were to show his face I would give him a piece of my mind for leading my poor husband—" She stopped abruptly, tears welling in her soft brown eyes.

Charity leaped to her feet and faced the soldier. "Go away! Isn't it enough that my pa won't be here for my own wedding?"

"'Twasn't my wish to upset the lot of you, folks. We just need to talk to the man."

"You won't find him here," said Zane, rising to his feet.

The shorter man looked up at Zane. "Lieutenant Benjamin Fellowes, sir."

Zane paused a moment. "Captain Rutledge."

The wonder was that nobody at the table fell over in shock.

"An honor, sir." Fellowes stepped back. "Sorry to be bothering you. I'll be on my way."

Zane motioned for conversation to resume as Rebekah saw the soldier to the door. They continued to talk and eat until the sound of horses' hooves faded away.

"I can't believe you did that," Emilie said after Zane flashed the all-clear sign. "What if he'd asked for some proof?"

"He didn't," Zane said.

"What do you think that was all about?"

"Trouble," said Andrew, reentering the room. He turned toward Rebekah. "'Twould be best if you knew nothing of the plans."

Rebekah nodded and shooed the children out of the room. She lingered for a moment in the doorway, casting curious glances at Zane and Emilie, then disappeared.

Andrew summed up the situation with an economy of words. The code system worked well. Unfortunately it would soon be of no use, for the spy ring had all but ceased to exist. Miller and Quick had been arrested, leaving Andrew as the only courier in the area between Princeton and the lighthouse where Emilie and Zane had met him.

"We are being thwarted at every turn," he said, his voice heavy with disappointment. "We had cause to believe we were near to discovering where Blakelee is being held, and now even that is but a dream." He met Emilie's eyes. "You tell me that we will win this bloody war, but I find no sign of it. Tonight I was to make an important contact and now I am imprisoned in this house with no hope in sight."

"There will be another night," Emilie said soothingly, trying to dispel the smell of desperation in the air.

"There are some things that cannot wait for the time to be right." A thousand shadings colored his words.

"I'll do it," said Emilie. "Who on earth would ever suspect a woman?"

Andrew started to protest, but Zane broke in.

"I'll go," he said.

Both Emilie and McVie turned to stare at him.

"This isn't the time for jokes," she said.

"I'm not joking."

McVie didn't think he was joking. But neither did he jump at the offer.

"'Tis a dangerous mission," he said.

Zane nodded. "Now tell me something I don't know."

Hope, crazy and improbable, sprang to life inside Emilie's chest. Maybe he was changing, she thought, looking at Zane's beautiful face. An experience like the one they'd shared had to have an effect on a person. Certainly she was vastly different from the woman she'd been back in twentieth-century Crosse Harbor.

Besides, it wasn't every day you got to be in at the birth of a nation. Maybe he really *was* beginning to care about the bigger picture.

She listened as Andrew explained the situation to Zane in blunt detail, not minimizing the risks involved. Her heart thundered wildly inside her chest as she watched Zane's expression. He looked so strong, so brave, so—

"Hell, yes, I'll go," Zane said. "It's not like I have something better to do, is it?"

Zane knew he'd made a mistake the second the words slipped out. The words were true, but that didn't mean they had any business becoming public knowledge.

Unfortunately there was no taking them back.

They were out there, hovering in the air between him and Emilie, and she looked as if she'd never forget them. He felt like a stupid teenager who'd gone out of his way to annoy the one girl he really cared about.

Trouble was, he wasn't a teenager. He was a thirty-four-year-old man who was throwing away his last chance for happiness with both hands.

McVie, however, didn't give a damn about his motives. All he apparently cared about was the fact that Zane was willing to put his ass on the line. They both knew Zane's memory would be an asset. People, places, conversations—he'd be able to commit everything he saw and heard to memory and add an extra dimension to a simple delivery.

"So what's the deal?" Zane continued. "I could use a blast of excitement." *Great going. Now she'll really think you're worthless.* He couldn't bring himself to look at Emilie and see the disappointment on her lovely face.

McVie had managed to gain a copy of the layout to one of the prison ships currently moored in New York Harbor. "A man will be waiting for this at—" He hesitated, growing obviously uncomfortable. His eyes rested on Emilie. "Perhaps you would leave, mistress Emilie. This is of a delicate nature."

She lifted her chin and glared at him. Of all the outdated, sexist notions. "I'm not going anywhere. I'm in this as deep as any of you now. I don't need your protection."

"'Tis not your safety I speak of," said Andrew. "It's something . . . a subject not usually—"

"Just say it," Zane broke in. "She'll find out anyway."

Andrew turned to Zane. "You will meet your contact at a . . . house south of Princeton, not far west from the cave where you spent the night."

"A house?" Emilie asked. "What's the big deal about a house?"

A grin twitched the corners of Zane's mouth. "I don't think he means a two-story Colonial."

Her jaw dropped. "You mean—"

Zane nodded, then met McVie's eyes. "A whorehouse. Am I right?"

Andrew couldn't bring himself to look at Emilie. "Officers from both armies congregate there."

"I'd heard this was a gentlemen's war," Emilie drawled, "but that's ridiculous."

"'Tis the nature of man," said Andrew simply.

Emilie snorted in disgust. "'Tis the nature of a beast," she mimicked.

"Knock it off, Em," said Zane. "This has nothing to do with you."

She glared at them. Two pigheaded, hormone-saturated examples of American manhood, separated by two hundred years but connected by testosterone. Why was it men accepted the most insulting institutions as both logical and natural? She could just imagine the screaming that would go on if some enterprising Yankee wife gathered together a score of handsome men and opened a bordello that catered to women.

Of course, neither one of them cared a fig for what she had to say about this situation. They continued making their plans for Zane's James-Bond-meet-George-Washington adventure while she continued to burn.

"You're wearing *that* tonight?" Emilie stared, eyes wide, as Zane walked into their shared bedroom with a Continental army uniform slung over his arm.

"McVie's idea," he said, tossing the uniform down on the bed. "Rebekah was making this with Josiah in mind and she said we're about the same size. McVie said you'd finish up the collar and cuffs."

"How nice of him to volunteer me for the job."

"Rebekah's busy with the wedding preparations." He shot her a sidelong look. "I thought you said you were in this with the rest of us."

"I am," she said. "It's just—" She stopped abruptly. She didn't want to think of what this bad mood of hers was really about.

He gestured toward the uniform. "Are you going to take care of it, or not?"

"Dusk is still hours away. What's the rush?"

"I'm not waiting for dusk. I'm leaving as soon as the uniform's ready."

"Such a patriot," she drawled, her tone etched with sarcasm. "Can't wait to give your all for your country."

"Give it a rest."

"No, I won't give it a rest. All this is to you is another excuse to risk your damn stupid neck."

"I suppose you think it's all flag-waving and moral outrage on McVie's part."

"He cares what happens to this country," she snapped. "He understands what's important."

"Grow up, Emilie," Zane growled. "He's running away from something and if you can't see that, you're not as smart as you think."

She bit her lip in dismay as she thought of Andrew's late wife and child. Andrew was running away from something but not in the way Zane thought. At least Andrew had managed to channel his pain and anger into a positive course of action, while Zane—

"You don't understand," she said after a moment. "Why don't we just forget it?"

"Are you going to finish the uniform?"

She nodded. "I'll finish the uniform."

"I'll be back for it in a half hour."

"Great," said Emilie dully. "It'll be ready."

For Zane, gold was the most valuable commodity he'd brought with him to the past.

For Emilie, it was pins.

The thought was laughable but true. Now that the war was raging, colonial women were at a loss for the basics of their existence. Items like sewing pins and needles were in short supply and Emilie found herself frequently thanking God that she had stumbled backward through time with her sewing kit intact.

She spread the uniform jacket out on the bed and took a good look at it. There really wasn't much left to be done, she noted. Josiah Blakelee was obviously a big man, taller even than Zane. She would have to hem the cuffs an inch or two. The edges of the collar were unfinished and the pewter buttons needed to be sewn on, but it wouldn't take her long to handle either job.

Her embroidered purse rested on the window ledge. She retrieved it, pulled out the sewing kit, then chose a needle. Threading it with a length of navy floss, she settled down to work.

As always, the rhythmic motion of the silver needle soothed her, linking her in time and space with all the women who had come before and all who would one day follow. She was rolling the edge of the collar between thumb and forefinger and placing a stitch when a feeling of déjà vu washed over her like a soft rain.

For a moment she felt as if the barriers of time and space were melting away.

Then, as suddenly as the feeling had appeared, it vanished.

"Strange," she murmured, continuing her work. She couldn't imagine what had brought about that odd sensation. She'd been working on uniforms intermittently for the past few weeks and she'd never felt anything remotely like that.

Zane returned just as she was snipping the last threads.

"Good timing," she said, determined to keep her emotions under tight control.

"Finished?"

She nodded, glancing up at him. Her breath caught in her throat. He wore a pair of buff-colored breeches that cupped his buttocks and molded themselves to his powerful legs, and his old white shirt of silky Egyptian cotton. His hair was freshly washed, slicked back into a ponytail, tied with a length of black ribbon.

He reached for the jacket, but she rose from the chair where she'd been working and approached him. Would she never get used to the sight and sound of him? He was like a drug to her and every bit as dangerous.

She held up the jacket.

"Where's your splint?" she asked as he slipped his arms into the sleeves.

"I took it off."

"Do you think that was a smart thing to do?"

"Why not?" he answered. "It's been a while."

"Only a month."

"Sounds long enough to me."

Of course it did. Zane did what he wanted whenever he wanted to do it. Nothing ever stood in his way. Not a broken arm. Not his marriage. Not the mission he was about to undertake for Andrew.

"I know this is a lark to you," she said, her voice fierce, "but it's vitally important to a lot of other people."

"Right," said Zane. "Like McVie. I'll keep that in mind."

She reached up to smooth the collar of his coat and a wave of dizziness overtook her. "My God," she whispered. "That's why..."

He turned to face her, a look of curiosity on his face. "What's wrong?"

"Remember?" she said, gesturing toward his outfit. "The uniform. The one you brought to me." The odd stitching on the collar, the hemmed sleeves...

She watched as the realization dawned on him.

"Jesus," he said, his voice low. "You don't think—?"

"You have to admit it's a possibility."

He found it hard to wrap his mind around the knotted puzzle that was the concept of time. "You telling me I'm my own ancestor?"

"I don't know what I'm telling you." All she knew was that she had the strangest feeling of having come full circle.

Andrew was waiting for them downstairs. He handed Zane a folded piece of paper that contained the detailed deck plan of the prison ship in Wallabout Bay, New York Harbor.

"Mark me well, Rutledge," he said, his manner stern. "One slip and all is lost."

Zane slid the deck plan into his coat pocket. "I won't slip."

Emilie met Andrew eyes. "What do you mean, all will be lost?"

"Each morning dead prisoners are buried in the mud flats. Those who survive live crowded together in the dark below deck with no light and little air and rancid food."

His eyes strayed toward the Blakelees, who were standing near the entrance to the front room.

"Josiah?" asked Zane.

Andrew nodded. "'Tis feared he has been sent to the Hell Ship."

"Wait a minute," said Emilie, struck by a dreadful thought. "I understand what will happen to other people if that map falls into the wrong hands, but what about Zane?"

The silence from the two men spoke volumes. She looked down at her hands, focusing on the gold-and-silver ring. The ring that was serving as her imitation wedding band. She covered it with her right hand.

"You are there to see Maggie," Andrew said. "She knows what you are about and will see to it that you connect with the necessary people."

Emilie was proud of herself. He'd handed her a perfect straight line and she'd resisted the urge. She didn't know anything about this Maggie, but she had a pretty good idea she wouldn't like her.

"Can you ride?" Andrew asked Zane.

Zane nodded. "Won't that draw more attention?"

"You're an officer," Andrew said. "It's in keeping with your position."

And then it was time for Emilie and Zane to say goodbye.

Andrew stepped aside to allow them a moment of privacy, but he didn't look away. Emilie glanced over her shoulder and saw the entire Blakelee family, from Rebekah all the way down to Aaron, watching them with rapt attention.

A handshake just wouldn't do it. Rebekah was already curious enough about the two of them.

Zane met her eyes. "Come on, Em," he said, his voice low. "Let's give it our best shot."

He took her in his arms. The smell of soap and wool enveloped her as he held her close. Tilting her chin with his forefinger, he lowered his head and brought his mouth down on hers.

His kiss was bittersweet. Her tears were hot.

"Be careful," she whispered.

He smiled at her and, with a nod toward the others, he was off.

TWELVE

Emilie tried to throw herself into the frenzied preparations going on at the Blakelee house, but not even the excitement surrounding Charity's wedding could ease the feeling of disaster settling itself around her.

Saying goodbye to Zane, she'd wanted to throw herself into his arms and never let him go. But when she'd turned away from the door and met Andrew's eyes she'd felt embarrassed and confused and altogether positive that she was losing her mind. There was a connection between herself and Andrew, a deep and important connection, but she found it difficult to understand exactly what it was.

As it was, Andrew seemed restless. He'd wanted to go out into the fields and work off his energy, but he knew the farm was being watched and he dare not risk being seen.

And so he paced from one end of the farmhouse to the other, muttering to himself. Finally Rebekah could stand it no longer and she put him to work polishing the pewter service she'd dug up from the backyard where she'd had it hidden.

It was obvious he'd give anything to be in Zane's place, facing danger head-on, and Emilie found her own feelings on that subject surprisingly tangled.

At dusk Rebekah served a light supper of beans and brown bread with tankards of cider. Emilie found it hard to concentrate on her meal, and she ended up moving the food around on her plate with her fork. Afterward, she helped Rebekah and Charity tidy the kitchen, grateful to have something to occupy her mind.

Isaac had wanted help with something he was building for his sister's new home and Andrew had climbed up to the boy's attic room to help him. Emilie, Rebekah and Charity settled down in the front room to finish work on the girl's wedding linens by candlelight.

"Are you getting nervous, Charity?" Emilie asked as she put the finishing touches on a table runner embroidered with daisies and forget-me-nots. "Your wedding is less than forty-eight hours away."

"Charity is much like her father," said Rebekah fondly. "There is little in this world that can sway her from her course."

"Timothy's folks arrive tomorrow evening," Charity said. "I find myself wondering if I'll like them half as much as I love him."

Rebekah laughed out loud. "How like my girl to care not what they think of her but to worry if she will like them."

"I'd always wished for in-laws," Emilie said, more to herself than to Rebekah or Charity. "Zane's parents died years before I met him." She'd had but one chance to meet his grandmother Sara Jane during their brief marriage, and had longed to get to know the woman who'd meant so much to Zane.

"Poor man," said Rebekah. "'Tis no wonder he hurts as he does. He told me that he was sent away from home long before they met their untimely end."

Emilie's head shot up from her needlework. "He told you about his parents?"

Rebekah nodded. "The morning before last when he helped me hang the wash."

Zane Rutledge helped Rebekah hang the wash? Emilie found she could only stare at the woman in surprise.

"He is a good man," Rebekah continued, her needle dipping in and out of the open-weave fabric of the nightdress she worked on. "And he loves you very much."

Emilie looked back down at her own work again. If Rebekah only knew the truth: that Emilie and Zane had been married and divorced and were living a lie.

"You can always tell when a man loves a woman," Rebekah was saying. "'Tis the little things that give it away."

Charity smiled smugly. "Timothy gave me a tortoiseshell comb for my birthday."

"I don't think that's exactly what your mother meant," Emilie said. She looked at Rebekah. "Is it?"

Rebekah shook her head. "I always said I realized Josiah truly loved me the night he sat up with Charity when the girl was cutting her teeth." Rebekah, about to give birth to Isaac, had appreciated that unbroken night's sleep the way another woman might have appreciated a flawless emerald. "A man gives what he can," she said, meeting Emilie's eyes, "and he gives it in his own way."

Her thoughts went back to the warm tub of bathwater, scented with roses, that had awaited her in their room the other night. "Perhaps a woman ought not read more into a simple gesture than actually exists."

Rebekah smiled. "And perhaps a woman ought not read less into a man because he does not conform to the ideal."

"If I didn't know better, Rebekah, I would believe you spoke of me."

"Your husband is a good man, Emilie, and a kind one. I fear you do not always see that."

"He does not often allow that to be seen."

From the other room, baby Aaron started to cry and Rebekah motioned for her daughter to check on the infant. She waited until Charity was beyond earshot.

"When I spoke of Andrew some days ago, I spoke from concern for his well-being."

"I know that, Rebekah. I—"

Rebekah raised her hand to silence Emilie. "When I speak of Andrew now, it is from concern for all."

"I believe you see trouble where none exists."

"And I believe you do not see what stands before you."

"Rebekah—" Emilie stopped. What could she say? Anything she told the woman would sound either like a lie or a bad excuse. The truth was inconceivable.

She would more than likely find herself sentenced to an asylum somewhere.

The good housewife leaned back in her chair and considered Emilie, her soft brown eyes holding a subtle challenge. "Some would say you are a fortunate woman, Emilie Rutledge, to have two such men in love with you."

"Oh, Rebekah," she said on a sigh. "There are so many things you don't understand...." *So many things I can tell no one.* She met the woman's eyes.

"Zane—" She paused to collect her thoughts. "Zane is not a man like Josiah. Home and family are not uppermost in his heart."

Rebekah made a dismissing motion with her hand. "Nor were they in Josiah's heart. It takes time for a man to learn what is truly important in this world."

"That may be so," said Emilie, "but at least you have been given the luxury of a permanent home." She gestured toward the farmhouse and the land beyond. "A place to put down roots."

Rebekah's laugh was loud and full-bodied. "'Tis but a year that we have been back on our land. Josiah has led me on a merry chase these eighteen years past."

Emilie listened in shocked silence as Rebekah told of her vagabond marriage. Josiah was a crusader against injustice, a lawyer as well as a farmer, and he had combed the land from New Hampshire down to the Carolinas in search of a cause.

"I do not mean to make light of the grievous situation in which we find ourselves, but 'twas the first volley at Bunker Hill that gave me back my beloved home."

"Are you happy?" Emilie asked.

"What is happiness?" Rebekah parried. "I am content. I ask no more than that."

"I want more than that," Emilie said, unable to stop herself. "I want to be happy."

"And how will you accomplish that end?" Rebekah asked.

"Had I that answer, I should be at General Washington's side, conducting the war."

Rebekah laughed. "You must love your husband for who and what he is, Emilie, not for what you wish him to be."

The good woman had zeroed in on the root of her problem. "And what if that is not possible?" she asked, her voice little more than a whisper.

"Then you adjust," Rebekah said. "When you love, there is no other way."

Andrew stood to the left of the doorway and listened. When Emilie and Rutledge had embraced, he'd thought his heart would stop beating, so intense had been his anguish. Now he felt his spirits soaring upward like an eagle, freed from the bonds of a cruel captor.

Hope, elusive and wondrous, took root inside his heart. There was a chance to win her heart! That fact was undeniable. If she loved Rutledge, she would have stated thus to Rebekah.

He wondered how it was that only he saw how different, how amazing, Emilie was. How could Rebekah and the others not sense that she was as unlike the other good women of his acquaintance as night was unlike day? Her accent held a blend of the colonies and her voice, the melodious tones of music. The way she walked with her head held high, the strength in her voice, the youthful appearance of her skin— surely there was no other woman like her in this world.

He moved away from the door. It wouldn't do to be found there listening. Turning, he started for the attic stairs and Issac's project. His mind, however, remained with Emilie.

Was it possible all women were like her in the twentieth century? She'd spoken of strength and independence, and at first those notions had seemed unappealing when applied to the fairer sex. But as he watched and listened to Emilie and noted the way she rushed headlong into life, he felt a yearning for another time and place—a time and place he knew only through her eyes.

Rutledge spoke often of finding his way back to the world he'd left behind. Andrew had thought it a fool's errand. But now he wondered. Could it be possible that the same mysterious forces that had propelled them backward through the centuries could be waiting to shoot them forward once again?

What a miracle it would be if he could one day share her world with her....

"Did you hear a noise?" Emilie asked, tilting her head toward the doorway.

Rebekah shook her head. "Only the mice."

Emilie shivered. "There's a wonderful thought."

Rebekah looked at her curiously. "Surely you are accustomed to mice. I know not of a single house that hasn't known their company."

"That doesn't mean I enjoy their company."

"Most farm wives take little heed," said Rebekah. "You are an unusual woman, Emilie. Each time I believe I have come to understand you, I realize I have but scratched the surface."

More than anything, Emilie wanted to confide in Rebekah. Lately she'd been feeling puzzled and confused and more worn-out than she'd been at any other time in her life. The notion of having a woman friend was very tempting and she couldn't think of anyone more understanding or compassionate than Rebekah.

Unfortunately, the secrets Emilie had to confide were so unbelievable that she knew she could not open her heart. Besides, now that she and Zane were involved in the spy ring, she would do nothing that might compromise the Blakelees' already-shaky sense of security.

Emilie put down her sewing and stood, in order to stretch her aching back muscles. A wave of dizziness, unexpected and quite surprising, washed over her and she slumped back into her chair.

Rebekah was by her side in an instant, offering her a cup of water and a shoulder to lean on.

"As I figured it was," said Rebekah with a knowing smile. "You *are* with child."

"No," said Emilie, struggling to overcome the vertigo. "I'm not. Honestly."

Rebekah's gaze strayed toward the bodice of Emilie's gown. "The signs are there."

Emilie shook her head. "I'm retaining water," she said.

Rebekah looked puzzled. "Your monthly flow," she said with great delicacy. "Have you—"

"I'm fine," said Emilie. "Don't worry." They said travel could cause a woman's cycle to become irregular. God only knew what *time* travel could do....

The two women worked in companionable silence for a while longer, then Emilie again put down her sewing.

"Where is he?" she said, rising to her feet and walking toward the window that looked out across the moonswept farmland. "Shouldn't he be back by now?"

As if on cue, Andrew strode into the room.

Nodding politely toward Rebekah, he addressed himself to Emilie. "I would not expect him tonight, mistress Emilie. These matters develop at their own pace.''

Her cheeks flamed as she considered exactly where these matters were developing. "I hope he is safe."

Andrew chuckled. "As a babe against his mother's breast."

She whirled to face him. "I'm glad you find this matter amusing, Andrew. Zane is unfamiliar with the ways. Anything could happen—*anything!*"

"Hush, lass," he said, his voice low. "Rebekah listens intently." In truth he was experiencing his own measure of apprehension about Rutledge's safety, but to his chagrin, his feelings were not entirely unselfish. If Rutledge were to find comfort in the arms of a willing wench, he doubted if Emilie would look upon the man with fondness.

Aaron's cry pierced the air and Rebekah put aside her sewing and rose to her feet. "I must see to my son." She held out her arms to Emilie, who crossed the room for her embrace. "'Twill work out," Rebekah whispered against her ear. "I promise you."

"What was that about?" Andrew asked as Rebekah left the room.

"A personal matter," said Emilie, surprised that the circumspect McVie would ask.

"Rebekah Blakelee is a good woman," Andrew said. "Josiah is a lucky man."

Emilie sighed and sank wearily into her chair. "And you, Andrew?" she asked. "Were you a lucky man?"

Her question shocked him with its lack of delicacy.

"Elspeth was all a wife should be," he said after a moment. "Would that I could say such about myself."

She eyed him with curiosity. "I'm sure you were a wonderful husband."

"Nay, lass. I was many things, but I fear 'wonderful' was not among the lot."

"I know what the problem was," she said with a chuckle. "You always forgot to take out the garbage."

"Lass?"

"Pay no attention to me," she said, waving her hand in the air. "I'm overtired. That's an old twentieth-century joke. You wouldn't understand."

He walked over toward her. "I should like to understand."

She leaned forward, eyes glowing with intensity. "So what was it you did wrong, Andrew? How were you less than wonderful as a husband?"

Years of memories crashed over him and for an instant he found it difficult to speak. "I thought not of

Elspeth and David," he said slowly. "I thought only of my business."

"What was your business?"

"I am a lawyer."

"Like Josiah?"

"Like Josiah."

She shook her head in bemusement. "A colonial yuppie." Who would have imagined.

"A yup-pee?"

"Young urban professional," she said. "It was a disease in the 1980's. I had no idea it had started so early."

She listened to the familiar story of a man who sacrificed family and friends on the altar of career, knowing that the problem would only increase with time and grow to include women, as well.

"I rode the circuit," he told her, his mind far away. "For many months at a time, Elspeth was left alone with David to cope with a myriad of troubles."

"Did she complain?" Emilie asked.

He shook his head. "'Twas not in her nature." But he would never forget the terrible pain in her beautiful eyes each time he packed his satchel and walked out the door in search of the shilling.

"She should have," said Emilie. "People who accept mistreatment get what they deserve."

"Is that how it is in your time?"

She nodded. "The pursuit of happiness," she said. "That's a big part of what you're fighting for."

"I have never considered happiness a possibility in this world."

"You're wrong, Andrew. This world may be all we have. If you cannot find happiness here, then what is the purpose to life?"

Her intent was clear. Her words found their mark inside his soul.

He knelt down next to her chair and took her hands in his.

"Andrew!" Her voice went high with surprise. "What on earth—?"

"The pursuit of happiness," he said, heart beating loudly in his ears. "I have found it with you."

"Don't say that. I'm a—" She stopped. She had been going to say she was a married woman, but Andrew knew full well the lie to that statement.

"You are a free woman," he said. "There is no impediment to our happiness."

She leaped to her feet, almost knocking him down in the process. "You don't know what you're saying. I'm nothing like your Elspeth or the other women you know. I would fight you every step of the way on every issue imaginable."

"And I should welcome the challenge." He stood up next to her. "It is all the things you are that endear you to my heart."

She wanted to tell him that it wasn't Emilie Crosse whom he loved, it was some romantic image of the future. But something stopped her. Was this her destiny, she wondered. Could it be that Zane would never return and she would be left alone to chart a course through life?

"From the first moment, I have sensed that you hold my destiny in your hands," he said, his voice low and urgent.

"I know nothing of your destiny," she said, "beyond what I have told you." Once General Washington's life was spared, Andrew McVie's life—or death—was never mentioned again.

"Mayhap my destiny is yet to be written," he said. "Could it not be that you are the key to my future?"

"No," she said, suddenly terrified of what might lie ahead. "That cannot be! Your destiny and the country's are intertwined."

"I cannot lose you," he said, drawing her into his arms. "I have searched so long for the likes of you that we cannot be parted."

He was going to kiss her. She knew it by the questioning look in his eyes, the way his head dipped forward, and she stood there waiting for it to happen.

His mouth slanted across hers. There was wonder in his kiss and a hunger for something she knew she could never provide.

Turning her head she broke the kiss, but not before he saw the tears glistening in her eyes.

"Next time you will think twice before dallying with a whore," said the man as he opened the door to the jail and shoved Zane inside. "Some of the wenches prefer English swords to American sabers."

The door swung closed behind the English soldier and Zane found himself plunged in darkness. He sensed rather than saw the presence of other prisoners.

"Speak up, man," a voice called out. "Tell us who goes there."

"Rutledge," he said. "Who are you?"

"Fleming from Little Rocky Hill."

The name was familiar. "Who else is here?"

Names came fast through the darkness.

Miller . . . Quick . . . Hughes.

"Blakelee," he said. "Is Josiah Blakelee here?"

There was a moment's silence. Waves of distrust emanated from the other side of the cell. The only sound was his blood pounding in his ears.

"And how do you come to ask of Josiah?" asked one of the men.

"McVie," he said. "He asked me to—"

He never finished the sentence.

THIRTEEN

Daybreak came and with it no sign of Zane.

"Something terrible has happened," Emilie said to Andrew as the first light of dawn appeared beyond the trees. "He should have been back hours ago."

"There may be another explanation," said Andrew, "one you will not care to hear."

"I know all about sex," she snapped, scarcely registering the blush staining his cheeks. "That's not why he hasn't returned."

"How can you know with certainty?" They had married and divorced. Both were free to do with their lives as they wished without reproach.

"I know Zane and I know he wouldn't have left us." Certainly he wouldn't have left her alone with Andrew. Of that she was sure. "I have to find him, Andrew."

"You cannot do that."

"I *must.*"

"The hour is still early. He may yet return."

The noon hour arrived, followed by the main meal of the day. Neither Emilie nor Andrew could swallow a bite of beef stew.

"Aye, lass," he said after the dishes had been cleared from the table. "I fear Rutledge may be in trouble." Even the good wenches at Maggie's needed their sleep.

"Tell me where you sent him," she pleaded. "If you won't go for him, then I will." A wave of nausea, the result of fatigue, came, then blessedly went.

Andrew knew when he had met his match. Despite the precarious nature of his situation, he promised he would search for Zane. "I make no guarantees."

He dressed in the garb of a farmer, complete with concealing hat.

"I will return as soon as I am able."

He started for the door. Emilie was right behind him. "No," he said. "I cannot be responsible for your safety. 'Tis too dangerous an undertaking."

"You can't stop me," she said flatly. "I will go whether or not you allow it."

They stared at each other.

Andrew was the one who blinked.

"We go," he said. "I pray that I am not making a mistake."

They skirted Princeton proper, keeping to the paths worn smooth by tradesmen and Indians. The lush woodland scenery that had delighted her was all but invisible to her now. Keeping a steady pace, they reached the clearing at dusk.

"You can go no farther," Andrew said as the whorehouse came into view. There was no sign of the Blakelees' horse, a magnificent roan that Zane had ridden off the farm yesterday, but that meant nothing. "Your presence would draw suspicion."

She couldn't argue with his logic. "You won't be long?"

"As long as it takes to obtain the information."

She nodded, feeling as fragile and brittle as blown glass. "Please hurry," she said. She promised to wait beneath the towering pine tree that had lost a limb to a bolt of lightning.

She could stand anything more easily than she could stand not knowing.

Andrew had been gone no more than ten minutes when darkness fell. Each time she thought she'd grown accustomed to the swift finality of nightfall, she was again struck by the differences between the world where she'd grown up and the world she lived in now. The only light came from the three-story house where Zane had met his fate.

She shivered, although the night was warm. She had to stop thinking in these melodramatic terms. There would be a simple answer to Zane's absence.

Perhaps he'd drunk too much wine. Or, now that he had money, he might have found the temptation of a game of chance to be more than he could resist.

Of course, there were other more exciting temptations to be found in that gabled house. Temptations that only money could buy.

It's not as if you have any rights over him, she thought, keeping her gaze trained upon the establishment. Except for that one incredible interlude the night before the balloon accident, she had kept him an arm's length away, emotionally and physically.

Would it be so terrible if he decided to find comfort in the arms of another, more willing woman?

Yes.

She started toward the house. She had no idea what she would do once she got there, but there was no way on earth she could just stand there in the woods, waiting for Andrew to return. If something had happened to Zane, she needed to know.

And if he was happily ensconced in some upstairs bedroom with a brunette—well, she'd cross that strumpet when she got to her.

Good or bad. Right or wrong. Smart or crazy.

They belonged together. It seemed so clear to her now that she wondered how it was she'd fought so hard against the inevitable. They were two people with absolutely nothing in common except the fact that fate had destined them to be together.

How wrong she'd been when she'd said she wouldn't allow herself to be ruled by circumstances. She and Zane had shared an experience that few people, if any, had ever known. It was impossible to travel through time and not be changed in the process. And sharing that incredible event with the man with whom you'd once shared your life—how could she have thought that wouldn't make a difference?

Of course, that was only one of the mistakes she'd made along the way. Strange that Rebekah had been able to see so clearly the things that Emilie couldn't see at all. She had been so busy sympathizing with Andrew that she'd been blind to all that Zane must be feeling.

You accepted your spouse for what he was, Rebekah had said, and then you learned to adjust. A few months ago Emilie would have argued the point. Now she wondered if there wasn't a touch of eighteenth-century wisdom at work in the woman's simple words. She'd been so busy trying to change Zane into her image of the perfect man that she had overlooked all the things about him that were wonderful. His strength. His love of life. His fearlessness.

The way he'd loved her....

Laughter spilled from the open windows as Emilie approached the house. She heard the deep rumble of men's voices and the high-pitched trill of women being coy. Her stomach knotted as a painfully clear image of Zane in bed with another woman rose up before her.

But, dear God, even that was preferable to the dark fear sending chills up her spine. Zane had to be safe. She refused to accept the idea that they had come so far only to let it slip through their fingers now.

"Why are you taking so long, Andrew?" she whispered as she knelt behind a hydrangea bush. Certainly he wouldn't dally with one of the women while she waited out here with bated breath.

A strangled laugh broke free and she covered her mouth with her hands to muffle the sound. She was losing it, that's what was happening. Her nerves were frayed to the breaking point. She'd been running on pure adrenaline. Too little sleep. Too little food. Too much excitement. Any moment now she'd march right up the steps, kick in the door and demand to see her ex-husband.

The front door creaked open and she ducked down into the shadows. The stairboards groaned as a man wearing heavy boots hurried from the house. Cautiously she lifted her head to see who it was.

"Andrew!" Her voice was an urgent whisper. "Over here."

He spun around, his expression hard to read in the darkness. "Who goes there?"

"Emilie."

He strode toward the bushes. She didn't need to see his face to know he was less than pleased. "You were to wait near the tree."

"I couldn't stand it. Zane—where is he?"

He grabbed her by the wrist and yanked her from her hiding place. They headed down the pathway at a fast clip. Although they were close in height, Emilie had difficulty keeping up with him.

"Say something, damn it!" she snapped as they reached the shelter of the woods. "If you don't tell me where Zane is, I'll—"

He spun her around to face him. "A score of prisoners were rounded up soon after midnight last night," he said, his voice tense.

"Zane?" The word was little more than a whisper.

McVie's expression was tender and infinitely sad. "He was one of them." The whore, Maggie, had turned Loyalist and, as luck would have it, Zane was the last member to join the spy ring and the first to be betrayed.

She sagged against Andrew as her knees gave way. "Oh, God." All the dreadful things she'd heard about the British prison ships in New York Harbor came back to her. "The *Jersey?*"

He shook his head. "Tomorrow morning they will transport the prisoners from a temporary jail to one of the prison ships."

"Then we have to do something tonight."

"I will take you back to the Blakelee farm, then consider the next step."

"The hell you will!"

He stared at her as if she'd grabbed the devil himself by the tail.

"Stop looking at me like that, Andrew. We have no time to spare."

He struggled to ignore her unladylike language. "This is a dangerous business, mistress Emilie. I cannot allow you to risk your person in a venture with little hope of success."

"I make my own decisions," she said, lifting her chin. "And I say we must do something now."

He raised his hand. "Quiet," he said, his voice low. "Someone approaches."

They crouched behind the wide trunk of a maple tree as two portly gentlemen, obviously in their cups, stumbled down the road.

"I would sell my soul for an hour of that lass's time," said the taller of the two.

"Aye," said the other. "There's little a man won't do for a willing wench...."

She turned to Andrew when the two men disappeared down the lane. "How big is the jail?"

"'Tis a small one," said Andrew, looking at her curiously. "A stone building with but one room."

"And many soldiers guarding it?"

"One soldier," said Andrew slowly. "There is a party tonight south of Morristown for the regiment."

"We could do it," she said, gripping his forearm tightly. "You have your pistol with you and I know you are never without your knife."

He said nothing.

"Think of it, Andrew. If you don't care about Zane's safety, think about the other men...think of Josiah Blakelee and his family."

"The chances of victory are slight."

"But if we do not try," reasoned Emilie, "they have no chance at all."

The prison ships were a death sentence as surely as a trip to the gallows.

He touched her cheek with his forefinger, as if commending her visage to memory against the day when they would ultimately be parted. If they succeeded in rescuing Rutledge, he would lose the red-haired lass forever.

But, looking at the expression in her eyes, the sound of her voice as she pleaded Rutledge's case, he feared in his heart that he had already lost.

"Over there," said Andrew, pointing toward a structure on the north side of the trail.

Emilie's spirits soared. "It *is* small," she said. "We should have no trouble at all."

Andrew shook his head in dismay. "You speak as if we have accomplished the task and, in truth, we have yet to begin."

"It's called a positive attitude," she said. Or Dutch courage. "If you believe you can do it, you can."

"Is that how men think in your time?"

"Some men and *women* make a lot of money teaching others to think that way."

"Then teach me those ways quickly, mistress Emilie, for what we attempt might lead to disaster."

She refused to believe failure was even a possibility. Zane was in mortal danger. Nothing else mattered.

"The moon is full," said Andrew. "We will not have the benefit of darkness to conceal our actions."

Emilie took a deep breath and loosened the top two laces of her bodice. "That will be no problem for me." Her heart was pounding so wildly that she was surprised only she was aware of it. "I will keep the guard occupied. The rest is up to you."

"I fear that you are in the more dangerous position," he said. "I cannot guarantee how long I will allow you to be at risk."

"That's my business, Andrew, not yours," she said. "If you're so worried, then give me a weapon."

To his credit, he didn't hesitate. He handed over his pistol and told her how to use it.

Emilie nodded, then tucked the weapon into the garter that held up her cotton hose. Obviously no one would be able to call her Quick-Draw Crosse, but there was a measure of comfort to be gained in knowing that the gun was there.

The plan was simple. Emilie was to distract the guard long enough for Andrew to speak to the prisoners through the barred window they'd noticed on the side of the small building. When he gave her the signal, Emilie would step aside, Andrew would leap forward and knock the guard unconscious. Once they had the key to the jail, they were home free.

"'Tis time," said Andrew as a cloud drifted across the face of the moon.

Emilie squared her shoulders and met Andrew's eyes. "You have been a good friend," she said. "I could not have asked for a better one."

It wasn't enough and he could not pretend otherwise. "Godspeed," he said, kissing her hand in a gesture of luck and farewell.

"Godspeed," she said, then whispered a prayer that the end would be a happy one for them all.

The guard, a ruddy-complexioned man in his fifties, was dozing when Emilie first approached. A musket lay across his lap. A jug of Jamaican rum rested at the ground near his booted feet and it was obvious by the way he was snoring that he had enjoyed every drop. Her hopes soared. *Let him be drunk,* she thought. Then she could heft the musket and render him unconscious and not have to go through with part of her plan.

But that wasn't meant to be. On a loud snore the guard roused and turned his bloodshot eyes on her. "Who goes there?" he called.

Not answering, Emilie resignedly sashayed over to him, swishing her skirts the way heroines did in old costume-drama movies. He eyed her appreciatively. Lustily.

She stopped a few feet away from him, her eyes drawn to his nasty-looking beard with God knew what disgusting substance clinging to it. She prayed her roiling stomach would settle down long enough for her to act seductively.

She stepped closer. She'd never been much of a flirt. All of that simpering and eyelash batting had seemed an incredible waste of time and effort. Now she wished she'd paid more attention.

"'Tis a fine night," she said, summoning up a saucy smile.

He nodded and sat up straight on the wooden bench.

She leaned forward, allowing him a view of her cleavage. "Poor man," she said, tapping him on the top of his head with her forefinger. "Left all alone while the others dance and make merry. 'Tis a shame to let a full moon go to waste."

His hot gaze trailed across her bodice, lingering along her shadowy cleavage. It took all her self-control to keep from shuddering.

"You're a fine-looking wench," he said. "Has Maggie taken to sending her girls in search of work?"

"Nay," she said with a toss of her head. "But our hearts go out to a man who isn't free to search for his own pleasures."

He licked his lips and bared his teeth in a leering smile. "And do you have a name, mistress?"

She gave him what she hoped was a sultry look. "Bonnie."

"Aye," he said, "and it's a bonny girl you are." He removed the musket from his lap and leaned it against the bench. "Sit with me."

She dimpled prettily. "There is no room for me on that bench."

He patted his lap. "I have a spot for you."

Casually she glanced about to see if Andrew was anywhere in sight. "You presume much, sir," she said coyly. *Where are you, Andrew?*

The guard reached out and clasped his fingers around her wrist. "Give us a kiss," he said, pulling her down onto his lap.

Her skin crawled as he toyed with the laces on her bodice. *Think of Zane,* she ordered herself. *Anything is worth his life. Even this.*

She leaned over and retrieved the jug. "How ungenerous you are, sir. Fine Jamaican rum and you do not offer me a drop."

"There are better things to do than drink rum, lass." His fingers traced the swell of her breasts. "We can drink after."

What she wouldn't give for a scalding tub of water and a bar of lye soap. "You're a randy one," she noted, striving for lusty enthusiasm. "I hope you won't be in too much of a rush."

He threw back his head and laughed heartily. "You need not worry," he said, placing a hand on her thigh, "for there is plenty more to be had."

A slight motion caught her eye, and to her relief she saw Andrew crouched at the corner of the building. He met her eyes and flashed the signal.

She made to stand but the guard held her fast.

"Patience," she said, trying to get free. "I promise it will be worth your wait."

He leaned forward and she gasped as his hand slid under her skirts. His rough fingers snagged the fine cotton of her stockings as his hands roamed unerringly up her legs. She could only imagine how they would feel against her skin. She struggled against him, praying he wouldn't find the pistol.

He groaned with pleasure. "You're a fine piece," he said. "Jack knows how to pleasure the women—" Suddenly he stopped. His hand had no doubt found the gun. "What the hell—"

There was no time to think. If he grabbed Andrew's pistol, it would be all over. For all of them. Andrew was still several yards away. Emilie grabbed for the musket leaning against the bench and brought it down sharply on the back of the guard's neck.

He yelped in pain. "You bloody bitch!" He reared back and struck a blow to her cheek. She fell to the ground at his feet. "I'll teach you to—"

Andrew was on him like a mountain lion. Emilie, cheek throbbing with pain, lifted her skirts and pulled out the pistol. With trembling hands she aimed it at the guard as Andrew's next blow sent the man tumbling into unconsciousness.

"Thank God you showed up when you did," she said to Andrew as he threw the guard to the ground.

"The keys," he snapped. "Hand them to me quickly."

She did as he asked, her stomach twisting at the sour smell of the guard's flesh.

"Do not let him go," Andrew warned. "If he awakens, do what is necessary."

The next few minutes were the longest of her life. Voices emanated from inside the jail, but none of them were Zane's. Beads of sweat trickled down her back. He had to be there. *But what if he's sick,* a small voice worried, *or injured?*

"Just let him be alive," she whispered. They could handle any other eventuality together.

Two men stumbled from the jail, stiff legged as if they hadn't walked in a long while.

Neither one was Zane.

Her mouth went dry with fear. *Dear God, please let him be in there. If he is, I'll never ask you for another thing....*

A tall man with a head of red hair even brighter than her own staggered out.

She bit her lip as tears stung her eyelids.

And then she heard his voice, that low and thrilling voice that had first captivated her years ago, and she felt as if someone had handed her future back to her, all golden and shining and wonderful.

"Emilie."

She turned, unable to control the tears that fell freely down her cheeks. So tall, so strong—the one man she'd ever loved.

The only one.

Somehow she was in his arms. There was no other reality beyond the sight and sound and feel of him.

"I thought I'd lost you," she murmured against his lips.

"McVie told me what you did. If you ever try a stunt like that again, I'll—"

His words were lost in the kiss they shared, and when he broke the kiss she felt bereft.

"Emilie was right," he said as McVie approached. "There's a plot against Washington."

McVie looked puzzled. "I have talked to the others. They mention no such intrigue."

"They don't know about it," said Zane. "I found out about it at the whorehouse. They thought they'd knocked me out cold, but I heard every damn word they said." Sometime in the next ten days an attempt would be made on the general's life and it would be made at close range.

"Who is behind it?" asked McVie, still skeptical.

"Talmadge," said Zane. "Does that name mean anything to you?"

McVie paled visibly. "Talmadge is one of the general's closest advisors."

"We have to move fast," said Zane. "These guys mean business."

McVie called two of the other prisoners over. "Where is the general?"

"Long Island," said the man with the red hair.

"And Talmadge?"

"With the general," said the man.

McVie began barking orders at the assembled men. "Spread out into the countryside," he said. "Alert the others to the imminent danger."

"What about Washington?" asked Zane. "He has to be told."

"I am most familiar with the territory of Long Island," said McVie. "'Tis a dangerous trip and I have the least to lose." The other men had sweethearts and families. Andrew had nothing but regrets.

"I left the Blakelees' horse with a blacksmith at the edge of town," said Zane. Ten shillings and the man had been ready to adopt the roan. "Tell him Captain Rutledge granted his permission."

Emilie listened to the exchange with a growing sense of bewilderment. The trip to Long Island was everything Zane loved: long, difficult and extremely dangerous. Yet there he was, literally handing the reins over to another man.

The guard began to stir and Andrew motioned for the other men to scatter.

"Wait until first light, then return to the Blakelee farm," said Andrew. "I will see you there again."

"Take care, Andrew," said Emilie, "and come back safely."

He nodded. There was a world of sadness in his eyes and it tore at her heart that once again life had seen fit to deny him the happiness he deserved.

Zane, too, noticed the darkness in his countenance as he extended his hand to Andrew.

"Mark me well, Rutledge," he said, taking the hand and meeting Zane's eyes with fierce determination. "I would fight you if I believed there was a chance of victory."

With that, McVie vanished into the darkness.

FOURTEEN

For the second time in as many days, Zane found himself a prisoner. This time, however, it was not the British army who held him captive; it was Emilie.

The woman he loved.

All around them the members of the spy ring were vanishing into the night. Their movements barely registered on Zane. There was only Emilie. Once again he was struck by her beauty, but for the first time he saw her soul, as well.

A bruise, purple and angry, was blossoming along her temple near her hairline, and a murderous rage filled him as her gaze strayed toward the guard slumped on the ground by the door.

"Don't," she said, reading his mind. "It doesn't matter."

Gently he cupped her chin and tilted her face until it was bathed in moonlight.

"Why the hell did McVie let you pull a stunt like this?"

"He couldn't stop me," she said, cradling his face in her hands. "I had to find you."

She had risked her life to save his. The enormity of what she'd done hit him full force in the middle of the chest. There was so much to say, so many things to tell her, and no time to say any of it.

The guard was coming to and they had to escape.

"We're near the cave," Zane said, grabbing Emilie's hand. "Come on."

Swiftly they blended into the forest, away from the revealing moonlight. Zane cleared his mind of everything but the location of the cave where they'd spent the night many weeks ago. A small stream, a stand of towering pine trees, and a fifteen-degree slope to the land, give or take a degree or two. It wasn't much to go on, but he'd worked with less before.

Faint shafts of moonlight penetrated the canopy of trees, casting an eerie glow. From somewhere an owl hooted and it seemed as if the Christmassy smell of pine was all around. He let instinct and memory guide him and, to his amazement, Emilie never hesitated.

She was with him every step of the way, his partner, his soul.

His wife.

"Over there," he said, pointing to an outcropping of rocks to their right.

"Your memory is amazing," Emilie said as they found shelter inside the velvety darkness of the cave. "Rand McNally couldn't have done better."

"I remember a lot of things, Em." He drew her into his arms. "Everything about you." The little freckle on her left shoulder. The sound of her delighted laughter when he kissed her unexpectedly. Her strength and goodness and absolute certainty that happiness was theirs for the taking.

She rested her head against his shoulder. He could feel her heart thundering inside her chest, its wild pulse beat matching his own.

"You were wonderful," she whispered, her lips brushing the side of his throat. "Brave and selfless. I was so proud of you."

"You sound surprised."

She chuckled softly. "I was."

"I don't think anyone's ever been proud of me before."

"How does it feel?"

"Good." He found her mouth with his. "But not as good as this."

Their kisses held another dimension, a sweetness that transcended the purely sexual. He felt as if he'd been living behind a wall of glass and now that glass was shattering before the force of something greater—

and more dangerous—than anything he'd ever imagined.

"It's so dark in here," she said, laughing softly. "I can't see your face."

"I can see yours," he said.

"That's impossible."

He traced the contours of her chin, her mouth, her cheekbones with his fingertips. She was part of him, burned into his heart, half of his soul. "I know every inch of you."

A voluptuous shiver rose up from the center of her being. There was nothing beyond this moment. No one except this man. Everything that had come before, every dream, every fantasy, all of the endless days and nights of wanting something that danced just beyond reach—all of it vanished before the feeling of destiny that held them in its embrace.

He used their clothes to cushion the ground where they lay together, limbs tangled, hearts beating wildly. There was no hesitation. There were no missteps. They moved together as if they had spent their lives waiting for this night.

She gloried in his strength. He took comfort from her softness. The act of love became a sacrament.

This was the secret that had always eluded him, the secret that was at the heart of a marriage, at the center of life.

"All those years," he murmured against the curve of her breast. "All that time wasted...."

"We're together now." She arched against him, all softness and strength. "That's all that matters."

"This is forever," he said, moving slowly inside her. "Nothing can tear us apart."

"Don't say that." She kissed his mouth as if to erase his words.

His laugh rumbled against her lips. "Don't tell me you're superstitious."

"Why tempt fate?" she said. "We have so much. If I lost you I would die."

"To hell with fate," said Zane fiercely. "This is forever."

It was a night of wonder, of promises made and pledges given.

"We're getting married again," Zane said, holding her close to his heart as dawn broke beyond the cave.

"How on earth will we explain that to the Blakelees?" she asked, listening to his heart beating beneath her ear. "They'll be scandalized."

He looked at her, his blue eyes twinkling with a wicked light. "Are you suggesting we live in sin?"

Emilie traced the line of his muscular calf with her bare toe. "I'm suggesting we use some discretion."

"You mean no Elvis impersonator officiating?"

She laughed out loud at the memory. "I haven't thought about that in years." She shook her head in amazement. "I can't believe we were married by the King."

"Bet nobody around today can make that statement."

"Unless it's King George," she said dryly.

"You haven't given me an answer."

"I haven't heard a real proposal."

"You'll marry me."

"That's not a question."

"Damn right," said Zane, rolling her onto her back and straddling her hips. "There's only one answer I'll accept."

"I love it when you're macho."

He moved against her and her back arched in response.

"I also love it when you do that."

He leaned forward, drew one nipple into his mouth and sucked deeply.

Her eyes closed as a slow wet heat suffused her body.

He shifted position, parting her thighs and positioning himself between her legs. He cupped her with his hand and she moved against him as the need built inside her.

"You're ready for me." He brought his hand to her lips, letting her taste herself on his skin. "Hot and sweet."

"Oh, God...Zane—" She wrapped her legs around his waist and fiercely drew him into her body, demanding all that he had to give and more.

And neither was disappointed.

The sounds of laughter and music reached them as they crested the hill near the Blakelee farm a few hours later.

"The wedding!" said Emilie. "It must be today."

The events of the past few days were all jumbled together in a crazy quilt of fear and joy, and it came as a surprise to see that the regular patterns of life were exactly as they'd left them.

"There must be a hundred people down there," Zane said, whistling low. "I guess big weddings were always in style."

It was something out of a dream, Emilie thought, as they made their way down the gentle slope then headed toward the revelers milling about. The harshness of their life and the realities of war were not visible today as friends and family gathered together to celebrate the marriage of Charity Blakelee and her Timothy. A fiddler sat atop the porch railing, his spirited music perfectly capturing the mood of the crowd. Long tables had been set up in the front yard, and they groaned with the weight of smoked hams and hearth-roasted chickens and bowls of salads and fresh vegetables.

She gestured toward the scene below them of family and friends, little children and tiny babies. The whole spectrum of life in all of its aspects and all of its beauty.

A life without the walk-on-the-highwire intensity Zane thrived on.

"Look, Zane," she said softly. "That's all there is. Will that be enough for you?"

"I have you," he said, ruffling her hair with a gentle hand. "And one day we'll find our way back where we belong."

"That's not going to happen."

"I think it will."

"And in the meantime?"

"Hell," said Zane, looking young and filled with hope, "there's a whole world out there for us to discover."

"There's a war going on," she reminded him.

"That's the best part," he said. "We've helped save George Washington's life. Who knows what else is in store for us before we leave."

"We haven't exactly saved George's life," Emilie corrected him. "That's Andrew's job."

"We made it possible," said Zane with a snap of his fingers. "We'll clear up the confusion in the history books when we get back where we belong."

Why argue the point? If he needed to believe they'd return to the future one day, it was no worse than believing in Santa Claus or thinking that calories really didn't count.

So what if they had no home, no family and no steady source of income? Things would work out for the best. She had to believe that. After all, this was everything she'd ever wanted. The man she'd always loved had become part of the world she'd always longed for. The puzzle pieces that had been her life had finally joined into a beautiful picture.

So why did she have the feeling that one piece of that beautiful puzzle was still missing—and that that one piece might change everything?'

It wasn't as if he could click his heels together three times and wake up in the future. Things didn't work that way. The best they could do was build a life for themselves in the here and now. It was all that anyone could do, no matter what century he lived in.

Zane took her hand and they walked across the meadow to mingle with the wedding guests.

"Look over there," Emilie said, gesturing toward Charity, who was dancing with a handsome young man. "The bridal couple."

"They look awfully young," Zane said after a moment. "Do you think he's old enough to shave yet?"

"It's a different world now," Emilie said. "Real life starts a lot earlier. Let's go over and wish them well."

"Emilie!" Rebekah's sweet voice rang out across the yard. "Zane!" The woman, dressed in a pretty pink muslin gown with flowered trim, hurried toward them. She embraced Emilie warmly, then her brown eyes widened as she noticed the bruise near Emilie's hairline. "What on earth—?"

"I am fine," said Emilie, returning her hug. "Truly."

"You cannot know how worried I was for your safety. When you did not return the next morning I feared the worst." Rebekah glanced about. "Andrew...?"

"He is well," Emilie said quickly, "but he has been called away."

"And—and Josiah?"

"We discovered nothing," said Emilie. "I am sorry."

Rebekah whispered a quick prayer for both her husband's safety and Andrew's, then her narrow face lit up with a smile. She linked one arm through Emilie's and the other through Zane's. "Come and join the merriment,'' she said, leading them toward the tables laden with food and drink. "We are here to celebrate!" She lowered her voice conspiratorially. "Rumor has it we are to be honored with a most welcome guest."

"Anybody we know?" asked Zane.

"Of that I'm certain," said Rebekah.

Emilie gestured toward her wrinkled dress. "I must change into something more presentable."

"Hurry," said Rebekah, "for the dancing is about to begin!"

Zane followed Emilie into the farmhouse and upstairs to the second-floor bedroom.

"Oh, no, you don't," Emilie said, laughing as she eluded Zane's embrace. "Rebekah's waiting for us downstairs."

"She won't mind if we take our time."

"Patience, Mr. Rutledge," she said, reaching for her favorite mint green dress. "We have the rest of our lives ahead of us."

She changed quickly, then drew the comb through her tangled hair in an attempt to tame the fiery waves. She then gathered up the mane and twisted it into a loose Gibson-girl knot atop her head, securing it with a pair of ivory pins. She loosened a few tendrils around her hairline to hide the bruise and hoped for the best.

Turning, she saw that Zane had changed from the uniform and was dressed in black breeches and a black shirt.

"Very piratical," she said with an approving nod. "A nice blend of centuries."

"Everything else has to go to the cleaners."

"Remind me to explain the eighteenth century to you later on."

He pulled her into his arms and kissed her soundly. "Remind me to explain a few other things to you after that."

"Don't worry, Mr. Rutledge," she said. "You have my word."

Zane helped himself to several slices of ham and chicken, but Emilie found the mixture of smells off-putting and she instead accepted a pewter cup of sangaree. The sun blazed overhead and the cool blend of wine and fruit provided welcome refreshment.

"What's going on over there?" Zane asked, gesturing toward a crowd over near the barn.

"Maybe Rebekah's special guest has arrived. Is it me or did you think she was being awfully secretive about it?" She tilted her head as a thought struck her. "You don't suppose Josiah has returned?"

"Who knows," said Zane. "Let's check it out."

Zane put down his empty plate and Emilie was looking for a place to leave her cup of sangaree when

Charity and her new husband, Timothy, approached.

Charity, looking lovely in a white silk dress with embroidered roses along the curve of the bodice, smiled up at Zane. "'Tis our custom that each married man dance with the bride before the cake is cut."

Zane winked at Emilie, then cut a dashing bow. "And who am I to break with tradition? May I have the honor, mistress?"

Smiling, Charity stepped into his arms.

Her husband, a pleasant-looking fellow with dark auburn hair, bowed toward Emilie. "It would please me greatly, mistress, if you would honor me with a dance."

"I would very much enjoy that—" She paused. "Timothy, isn't it?"

His smile was as sunny as the day. "Timothy Crosse," he said, offering his hand.

She gasped, feeling as if the breath had been knocked from her body. "What did you say?"

"Timothy Crosse," he repeated, looking at her curiously.

She couldn't breathe. The heat of the day seemed to press upon her chest, making it impossible for her to draw breath into her lungs.

"Mistress Emilie..." Timothy's voice seemed to come toward her through an airless tunnel. "You look unwell. Let me see you to a chair."

She sank onto the porch step and closed her eyes against a wave of dizziness. "Please," she managed as the young man peered at her worriedly. "I—I am fine. It's only the heat."

He waved his arm in the air, motioning for Zane and Charity to stop dancing and join them.

"I do not know what happened," Timothy said to Zane when he approached. "One moment she was fine and the next—"

He shrugged his shoulders.

"I could use some water," she said. "If you would—"

Timothy and his bride went off to fetch a cup.

Zane helped her to a chair inside the cool darkness of the house. "You look like you've seen a ghost."

"I did," she said, a wild laugh breaking free. "And his name is Timothy Crosse."

Zane stared at her. "You've got to be kidding."

She shook her head. "That why I've been so comfortable here, so at ease." She gestured broadly. "In a way, they're family."

"We're getting into weird territory here. How can you meet your own ancestors?"

"I don't know," she said. "How can you travel back in time?"

"Don't look at me," he said. "You're the one with all the answers."

She thought of the other wedding guests for the first time. The laughing woman in the yellow brocade dress...the portly gentleman in the snuff-colored waistcoat...that beautiful towheaded baby who sat playing in the grass. She was related to half of these people by blood and to the other half by marriage.

A lifetime of familial history rushed in on her, making her dizzy. She heard her mother's voice and her grandmother's, each story forging a link in the chain that wound through the centuries.

Sweat broke out on her brow. "I can't think." She struggled to find the words, but they eluded her. "There's something...something, but I can't seem to remember what."

"Don't worry about it," he said, his gaze drawn to the bruise near her temple. "Whatever it is, it can't be too important."

"I know it sounds crazy," she said, shaking her head, "but I can't stop thinking about George Washington."

"Okay," he said carefully, "that's not too hard to figure out." McVie was on his way to Long Island to warn the general of the assassination plot. It had to be on her mind. "You're concerned."

"It's more than concern." She looked up at him, green eyes wide and puzzled. "I'm afraid something terrible is about to happen."

"Even if that's true, there's nothing you can do about it," Zane said with one of those displays of logic men pride themselves on. "You're in New Jersey. General Washington is in New York."

"But all those family stories—" she persisted.

"You did your best," Zane said. "Don't worry. History will bear you out."

Isaac burst through the front door, his narrow face bright with excitement. "My ma says to come on outside fast as you can! He's about to leave."

Zane and Emilie looked at each other.

"Who's about to leave?" Zane asked.

"General Washington," said Isaac, heading for the door. "He came to the wedding to deliver a letter from my pa. My pa's a hero! He—"

His words faded as it all came into terrifying focus for Emilie. The answers had been right there in front of her all the time. Her family. The wedding celebration with the fiddle music and laughter. She looked at Zane. *The man dressed in black who saved the general's life....*

"Oh, my God!" She started for the door, fighting down a wave of nausea. "This is it!"

Zane grabbed her by the arm. "Are you sure?"

"Yes!" Her voice was high and tight. "Andrew's not the hero. It's—"

He bolted for the door, knocking Isaac onto his behind. There'd be time enough for apologies.

Rebekah stood on the front porch, clutching a letter to her heart. "Zane!" Her smile was radiant. "We tried to find you. I so wanted to introduce you to His Excellency."

He grabbed the woman by the arm. "Where is he?"

She pointed toward the barn, where he saw a man in uniform astride a horse. "He leaves now for Philadelphia."

"Is he alone?"

Rebekah shook her head. "He travels with his aide." She frowned. "Now, what is his name? Ah, yes . . . Talmadge."

Zane vaulted the porch railing and hit the ground hard. A sharp pain shot through his right arm and it occurred to him that he'd probably broken it again. It didn't matter. Scrambling to his feet he headed full speed toward the barn.

One hundred yards . . . fifty . . . faster . . . he had to run faster. . . .

The assassin could be anywhere. The musket could be trained on Washington right now.

He kept running. Somewhere behind him he heard Emilie's voice. Whatever happened, however it ended, he wanted her to be proud.

"Get off that horse!" he roared at the general. "Now!"

Washington turned slowly and looked toward Zane. The man was a dollar bill come to life, the face on a thousand President's Day circulars. The impact stopped Zane in his tracks.

But not for long. If he didn't do something in the next ten seconds, the future he and Emilie took for granted wouldn't stand a chance, and that dollar bill would be a pound note instead.

The general's hand moved toward the hilt of his sword.

Behind him, he heard Emilie scream.

Sorry, George. This is gonna hurt me more than it hurts you.

And with that thought, Zane Grey Rutledge threw himself headlong into history.

FIFTEEN

Rebekah stood in the doorway, watching as Emilie collected the last of her things from the second-floor bedroom that had been their home. "Are you feeling better?"

"I'm fine," Emilie said with a smile. "Truly."

"The nausea?"

"Gone," said Emilie. "The lemon crackers did the trick." She could no longer deny the symptoms. She had tried to attribute the dizziness and nausea and skipped period to everything but the truth: she was pregnant with Zane's baby, this miracle child conceived in the future on that moonlit night when she'd thrown caution to the winds and followed her heart.

"'Tis a good sign. Misery now means a healthy babe when your time comes."

"From your mouth to God's ear."

Rebekah looked at her curiously. "I have not heard that expression before."

Emilie folded Zane's black shirt and added it to the small pile of clothing. "It's a very popular expression in New York."

"So you say. Still, there is something about you and your husband that sets you apart."

"Our accents?" asked Emilie.

"How I wish I could pinpoint it with precision. I have never known a friend such as you."

Emilie gave the other woman an impulsive hug. "I'm going to miss you, Rebekah. Especially now."

Rebekah nodded, her brown eyes wet with tears. "I am afraid I do not know how I will manage without your friendship."

"The friendship will not end," said Emilie, meaning it. "Only the proximity."

They heard the sound of Zane's footsteps on the staircase.

"Not a word about the baby," Emilie warned.

"You still have not told him?"

Emilie shook her head. "He has had enough to think of this week."

Zane had rebroken his arm during his heroic rescue of General Washington. Between that and all the excitement the rescue generated, there had been little time to break news of such a delicate nature. As soon as they were settled in their new home near Philadelphia, she would tell him.

It wasn't that she was nervous about telling him. Not really. Just because they hadn't gotten around to talking about children didn't mean he didn't want any. Sure, during their first marriage he'd made it clear that reproduction was near the bottom of his list of priorities. But that was a long time ago—and this was a different Zane.

As if on cue, Zane appeared in the doorway. "It's time, Emilie. We have a long trip ahead of us."

As always, the sight of him tugged at her heartstrings. "Is the wagon loaded?"

Zane nodded, then turned to Rebekah, a stern look on his handsome face. "You've given us enough food to last a year."

"'Twas the general's orders," Rebekah said with a saucy grin.

"How will you feed your family?"

"His Excellency said that will no longer be a problem for us."

"You must be so proud of Josiah," Emilie said. "Working behind British lines the way he has been doing must take a great deal of courage."

For the past three months Josiah Blakelee had been collecting valuable information for the patriots' spy ring that General Washington devoutly prayed would lead them to their first decisive victory of the war.

It was all Emilie could do to keep from telling them that the victory they so desired was in sight. In just a few short months, on a cold winter's day in January, the Battle of Princeton would be fought and won, setting the Continental army on the road to glory.

Zane turned to Emilie. "I'll meet you downstairs."

Emilie's eyes filled with tears. "Will we see each other again?" she asked Rebekah. "Now that Zane and I are both part of the spy ring—"

"Life is filled with surprises," Rebekah said. "That is one thing that eighteen years of marriage to Josiah Blakelee has taught me."

Emilie glanced about the room, suppressing a smile as her gaze fell upon the copper tub. "It appears that I have everything."

"You came with so little," Rebekah said. "I have often wondered how it was you and your husband came upon Andrew."

Emilie sighed. "It seems a lifetime ago, Rebekah. So much has happened since." She gathered up the satchel of clothing from the bed.

"Do you have the letter of protection from General Washington?" Rebekah asked.

Emilie patted the pocket of her gown. "The most valuable item in our possession." She had placed it in the embroidered purse, along with the items she'd retrieved from their hiding place near the barn. She could just imagine the uproar if Rebekah had discovered the money with the general's picture on it.

Washington's gratitude had been sincere and overwhelming in its generosity. In addition to the letter granting them safe passage, he had procured for them a wagon and horse, the eighteenth century equivalent of a BMW and free gasoline for life. They had been asked to join the Philadelphia branch of the spy ring, where Zane's powers of observation and Emilie's skills with a needle and floss would be put to their best use.

What Washington had done, in effect, was to hand them their future—the one thing they'd been unable to do for themselves. And now, with their baby growing beneath her heart, that future took on new importance.

Zane waited near the wagon with Rebekah's children. Even Charity and Timothy, home from their wedding trip to a cousin's house in Delaware, had returned to say goodbye. Emilie was deeply touched, and she hugged the two young people warmly. The thought that her life would be forever intertwined with the lives of these good people made her feel part of that invisible chain that linked her still with the world she'd left behind.

"The post runs well between Philadelphia and Princeton," said Rebekah. "You must write and tell me how you fare in your new home."

"No sister has ever been more kind," said Emilie as the two women hugged one last time. "We'll never forget you—not any of you."

Isaac, looking terribly adult, offered his hand, which Zane shook with great solemnity. Emilie detected a certain mistiness in Zane's eyes, which only made her love him more.

Finally they could delay no longer. Emilie took her seat next to Zane on the wagon as he took the reins in his left hand.

"Do you know how to drive this thing?" she whispered.

"How hard can it be? The horse does all the work."

"Godspeed!" cried Rebekah and her children as Zane urged the horse forward.

Emilie sniffled loudly for the first hour as they skirted the town of Princeton and headed south.

"We'll see them again," Zane said. "Our paths are bound to cross."

"How can you be sure?" she asked, her green eyes brimming with tears. "It's not like we can jump in the car and zip over for coffee."

He started to laugh. "What's that I hear? The sound of a woman longing for modern conveniences?"

"Don't make fun of me," she said, glaring over at him. "I miss Rebekah."

"You haven't been gone long enough to miss anybody."

"I don't care. I miss her and that's that."

Zane shot her a quizzical look. Apparently her familiar redhead's temperament had a few variations he'd yet to discover.

He'd seen Emilie furious, he'd seen her jealous, he'd seen her indifferent. But the one way he'd never seen her was weepy.

"Don't look at me like that!" she snapped. "I hate it when you look at me like that."

"I'd tell you to count license plates, but I don't think we're going to see any."

"I don't think you're funny."

They rode on in silence for a while, stopping once so an aggrieved Emilie could disappear behind a large bush only to return moments later complaining loudly of brambles.

Andrew had envisioned himself a hero.

In his mind, his return to New Jersey was as the hero Emilie had claimed he would be. But, instead, he was returning once again in anonymity.

When he'd reached Long Island he'd discovered that George Washington had left suddenly for New Jersey, leaving Andrew feeling like a fool as he spoke of assassination plots and daring rescues.

The men had looked at him as if he were crazy.

But then maybe he was.

The torch had been passed. Even he could see it. There were new men to take his place. Younger men. More impassioned men. Men with brains and vision who could do things for the cause that Andrew hadn't dreamed. Rutledge, for one. Even Emilie had more fire in her belly for independence than he had today.

He had stayed on Long Island only long enough to visit with Elspeth's mother. Then he had set out on the journey back to New Jersey. Back to what, he did not know.

Lately he had found it difficult to concentrate on the matters at hand when his mind was drawn again and again to the world that Emilie had described to him.

He could imagine the riotous cacophony of noise on a city street. When he closed his eyes he conjured up a gigantic silver bird that streaked through the sky like a shooting star. Nothing was more real to him now than those images Emilie and Rutledge had painted for him.

He had made up his mind that when he saw them again at the Blakelee house, he would tell them that he wanted to see their world. At least, that was, if they ever figured out a way to return.

Of course, that didn't seem very likely, but then neither did anything to do with the whole amazing enterprise.

Why he had bypassed Princeton and continued southeast until he reached the lighthouse puzzled him. Strange, but the need to see the lighthouse again had been too strong for him to resist. Like some unrelenting call of nature, he'd found himself going miles out of his way just so he could row across the harbor and spend the night listening to the waves crashing against the shore.

Just one night, he thought as he gazed out at the harbor. Just one night and then he'd move on.

After a few more miles of silence, Emilie leaned over and placed her hand on Zane's leg.

"Sorry I've been so disagreeable."

"I'd rather have you cranky than crying." He met her eyes. "You'll see Rebekah again. I promise you."

That brought about another few minutes of sniffling.

"You're not acting like yourself," he observed.

"Yes, I am." Her tone of voice brooked no discussion.

They approached a fork in the road and he guided the horse to the path on the right.

"I think you're making a mistake," Emilie said.

He gritted his teeth. Why hadn't someone told him this was going to be the ride from hell? "The directions said to bear right."

"I think you're wrong."

"I'm the one with the photographic memory."

"And the lousy sense of direction."

Zane bristled. "I seem to recall *I*'m the one that found that cave not so long ago. I didn't hear a sound from you then about my so-called lousy sense of direction."

Emilie flushed at the memory of that night—the daring rescue . . . the passion that followed. No, the only sounds Zane had heard then were her sighs of pleasure.

Still, she said, "Well, that only proves you can find places the *second* time around, Zane. The first time is the problem."

He just shook his head.

But after a few more miles even Zane had to admit things were looking a little bleak. He was supposed to be watching for an ancient weeping willow tree adjacent to an abandoned well. Unfortunately, there was nothing even remotely like that on the horizon.

They'd been on the road for hours. They were tired, hungry, and their butts were sore from bumping around on the wooden bench.

"I thought we were supposed to stay at an inn tonight," said Emilie.

"We are," he said, his teeth still clenched.

"So where is it?"

"We're getting there."

"I don't see it."

"If you tell me to pull in to a gas station and ask for directions, I'll—"

He never finished the sentence. He and Emilie took one look at each other and burst into laughter.

"We're gonna be okay," he said, ruffling her hair in an affectionate gesture.

"I know," she said. But even as she said the words, she felt a pang of guilt. This was the man she loved, the man who loved her. If they were going to build a life together, he should know about the tiny life growing inside her. Waiting until they reached Philadelphia suddenly seemed ridiculous. "Zane," she began slowly, "there's something I have to tell you."

No response.

"Zane?"

She followed his line of vision. "What is it?" she asked, straining to see over the trees.

"Over there." He directed her to the right. "Do you see it?"

Suddenly she felt dizzy, chilled as if by a gust of icy wind. "My God," she murmured. "The lighthouse."

"How the hell did I screw up like this?" he asked, jumping down from the wagon. "Only a moron could mistake east for west."

"I don't think it was a mistake."

He looked up at her. "What was that?"

She couldn't control her trembling. "Let's go," she said, her voice thin. "Let's get out of here."

"What's the matter, Em? This is as good a place as any to spend the night."

A sense of dread gripped her and would not be denied. "This could be dangerous."

He made a face. "No one expects us to be here. If anyone sees us, we're just another couple."

But they weren't just another couple. They were a couple from the twentieth century.

"Come on," he said. "Let's take a look around. We didn't have time to check it out when McVie found us."

She wanted to grab the reins and speed away as fast as she could, but she couldn't do it. Not without Zane. Reluctantly she allowed him to help her from the wagon.

"This is old hat," she said as they strolled toward the water. "There are so many new things to explore. Why should we bother with reruns?"

A rowboat bobbed at the water's edge, loosely tied to a post. Goose bumps danced over her flesh. If you asked her, it was all too damned convenient.

She tugged at Zane's sleeve. "Have you seen enough?"

He headed toward the boat. "Let's row over to the lighthouse."

"We can't do that, Zane. You have a broken arm."

"So what? I'll use the left oar, you use the right."

"I don't want to row across to the lighthouse."

"Then you wait here."

"Why are you so interested in checking out the lighthouse? You already know what it looks like."

He stopped, considering her words. "I don't know why I'm so interested," he said slowly. "I feel—I feel drawn to it somehow."

"I don't like this," she said. "I'm getting really bad feelings about this whole thing."

Nothing she could say, however, was enough to dissuade him. She climbed into the rowboat next to him.

"Let's get it over with quickly," she said, manning her oar. The wind was picking up. Unless he intended to sleep in the wagon, they still had to find a place to spend the night.

When they reached the island Zane helped her from the rowboat and she tied it to the dock.

"Look," she said, pointing to her left. "Another boat. Do you think they're manning the lighthouse again?"

"No," said a familiar voice from behind them. "We're all alone here."

Both Zane and Emilie spun around to see Andrew McVie looking at them.

"Andrew!" she exclaimed. "What on earth—?"

"I was on my way to the Blakelees'," he said.

Zane met his gaze. "We were on our way to Philadelphia."

Neither man commented on the obvious, that they had both gone considerably out of their way to get there.

"We look like a local meeting of the New Jersey spy ring," Emilie observed, struggling to sound calm and unconcerned. "Perhaps we shouldn't be seen like this. It would only—"

She stopped. Both men were looking off toward the horizon. She followed their line of vision. Spirals of icy gray cloud cover moved swiftly toward them. She gripped Zane's arm. "I know that cloud cover," she said urgently. "I knew I should've tried to put together a balloon. Anything that would give us a chance to—"

"Look over there!" Andrew broke in. "Down on the beach."

"That's it!" Zane yelled over the roar of the wind. "The balloon!"

Emilie knew without looking that the balloon and the gondola were in perfect shape. How could this be happening?

"This is our chance, Em!" Zane grabbed her by the waist and swung her around lamely with his one good arm. "We've done whatever it was we were supposed to do. Our job is done and we can go home."

"It's an illusion," Emilie said, grasping at straws. "This isn't really happening."

Zane started toward the balloon with a reluctant Emilie close behind. "I was beginning to think it wasn't going to happen, that I'd missed the chance somehow. This is a miracle, Em!''

No, she thought. *The miracle is that I ever thought you and I had a chance.*

That icy silver-gray cloud cover blanketed the entire island. The clouds were so low they obscured the top of the crimson hot-air balloon.

"Come on, Em. We don't have much time."

"I—I can't go." She felt paralyzed by a feeling she could not even identify.

He stared at her as if she were a stranger. "We're not going to get any second chances, Emilie," he pleaded.

"It might be a trick. What if something happens?"

"Then at least we know we gave it a shot."

She shook her head. "I can't do it."

"Sure you can."

She stepped back. "Not this time." Earlier, she'd vowed she would follow Zane to the ends of the earth and beyond, but now... Now there was another life to protect. She couldn't risk the safety of their unborn child. Her heart ached with pain. She knew if she told him about the baby he would let that balloon fly off without him. But she wanted more than that for him.

"I love you," she said softly through the tears that constricted her throat, "but I just can't do this."

He felt as if he were trapped in the middle of a nightmare with no beginning and no end. She couldn't be saying no.

"You can't stay here, Emilie," he said frantically. How would he convince her of that when the clock was ticking away those precious few moments they had to reach the balloon? He grabbed her shoulders. "Emilie, please, we belong together."

"Go," she said, breaking his hold and gesturing toward the balloon. "Don't lose your chance at happiness because of me."

This way of life was harsh. Without his crutches of money and power, Zane Grey Rutledge was just another man. He wasn't entirely sure he could make a living at that.

"The balloon is beginning to rise," Andrew shouted. "It's now or never!"

Zane realized he couldn't convince her. This had to be her choice. "What is it, Em?" he asked her. "Are you coming or aren't you?"

"I can't, Zane," she whispered on a sob. "Dear God, how I wish I could...."

Tossing him her embroidered purse with the money and credit card, she ran toward the lighthouse. She threw herself down across the bed and did the only thing she could—she cried as if her heart would break.

You did the right thing, her heart consoled her. *You let him make his choice without telling him about the baby.* He had the right to return to the world he knew and loved, the same as she had the right to opt in favor of their child. The thought did little to comfort her.

A few minutes later she heard the front door creak open.

Andrew, she thought dully. Zane must be gone now.

She lay there listening to the sounds of the lighthouse. Then she heard a voice.

"Emilie."

How cruel, she thought, for the Almighty to fill her heart and mind with the sound of Zane's voice when he was so far away from her.

But then the bed dipped low on the right and a strong arm pulled her close until her cheek rested against a broad chest that could belong to only one man. The steady beat of his heart was a benediction to her soul.

She looked up into his eyes. "It didn't work?"

"I didn't try."

Her breath caught in her throat. "I—I don't understand." *Please let this be real...please let him stay here with us....*

"This is home," said Zane Grey Rutledge, the man who had never understood the meaning of the word. "It doesn't matter a damn if it's the twentieth century or the eighteenth. The only place I want to be is with you."

They were the words she'd always longed to hear, but she had to be sure. "It's not too late," she said. "I want you to be happy. I—"

The thought struck them simultaneously and they raced for the window.

"Oh, my God!" she whispered. "Andrew!"

There, in the wicker gondola suspended from the crimson balloon, was Andrew McVie.

"I'll be damned," said Zane as they watched the clouds wrap the balloon and gondola in their icy embrace. "He's going for it."

Tears filled her eyes. "There's so much he doesn't know...so many things he'll need to learn."

"He'll manage," said Zane, putting his arm around her as the balloon vanished from sight. "McVie's a survivor."

She shivered at the words. "I hope he makes it."

"So do I." He kissed the top of her head. "Is that why you wouldn't go?"

"It's a little more complicated than that."

"You like the eighteenth century better than the one we left behind."

"That's only part of it." She took a deep breath, then met his eyes. "There's someone else to consider."

And then he wondered how it was he hadn't known. The easy tears, the secret smile, the way she looked at him as if he'd helped create a miracle. "A baby," he said, his voice filled with wonder.

"A baby," she said, her hands resting protectively across her belly.

"That first night," he said, struck by the enormity of it all. Not only was this child the visible proof of their love, but he was also the product of two centuries.

"Do you need to sit down?" Emilie asked with a soft laugh.

He shook his head. "I think I'm supposed to say that to you." He drew her into his arms. "How long have you known?"

"I had my suspicions, but I've only been sure for a week."

"You should have told me."

"I— To tell the truth, I wasn't sure how you'd feel about the whole thing."

"I can't think of anything I'd like more than a little girl with your eyes and your zest for life."

Those beautiful green eyes shimmered with tears. "I have my heart set on a little boy who's as adorable as his daddy."

Blinking rapidly, he glanced away for an instant. "We're going to do this right, Em. We're going to be there for our kid . . . let him know he's loved."

"And we have to get married."

"We'll make it legal as soon as we get to Philadelphia, but no piece of paper could make us any more married than I feel right now." The kiss he gave her was one of communion and she felt it all the way through to her soul. "This time it's forever."

EPILOGUE

"Sit down, Rutledge," Josiah Blakelee ordered. "You're wearing out the floorboards."

Another groan issued from the birthing room next to the kitchen and Zane shuddered.

He stopped pacing and looked at Josiah. "You have six children," he said. "Is it always like that?"

"Sometimes it is worse," said Josiah. "'Tis a woman's lot."

"Why do they do it?" Zane asked as his wife's pain ripped into his heart.

"For love," said Josiah. "Rebekah claims not to remember the pain once the babe suckles against her breast."

"Never again," said Zane, resuming his pacing. "I won't put her through this again."

Josiah simply smiled. The entire Blakelee family had been uprooted by the cause from their home in Princeton to begin again on a small plot of Pennsylvania land not far from where Emilie and Zane had settled. The two men had become close friends through their shared work in the spy ring, while their wives had simply picked up their friendship where they'd left off.

Right now Zane didn't know what he'd do without them.

Every time Emilie groaned he felt waves of pain tearing at his gut. When she was silent, beads of sweat broke out on his brow until he heard the sound of her voice again.

Josiah rose from his seat and handed Zane a bottle of rum. "Drink up," he ordered the younger man. "'Twill be a long day."

Morning became night and still she labored.

He might as well have been drinking water for all the good the rum did. His wife's agony was his own.

Zane wanted to be with Emilie the way he would have been in the future, but the shocked look on Josiah's face each time he broached the topic held him back.

Finally, he could take it no longer.

"She's my wife, damn it," he said. "This whole damn thing is barbaric. I'm going in."

He strode toward the birthing room and pushed open the door.

"Zane!" Rebekah was horrified. "This is no place for a man."

"Let him in." Emilie's voice was weak. She looked small and pale and exhausted against the plain white bed sheets. Suddenly her back arched and she reached for his hand, gripping with a strength that threatened to break his bones.

"The baby's crowning," said Rebekah. "Push, Emilie! Push!"

The room echoed with his wife's pain as she strained to deliver their child. He found himself horrified, scared, elated and every emotion in between.

"A little more," Rebekah urged. "Just . . . one . . . more . . . push!"

"Come on, Em," he pleaded.

"I can't . . . I'm tired. . . . It's too much . . . I—"

"You can do it, Em. You can do anything."

From some hidden wellspring she summoned the strength to try one more time. Her face contorted from the effort. "It's coming . . . I can feel it. The baby's coming!"

And then their child's first cry rang out, strong and lusty and miraculous.

"It's a girl!" Rebekah shouted joyously. "A beautiful baby girl!"

"Oh, God—Zane!" Emilie turned her face toward him, tears sliding down her cheeks and mingling with his own.

He thought he had known what love was about. He thought he had learned the secret to it all, thanks to this woman in his arms and their incredible journey through time. But when he saw that beautiful squalling infant placed in her mother's arms, he realized he'd known nothing at all.

Suddenly Emilie's back arched again and she cried out.

"'Tis the afterbirth," said Rebekah, still positioned between Emilie's legs. Rebekah placed her hand on Emilie's distended abdomen and an odd look passed across her features.

"What is it?" asked Zane, fear striking his heart. They couldn't have come this far for something to happen to Emilie. "Is something wrong?"

"Take the baby," she ordered in a clipped voice. "It seems Emilie's labors are not yet over."

Take the baby? He stared at the tiny, fragile infant in Emilie's arms. He couldn't take the baby. He didn't know the first thing about—

"Take the baby!" Rebekah's voice brooked no argument.

Long ago he'd heard someone say you scooped up a baby the way you scooped up a football. Since no one was offering any new suggestions, that's what he did, and to his relief it worked. She was so little, so perfect, so—

"Push!" Rebekah barked, sounding like a twentieth-century drill sergeant.

"I can't," said Emilie, gripping the bedpost with white-knuckled hands.

"You must."

Emilie's back arched.

"Push...push...sweet Jesus!" Rebekah's tears were mixed with laughter. "You have a son."

"A son?" Zane stared down at the child in his arms. "I thought we had a daughter."

"Twins?" asked Emilie, sounding both exhausted and triumphant. "We have twins?"

"'Tis a wonderful day," said Rebekah, wrapping the second newborn in a receiving blanket and handing him to his mother. "The Almighty has seen fit to bless you twice."

She turned, tears of joy running down her cheeks, and left the room to announce the exciting turn of events.

"We're a family," Emilie whispered, meeting Zane's eyes. "A real, live family."

He looked at his wife and their children and knew that he would lay down his life for them. Their way would be rocky in this new world, this new century, but Zane knew he'd do whatever it took to keep them safe from harm.

For the first time since he'd slipped through time—what seemed like a lifetime ago—his future seemed clear. He threw back his head and laughed with joy.

"I love you," he said, wishing the words didn't seem so inadequate when it came to describing the wondrous feelings that lived inside his heart. "I couldn't live without you."

"Poor Zane," she said as he bent to kiss her lips. "This isn't the life you planned on, is it?"

"No," he said without hesitation. "I got lucky."

"No regrets?"

"Not a one."

It's about time you realized it.

Emilie's eyes widened. "Did you hear something?"

He grinned. "I was wondering when she'd come back."

"Who?"

"Sara Jane."

"Your grandmother?"

He nodded. "In a way, she's responsible for this whole thing."

"I don't understand."

"You will," he said. "One day I'll explain the whole thing."

I'm proud of you, Zane. You've become a fine man—a true Rutledge.

"I heard her again," said Emilie, glancing around the room, "but I couldn't make out the words."

He smiled as a feeling of peace settled itself inside his heart. "I think she just said goodbye."

The door to the room swung open and in burst Rebekah and Josiah, Charity and her husband, Timothy, Isaac and Stephen and Benjamin and Ethan and even baby Aaron, who was beginning to walk.

The babies were proclaimed absolutely beautiful and as clever and brilliant as their besotted parents.

"But they don't have names yet," said Rebekah. "What are you going to call them?"

Zane met Emilie's eyes and she nodded.

"His name is Andrew," said Emilie as their newborn son yawned. For their friend, wherever he might be.

Zane smiled as their daughter waved her tiny fist in the air. "Sara," he said. "We'll call her Sara Jane."

And so it began....

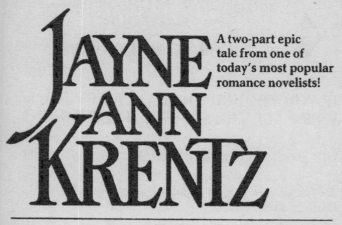

JAYNE ANN KRENTZ

A two-part epic tale from one of today's most popular romance novelists!

Dreams
Parts One & Two

The warrior died at her feet, his blood running out of the cave entrance and mingling with the waterfall. With his last breath he cursed the woman— told her that her spirit would remain chained in the cave forever until a child was created and born there....

So goes the ancient legend of the Chained Lady and the curse that bound her throughout the ages—until destiny brought Diana Prentice and Colby Savager together under the influence of forces beyond their understanding. Suddenly they were both haunted by dreams that linked past and present, while their waking hours were filled with danger. Only when Colby, Diana's modern-day warrior, learned to love, could those dark forces be vanquished. Only then could Diana set the Chained Lady free....

 Available in September wherever Harlequin books are sold.

JK92

HARLEQUIN SUPERROMANCE®

A PLACE IN HER HEART...

Somewhere deep in the heart of every grown woman is the little girl she used to be....

In September, October and November 1992, the world of childhood and the world of love collide in six very special romance titles. Follow these six special heroines as they discover the sometimes heart-wrenching, always heartwarming joy of being a Big Sister.

Written by six of your favorite Superromance authors, these compelling and emotionally satisfying romantic stories will earn a place in your heart!

**AVAILABLE WHEREVER
HARLEQUIN SUPERROMANCE
BOOKS ARE SOLD**

BSIS92

WELCOME TO

The quintessential small town where everyone knows everybody else!

Finally, books that capture the pleasure of tuning in to your favorite
TV show!

GREAT READING...GREAT SAVINGS...AND A FABULOUS FREE GIFT!

Each book set in Tyler is a self-contained love story; together, the
twelve novels stitch the fabric of the community. The covers honor
the old American tradition of quilting; each cover depicts
a patch of the large Tyler quilt.

With Tyler you can receive a fabulous gift ABSOLUTELY FREE by
collecting proofs-of-purchase found in each Tyler book. And use our
special Tyler coupons to save on your next TYLER book purchase.

Join your friends at Tyler for the sixth book, SUNSHINE
by Pat Warren, available in August.

*When Janice Eber becomes a widow, does her husband's friend
David provide more than just friendship?*

Fall in love with

Harlequin Superromance®

Passionate.
Love that strikes like lightning. Drama that will touch your heart.

Provocative.
As new and exciting as today's headlines.

Poignant.
Stories of men and women like you. People who affirm the values of loving, caring and commitment in today's complex world.

At 300 pages, Superromance novels will give you even more hours of enjoyment.

Look for four new titles every month.

Harlequin Superromance
"Books that will make you laugh and cry,"